With Aristotle
online

Georgios E. Manousakis

Emeritus Professor

With Aristotle
online

———

a student chats
with the great philosopher
through the Internet
about Alexander the Great
and much, much more...

———

2016

Georgios Manousakis

With Aristotle online

Copyright © by Georgios Manousakis

Tel.: 0030 2310 341 597
www.gmanoussakis.gr
info@manousaki.com

ISBN: 978-618-82537-1-1

10 9 8 7 6 5 4 3 2 1

Translated from Greek by Janet Koniordos

For Vangelis
And Manolis

ACKNOWLEDGEMENTS

I am deeply grateful to all the friends and colleagues whose special skills and knowledge helped improve both the text and the appearance of this book. For the English edition in particular I wish to acknowledge especially the contributions of Tania Panagiotopoulos, Cece Rohwedder and Janet Koniordos, for the admirable translation of the text.

AUTHOR'S NOTE

My cyber-Aristotle knows everything that happened both before and after his own historic time. The student's questions and comments and the opinions are given in *italics*.

TABLE OF CONTENTS

PREFACE

FOR SOME YEARS NOW major publishing houses around the world have been bringing out old and new translations of Ancient Greek classics. The success of these editions shows that there is a broad general readership with a real thirst for accessible books on philosophical subjects. Handbooks like these are popular because they present the ideas of the great philosophers in a clear and intelligible way.

The general public interest in popular philosophy is also evident in the frequency of radio and television programmes on related subjects, and the success of the "cafés philosophiques", modelled on the Café des Phares, the original *café-philo* in the Place de la Bastille in Paris. Here, on a Sunday morning, people gather for coffee and an open discussion on some philosophical question. The idea was launched by French philosopher Marc Sautet, who wrote about the *café-philo* as a grassroots forum for philosophical discussion in his book *Un café pour Socrate*. In a parallel vein, when Dr C.L. "Max" Nikias, President of the University of Southern California, was awarded an honorary doctorate by the National Technical University of Athens (26 May 2015), he told the audience that he had made a seminar in Ancient Greek literature a requirement for first-year students. Why? Because he believed that the Ancient Greeks' way of reasoning would help students learn to think more precisely. Similar initiatives have also been taken at other institutions, from the University of Hong Kong to the Stevens Institute of Technology, one of America's oldest technological universities.

These currents, this climate, made me want to write a book that would paint a picture — however incomplete — of Ancient Greek philosophical literature for the ordinary reader.

Most of the text is a chain of questions and answers, conducted through the Internet, between Aristotle and a student called Alexander. I chose this way of presenting the material because I think it makes for easy reading. It also allows me to pick and choose the subject matter, to make Aristotle speak of things from before and after his own time, and to express my own views through the words I put in his cyber-mouth.

I hope that my effort will spur those who read it to try some less easily digestible works, books written by professional philosophers and containing original thoughts and interpretations. This book, in other words, is meant to whet the reader's appetite for more substantial fare. But even those who are not enticed to delve more deeply into philosophy will surely learn something new here about Alexander the Great and his place in history, about the life and work of Aristotle, about Socrates, Plato, Democritus, Thales and other ancient Greek philosophers. For those who want to look up the passages cited, I have in most cases provided the exact reference.

This book was written for the non-initiate, and especially for younger readers, in the hope that it will kindle their interest in Ancient Greek literature.

* * *

HOW IT ALL BEGAN

THE NEWS SPREAD like wildfire: Alexander Megas, a popular first-year chemistry student at the Aristotle University of Thessaloniki, was in hospital with a broken leg, the result of a skiing accident on a piste near Grevena.

Before long you could barely see his bed for visitors. Friends, relatives, fellow members of the Herakles swim team, classmates from the University all piled into the room. And even after he was sent home they still kept coming to see him every day, filling the house with their noise and laughter and the plaster cast on his leg with their autographs and silly messages:

"To Alexander the Great, conqueror of the world (except for the ski slopes!!!)", "Maybe you should have taken up riding!", "This is harder than the Gordian Knot!", and so on in the same style, mostly addressing him affectionately as Alexander the Great and alluding to the tales about his ancient namesake.

They had plenty of plaster to write on, for Alexander was a tall boy, with long legs. By the time they had finished, the cast looked like a marble column wreathed in arabesques.

Why did they call him Alexander the Great? It started because his surname means "great", in Greek, but it stuck because he was intelligent, well mannered, curious, and a born leader who was both liked and respected.

All the references to the story of Alexander the Great scrawled on his cast set him to thinking about that long ago King of Macedonia. The great commander was a figure he had always admired, not only for his invincibility on the battlefield but also for his success in spreading Greek civilisation halfway across Asia. He was impressed by the fact that Alexander had philosophers as well as generals on his staff — perhaps the only commander in history to do so. The respect he showed for his teacher, Aristotle, was another good quality, and he liked the way Alexander had kept in touch with him while on campaign.

It was Aristotle, he thought, who had made Alexander the Great the man he was. The more he thought about it, the more he wanted to know just what Aristotle had taught him and how he had gone about it. How he had shaped the boy's character, and how he had inspired such enthusiasm.

Still thinking about Alexander and his education, he settled down to try to sleep. But he was far too restless for that. Was it over-excitement from all the visitors? The ache in his leg? Being back in his own room again? A combination of all those things?

He kept changing position, moving as much of the rest of his body as he could to compensate for the immobility of the leg held rigidly in its cast.

As he lay there, he seemed to be floating in some in-between state. He wasn't asleep, but he couldn't be sure he was really awake. It was an odd sensation, and it began to bother him. A few minutes more and he'd had enough. So he swung himself over to his desk, pulled up a stool for his leg, and sat down at the computer.

He logged on and searched for "Aristotle". This produced literally millions of results, so he typed in "Alexander" to refine his search, and began surfing the boundless ocean of the Internet.

There were still thousands of results. He dipped into a few, but they were not what he was looking for. Scrolling down, he found a site headed "Aristotle and Alexander the Great". Which told him that Philip had chosen Aristotle to be his son's teacher, how old the boy was at the time, what the political situation in Macedonia was in those days, and a lot of other stuff that, again, was not what he wanted to know. What he was trying to find out was what *sort* of boy Alexander of Macedonia was when Aristotle came into his life, and whether Aristotle's teaching had changed Alexander's character and personality.

All the searching was making him feel queerer than ever, and by this time it was getting on for three in the morning. He was just about to log off when suddenly a bust of Aristotle appeared on the screen, although he couldn't remember calling it up.

He recognised it immediately. It was exactly the same as the one he saw every day, sitting on the top shelf of his bookcase, a copy of the portrait bust of Aristotle in the Museum of Art History in Vienna, made by modern Greek sculptor Paul Vrellis, the man who created the Wax Museum in Ioannina.

Suddenly, the marble head of Aristotle on the screen began to soften and take on the look of a living person. Alexander sat like a statue himself as the philosopher emerged from the image of his marble effigy. Sat awestruck, for there before him was one of the greatest intellects of all time. He rubbed his eyes, shifted position, even pinched himself to make sure he was awake. But the image was still there on the screen before him. Aristotle, alive and … speaking to him in a soft, sweet voice!

"What are you looking for, lad? I've been watching you search for hours. Is there something I can help you with?"

As if this conversation was the most natural thing in the world, he answered:

—I'm curious about Alexander the Great, sir. He achieved so much, and you were his principal teacher. I'd like to know what went into the making of the extraordinary phenomenon that we call Alexander the Great. From what I know, it was you and your teaching that moulded his character. Was it also you who gave him the idea of conquering the world? Was it you who taught him how to rule his kingdom?

Let's see if I can paint a picture for you. I'll tell you what I can about his life and work, focusing on details that illustrate his character and personality —that's the sort of thing you want from me, isn't it? But let's start with his physical appearance.

ALEXANDER THE GREAT IN HIS YOUTH

Alexander was a handsome lad, with a head of thick, curly, blond hair that fell to his shoulders like a lion's mane. His skin was fair and his eyes were blue. He had a strong face and a haughty gaze. He looked, actually, like a cross between Hermes and Apollo. He was always clean-shaven, a fashion that —perhaps because of him— most men followed for centuries afterwards. He had the well-knit body of an athlete, and he carried his head cocked slightly to the left —a trick that many of his friends tried to imitate.

He was endowed with many natural gifts, among them courage, nobility, and a keen intelligence. And he knew to how to listen to people. Open-minded, you would call him today.

His skill, courage and intelligence were obvious from a very early age. This was evident in things like the way he handled Bucephalus, a horse no one else had been able to tame. A number of experienced and battle-hardened warriors from his father's court had tried to break the animal in, but each one had eventually given up.

Alexander, however, had noticed that Bucephalus became nervous every time he caught sight of his shadow. He realised that if he kept the horse facing the sun, his shadow would fall behind him, and what he could not see could not spook him. So that is what he did, and having soothed the frightened animal was able to mount and ride him. He was just twelve years old. That was only the first of many episodes suggesting that he was destined for great things.

When King Philip was away on campaign, he left Alexander in Pella as regent. And he served his father very competently. On one such occasion, when he was sixteen, he received an embassy from Darius, the great king of Persia. The Persian officials were struck by the kind of questions he asked them. He wanted to know about where the king placed himself in battle, about the organisation of the army, about communications, about methods of governing, and in general about matters of strategic importance. The Persians were so impressed with Alexander that upon leaving they observed that he was already a gifted king, whereas their own master was merely a wealthy one.

That same year, when he was still only sixteen, Alexander as regent had to suppress an uprising in Thrace. This he did, and sealed his accomplishment by founding a city with a mixed population of Macedonians and barbarians.

THE LEAGUE OF CORINTH

When Philip was assassinated in the autumn of 336 BC and Alexander ascended the throne of Macedonia, he was already a seasoned ruler in the eyes of his subjects. The southern Greeks, who initially thought little of him, were soon forced to acknowledge his military, political and administrative abilities.

He summoned an assembly of the Greek League at Corinth, which duly appointed him its head, in his father's stead, and made him supreme commander of the united Greek army that was gathering to march against the Persians. The city, Plutarch tells us, received Alexander with great pomp and ceremony, while important politicians and renowned philosophers hastened to greet him.

The only Greeks who did not join the expedition were the Spartans; and while Alexander imposed no penalty on them, he made sure that all sacrifices were done and all votive offerings made in the name of all the Greeks except the Spartans.

—*What was this League of Corinth?*

That is a long story, but I will try to tell it briefly. The commonest political formation in Ancient Greece was the city-state. Two of the most important ones were Athens and Sparta, which were constitutionally hostile towards one another. While Alexander was still a boy, a number of prominent Greeks, including Isocrates, one of the most famous Attic orators, had become very worried about this situation, because things had degenerated to the point where Athens and Sparta were making war on each other rather than against the common enemy, Persia. Persia had already seized the most important Greek cities in Ionia, and its armies were laying waste everything in their path.

Many Greeks thought that, in the face of this common enemy, all the Greek cities should unite in an alliance under a single king, who would lead an expedition into Asia.

This would be a difficult undertaking, but not impossible. It had seemed that having Philip of Macedon plan and lead the campaign was the solution to the problems. Although the southern Greeks considered the Macedonians to be little better than barbarians, Philip's strong personality, and the fact that Macedonia was a kingdom, not a city-state, made it easier for them to accept him as leader of the expedition against the Persians.

That is something to remember: Philip's Macedonia was the first nation-state in European history.

PHILIP II OF MACEDONIA

By the age of fifteen Philip had spent three years as a hostage in Thebes, one of the leading political and cultural centres of the age. Those years made him thoroughly familiar with Greek culture and the Greek mentality, and when he inherited the throne of Macedonia he adapted his country to the cultural model of the Greek cities.

In another decisive move, he used the gold of Mount Pangaeum to create a professional army of select warriors, including the famous Macedonian phalanx of foot-guards, while the ranks of the infantry were filled with well-trained men from the class of farmers and stock-herders. The cavalry came from the higher social classes, and were known as the "Companions".

Those gold mines also allowed Philip to purchase support in various Greek cities.

When Philip captured a city or region, he did not make

it a colony but absorbed it into his kingdom. In 357 BC he sought to do this with Amphipolis and other Athenian colonies. Athens objected, declared war on him, and lost —a defeat that cost her the support of a number of her allies.

Meanwhile, the Greeks had engaged upon a Sacred War to liberate Delphi, with its oracle of Apollo and its store of treasure, from the Phocians.

THE SACRED WAR

In Ancient Greece wars waged for religious reasons, or on religious pretexts, were described as sacred wars.

With the treasure plundered from Delphi the Phocian general was able to hire a sizeable mercenary army, which he then used to conquer Locris, Boeotia and part of Thessaly.

This so offended public opinion that all the Greek cities, including Athens and Sparta, were united in condemning such conduct. The Thebans were the first to declare a sacred war against Phocis, and almost all the Greek city-states joined in. But it was Philip's intervention that finally brought about the Phocian defeat.

This, of course, added to his fame; and that worried the Athenians, who saw him as a threat to their primacy. The famous Athenian orator Demosthenes, a young man in those days, made a series of fiery speeches warning against the dangers - for Athens - of Macedonian imperialism; these speeches were known as *Philippics*.

Two years later, Philip began to seize other Athenian colonies. Soon he was the undisputed master of all the territory from the Hellespont to Thermopylae, and controlled a number of cities farther south through political appointees.

In the face of this new reality the Athenians sent a distinguished politician called Philocrates to conclude a peace treaty with Philip and to seek a new defensive alliance. The Phocians were forced to restore what they had stolen from Delphi and were excluded from the Delphic Amphictyony; their two votes were transferred to Philip. This made Philip an official player in Greek affairs, and recognised him as Greek. More than that, as the defender of Delphi he was considered, and in some way had become, the regulator of Greek affairs.

What was an amphictyony, you ask? It was an association of neighbouring states formed around a religious centre, usually for religious purposes.

After all this, Philip decided that the time had come to lead a great expedition against the Persians, in which all the Greeks would take arms against their common enemy. First, however, he wanted the Athenians to approve his plan. Why? Partly because Athens was the heart and soul of Greece, but mostly because it had a powerful navy, which Macedonia did not.

Once again, however the Athenians reacted negatively, for they felt that they were losing their autonomy. The first thing they did was to exile Philocrates, a realist who had agreed that Philip should lead the expedition. The second was to accuse Aeschines, who was of the same opinion (and a bitter political opponent of Demosthenes), of having been bribed by the Macedonians with a gift of lands at Olynthus. But it was no use: most of the Greeks had already accepted Philip as their leader.

Seeing that matters had come to a head, the Athenians allied themselves with Thebes, confronted Philip at the famous Battle of Chaeronea, and were soundly defeated.

Philip left a Macedonian garrison in Thebes, but took no measures against Athens. Respecting its history and prominence, he even left it its colonies in Samos, Lemnos and Delos.

Immediately after this, Philip began organising his campaign against the Persians. In 338 BC he summoned the representatives of all the cities in Greece to a meeting and founded the League of Corinth. The assembly duly voted to wage war against the Persians with Philip in command.

But while everything was going so well for Philip on the broader political stage, back home in his capital of Pella people were plotting against him. One of them, apparently, was Alexander's mother, Olympias, who, jealous of Philip's younger wives, is suspected of arranging to have him killed.

The assassination took place at the palace in Pella on the day of his daughter's wedding to Alexander of Epirus, before the eyes of the assembled guests and of their son, Alexander. That is how our Alexander came to be proclaimed the head of the League of Corinth and the leader of the expedition against the Persians. He was then just twenty years old.

—*What exactly was a city-state, in Ancient Greece?*

THE CITY-STATE

The city-state was a sort of partnership,[1] a cooperative social organisation in which people lived together in order to pursue the supreme good, which is the satisfaction of their spiritual needs.

Within the framework of that society children had a natural obligation to submit to their parents and wives to their husbands, although within the household the women were in charge. The men formed the political community. Political action was the privilege and the obligation of the men in the city, and it was a serious matter, since their activities spanned a great many areas and required a wide range of general and specialised knowledge.

Democracy in Ancient Greece was direct, meaning that every citizen was obliged to take part in the work of the council, which deliberated on civic matters, and could also be required to act as a judge. As you can see, this meant that people had to have a good general education[2] and be well informed in many different areas in order to be able to assume their responsibilities as members of the community. To me, a *polity*, a civic state is unworthy of the name *polis* (=city) if its citizens are not able to take part in public discussions, where opinions often conflict. For these discussions sharpen people's minds and in some sense make them intellectually self-sufficient.[3] Absolute self-sufficiency is, of course, only for the gods,[4] while the lower animals can be materially self-sufficient.

Intellectual development requires the stimulation of political fellowship, for even a man perfectly formed in mind and body becomes worse than a beast when he is cut off from his fellows, from the city, from law and justice.[5]

Let me add here that children who live in semi-savage tribal groups in the jungle do not know how to speak or think; but if they are removed and placed with a family in society they adapt, they develop normally, and sometimes achieve great things.

For me, the *polis* is the ideal social partnership, the place where man can best attain happiness, the supreme good of "living-well", which is a life that is self-sufficient in intellectual as well as in material goods[6.7]. Very small cities cannot meet all the needs of those who live in them.

Another equally essential condition for the proper functioning of the city-as-institution is the existence of an authority to organise and regulate the relations between the social entities that co-exist within it.

In other words, the creation of the city is a natural necessity for man, for he is by nature a political animal[8.9], suited to living in societies.

—*Would men not be happier living alone and independent, living freely in a natural environment, and not subject to the forced discipline imposed by the laws on those who live in cities?*

No, quite the opposite, I think. Man is by nature a pairing creature.[10] He cannot live alone. The union of man and woman, which is a natural imperative, may be said to be the germ of the fundamental social unit, which is the family.

HUMAN PARTNERSHIP

The union of male and female occurs primarily for the continuance of the species.[11] This does not, of course, mean that it serves no other purpose. Human beings live together not only for the sake of reproduction, but also for the satisfaction of the various purposes of life. The proof of this is that whereas animals remain together only for as long as required for generative act,[12] human couples live together for years.

Another thing that makes man different from the animals is the capacity to express his thoughts and feelings[13]. Man alone possesses reason and speech, which in Ancient Greece were considered two sides of the same coin and expressed by the same word, *logos*. And because nature does nothing without purpose, man is endowed with the gift of speech so that he can communicate with his fellow men.

Communication, however, presupposes the existence of a community. It is only within society that man can achieve his fullest development, mental and spiritual, and fulfil his mission. It is then that he truly becomes a man. He cannot fulfil his true potential within the narrow confines of the family circle, because it limits the development of his mental and moral capacities. These can only be developed in civic society, within the framework of the city[14]. That is, without civic fellowship man remains incomplete.

Another thing that develops within society is friendship, which I consider a very important *good* for man, because it makes him happy. Friendship simplifies the problems that arise out of community living.

People desire to live together even when they have no immediate need of one another, but in most cases they do so from a common interest, because it allows them to help one another. Helping one another makes everyone's life better, and this creates social cohesion[15]. The communal life of a city is based on reciprocity: that is, we return the services that are rendered to us. Man is a social being, and thus it may be said that it is in his nature to create communities, and by extension civic polities[16]. I have said it before and I will say it again: man is a political animal[17]. And I definitely do not agree with the Cynics, and some of the Sophists, who say that societies and civic polities are legal constructs, to which man is constitutionally unsuited and which are harmful to him rather than beneficial. Nor do I agree that societies exist solely because men expect some immediate or long-term benefit from them.

Why do you say that man is the only "political animal", which seems to mean social animal? What about bees and other animals that live in colonies, where they communicate with one another, help one another and protect one another?

The big difference between men and animals is, as I have said, that man has the gift of speech and reason[18]. The sounds animals make to express pain or pleasure or to transmit some vocal message, which is usually concerned with their survival, are something quite different from human speech, which is vocalised thought. Human speech can express thoughts about what is good, what is bad, what is right and what is wrong[19]: That is, men can express opinions about things that concern the life of the community. Justice, for instance.

So, tell me please, what is justice and how did it operate in Ancient Greece?

JUSTICE IN ANCIENT GREECE

Justice is a social necessity. It is the guarantor of the communal life of the city. The concept of justice has no meaning outside the social partnership. Justice is always meted out on the basis of the rule of law, which presupposes knowledge of what is just and what is unjust.

Living in a community brings about changes in people's relations with one another. But which of these changes are beneficial and which are not? Which are just and which are unjust? The answers to these questions are a matter of rules and common consent. A matter of law. What is considered just in one place may be unjust somewhere else[20], just as different places use different units of measurement.

We must remember that any law, no matter how perfect, is inherently defective in that it is over-general. It is cold and austere, and does not enter into the specific conditions in which an offence was committed. That is why there are two views about how justice should be administered. One is that it should be administered by worthy, experienced judges who can understand the particularity of each case. The other is that justice should be administered by a collective body through a process of debate, from which a just result would eventually emerge, for each member of that collective body would have his own experience of life and thus be able to grasp different details of the dispute, and so the decision would be more correct. Which is why in your court system you have jurors.

With a collective body the impact of extreme situations, emotional appeals and simple indifference is moderated by the opinion of the many. The most suitable place for such deliberations is the assembly of citizens, where discussion of the arguments for both sides will lead in the end to the correct opinion.

One peculiarity of Ancient Greece regarding the rights of citizens was the practice of ostracism. This was a process by which a person could be banished for a period of five or ten years, if six thousand citizens voted for that. The voting was conducted by secret ballot, which meant that people you considered as friends could vote to have you ostracised, as happened to Aristides the Just. Ostracism was supposedly instituted to protect the people, the citizens as a body, from the arbitrary actions of a person in a position of power.

And while we're on the subject of justice, let me point out that advocacy is a Greek invention.

THE SOPHISTS

Up until the time of Pericles, accused persons had no one to speak for them in court; there were no professional advocates. They had to do the best they could on their own. But since the judges were ordinary citizens, and not trained jurists, they were more easily swayed by grandiloquent speeches than by real argument. So, as you can see, a person who could not speak persuasively was at a definite disadvantage.

The first person to see a business opportunity here was a

man called Antiphon, an Athenian who had been banished to Corinth. He had the idea of writing speeches for litigants, for a fee, of course; and he did it very well.

Those who, like Antiphon, wrote speeches for litigants to deliver before the courts were called speechwriters, and the service they provided was eventually officially recognised as a profession. Those who undertook to speak on behalf of another in court were called Sophists.

Because the Sophists charged a fee for their services, they were held to be selling the products of their mind and were despised by other philosophers, who considered them as men of no principle, who did not believe in truth and acted purely for gain[21].

Their services, however, were much in demand, and some of the Sophists became both wealthy and famous. Many of them became professional teachers and attracted many students. Their "schools", though, were nothing like the philosophers' schools, for, while they did teach their students many things, their sole objective was to make money, whereas the true philosophers had certain ideals and were devoted to the pursuit of truth.

Protagoras was the first to charge a fee for delivering a course of lectures, a practice that had adverse repercussions for him. But there were others who thought as he did. Philostratus, for example, said that the Sophists were right to take money, because all goods are bought and sold, and besides, everyone knows that we prize more what we pay for than what we get for free[22].

—If you ask me, Aristotle, I think Philostratus was right.

The spirit in which the Sophists wrote their speeches is well illustrated by the following story, which they tell of Protagoras.

One of his students refused to pay for his lessons, saying that he would pay when he won his first case in the courts. Protagoras agreed, adding that he was therefore certain of his fee: "I will collect my fee in any case," he said, "for I will sue you for it, and you will defend yourself. If you win, you will pay my fee because that is the agreement we have made; and if you lose, you will pay it because the court will order you to".

—*You mentioned earlier that the Cynics were anti-social. I have heard some weird stories about Diogenes, the best known of them. Were those guys serious? Were they really philosophers?*

Most of the Cynics were students of Socrates and pursued the supreme good, which for them was personal freedom. They believed that in order to be free, you had to reduce your needs to the minimum. You had to be self-sufficient and not in thrall to bodily or emotional needs —hunger, thirst, heat, cold, solitude, sexual appetites, money, fame, power. One might call them Socratic extremists.

THE CYNICS

The Cynics' thinking was based on two main precepts: detachment from any kind of dependency, and an aversion to work of any kind. It is true that their behaviour was often unconventional. The Cynic School was founded by Antisthenes[23], who was born in Athens in 446 BC. One explanation for its name derives it from the adjective *cynikos* (= 'like a dog'), a nickname given to Antisthenes because he was always wandering apparently aimlessly around the streets. The other is that Antisthenes lectured at the Cynosarges gymnasium, southeast of Athens. Antisthenes is famous for having said "I am happy because I sleep, I eat, I drink, I do what I want, and all the world is mine." Another of his sayings was that "no one who loves money can be good." That he liked his comforts is clear from a story told about him and his fellow Cynic, Diogenes. One day when Antisthenes was ill and in great pain, his friend Diogenes came to visit him. When he saw him, he groaned, "Ah, Diogenes, who will relieve me of this terrible pain?" But when Diogenes responded by offering him a sword, he snapped, "I said, who will relieve me of this pain, not of this life".

Antisthenes was the first Cynic, but Diogenes, who was

his pupil, is the best known. He was born in 404 BC in Sinope, a city on the south coast of the Black Sea. He lived in a barrel, and wandered around holding up a lighted lantern, even in broad daylight, saying that he was searching for an honest man. He lived on practically nothing, and wore the same clothes winter and summer.

Whenever he felt sexual desire he masturbated, wherever he happened to be, even when other people were around. If anyone protested, he would answer by saying, "I'll jack off when and where I like — I just wish I could satisfy my hunger by rubbing my belly". Plato called him a mad Socrates.

Diogenes could also be very sarcastic. One day, when he was watching a not very talented archer practising, he went and sat right beside the target. When asked why, he said that it appeared to be the safest place.

The only philosophical subject that interested the Cynics was ethics.

As I think I mentioned, another off-shoot of the Socratics were the Cyrenaics. (Their name comes from Cyrene, in North Africa, the city where their founder, Aristippus, was born.)

THE CYRENAICS

The Cyrenaics' approach to what is good was totally different from that of the Cynics.

You find that odd? You shouldn't, for it is no more unusual than to see two good men, children of the same parents, with totally different views on how to live their lives.

The philosophical difference between the Cynics and the Cyrenaics is illustrated by the following story[24]:

Aristippus was a cheerful man and not at all worldly. One day he found Diogenes, the Cynic, washing radish leaves in a fountain. Remarking the smirk on the other's face Diogenes said to him, "If you had learnt to eat these, you would not have needed to kowtow to tyrants". To which Aristippus replied, "And you would not be obliged to eat them, had you known how to behave among men."[25] As I said, two totally different choices of lifestyle.

In order to enjoy a comfortable life, Aristippus charged his pupils steep fees for the lessons he gave them. Once, when the father of one of his students complained about the cost, adding that for the same sum he could buy a slave, Aristippus replied, "Well, then, buy one, and you will have a pair"[26]. Aristippus spent lavishly on his pleasures and comforts. When he was reproached him for this he answered, "Better for the money to be wanting on account of Aristippus than Aristippus on account of the money".

Aristippus travelled a great deal. He wrote many dialogues and accounts of his travels. His philosophy can be summed up as "Live every moment, for it is soon gone." Live for the present. He also said that "Pleasure is like a gentle breeze, pain a storm, and everyday existence a flat calm". There can be no doubt as to which of the three conditions Aristippus preferred.

The Cyrenaics believed that pleasure is something to be pursued and enjoyed, as long as you do not become a slave to it. You always have to be able to walk away. When Aristippus was criticised for visiting the house of the famous courtesan Laïs too frequently, he remarked that "the shame does not lie in the entering of her house, but in the not being able to leave it." That is, you have to be able to control your actions and your desires and not overstep the line.

— *What made the Cynics despise society so? Can you tell me something about the organisation of society in Ancient Greece?*

I have already mentioned a few things, but since you want more, I will try to give you a concise outline.

THE STRUCTURE OF SOCIETY IN ANCIENT GREECE

There were three classes in Ancient Greek society: the rich, the poor, and those in between.

The people in the middle class were the most reasonable and the most self-controlled, while the very rich and the very poor were much less disciplined. The poor frequently became insolent and cunning and prone to petty wickedness, the rich arrogant and prone to wickedness on a much grander scale. Moreover, people who have great power and many possessions are often unwilling to be governed, for they have never had to. Such people were spoiled as children, and never learned to submit to authority, even in school. On the other hand, those who have next to nothing tend to commit petty offences, feel oppressed, bow their heads to tyranny, and behave in a servile manner towards those who exercise the power of a tyrant over them.

If everyone belonged to one or the other of those two classes, then we would have societies of tyrants and slaves. There would be no free citizens. In such societies the poor would be envious and resentful and the rich contemptuous. That is, we would have a society inimical to friendliness and communication, which are values that need to exist among the members of a society if it is to prosper. Each would distrust the other, and —as I like to say— no one is even willing to walk in the same street as a man he mistrusts[27].

It is true that living in partnerships, living in communities, creates social problems. Social problems and political problems are, I think, interlinked. At this point I have to say that, whether we wanted it this way or not (and we probably did), Ancient Greek society included slaves, who in my view should have been treated better. Because mistreating those in an inferior position breeds plotting and hatred towards those who have more. There would always have been some hatred in the souls of the slaves, of course, simply because they were excluded from public life. That is why, in order to rule, the minority —and the free citizens in Ancient Greece were the minority— had to be stronger than the majority in their city. Sometimes, however, the minority imposes its views by force[28].

One more thing. I do not agree with Socrates' view, which you can read in Plato's *Republic*, that a state should be homogeneous. Because the composition of a state which is made up of citizens of differing capabilities, intellectual, financial, etc., is *de facto* pluralistic[29], and in such a society different opinions are heard and the decisions taken are thus more correct.

Nor do I believe that all things should be held in common, as Plato proposes. That is a utopia, because, as you may have noticed, people who own property jointly are more likely to quarrel than if each one had his own separate share.

—*You're right, I've seen it happen. But I want to get back to Alexander the Great now. What were his first actions as king of Macedonia and generalissimo of the Greek forces?*

THE FIRST ACTIONS OF ALEXANDER THE GREAT AS GENERALISSIMO OF THE GREEKS

After the assassination of Philip, Alexander assumed the overall command of the Greek forces. His first concern was to carry out the promise he had made to lead an expedition against the Persians. But he thought it wise, before setting out, to settle accounts with certain tribes that were in revolt on Macedonia's northern borders, so that he would be able to concentrate on the Asian campaign with a quiet mind. This operation took him as far as the Danube, but he successfully put down all the insurrections.

The Persians, meanwhile, had heard the news from their agents in Greece and were not sitting about twiddling their thumbs. While Alexander was busy suppressing the barbarian revolts, they were trying to buy allies among the Greeks and bribe Greek cities to drop out of the League of Corinth. Sparta, which was not a member of the League, accepted the Persians' gold. Athens, as a city, refused. But some Athenians felt differently: the famous orator, Demosthenes, for example, accepted a bribe of three hundred talents to stir up opinion against the Macedonians. It is said that he went so far as to produce a "witness" who said that Alexander was dead and that he had seen the body. Some of the larger Greek cities welcomed this news with a sigh of relief. They were not very happy with the alliance, for the fact that all cities had equal rights worked to the advantage of the smaller ones.

In Thebes, the news of Alexander's supposed death sparked a revolt, which the powerful anti-Macedonian interests in Athens were happy to supply with arms. The anti-Macedonian faction in Thebes joined forces with the returned exiles and laid siege to the Cadmea, the Theban citadel, and killed two officers of the Macedonian garrison stationed there. Meanwhile, anti-Macedonian sentiment began to surface in other cities as well, and several of them began preparing to support Thebes.

Alexander the Great heard what was happening and his response was immediate: just two weeks later he was camped outside the walls of Thebes. His sudden appearance not only took the Thebans by surprise, it terrified them. The young king did not attack at once, but gave them an opportunity to reconsider their attitude and stop the revolt. He even offered an amnesty to the ringleaders. Unfortunately, however, the fanatics won the day and the Thebans launched an attack, killing several of the soldiers in the Macedonian outposts. Even then, Alexander waited a few more days. But it was becoming obvious that a battle was inevitable.

Arrian tells us that when the attack began it was not by Alexander's order. The command was given by his general Perdiccas, following a minor skirmish with the Thebans.

THE DESTRUCTION OF THEBES

The taking of Thebes was followed by looting, burning and massacre. Leading the sack of the once powerful city were the Phocians, the Plataeans and the Boeotians, who had suffered greatly at the hands of the Thebans and hated them bitterly. That, in fact, was their chief reason for joining Alexander's army.

It is true that Alexander consented to the destruction of Thebes, the reason being that he was not prepared to suffer defections on the eve of his campaign against the Persians and he wanted everyone to know it. That did not prevent him, though, from regretting the necessity of laying waste such an ancient and glorious city, and he made sure that the temples, the house of the poet Pindar and other historic monuments were not touched. It is also a measure of his regret that from then on he treated the Thebans with great courtesy and clemency.

Plutarch recounts an instance of this. In the general affray, the commander of the Thracian contingent in Alexander's army broke into the house of a woman called Timoclea, seeking plunder. Finding nothing, he demanded roughly that she show him where she had hidden her gold. She told him it was in the well. When he leaned over to look, she pushed him in and threw stones down on top of him, killing him. She was immediately seized by Thracian soldiers and taken to Alexander. Seeing her proud demeanour, he asked her who she was. Timoclea answered, "I am the sister of Theagenes, who did battle with your father at Chaeronea". To the astonishment of all those watching the scene, he ordered no punishment, but let her go free. The other cities that had joined in the revolt were treated leniently, and granted an amnesty.

After this most competent suppression of the insurrection, the Athenians sent an embassy to Alexander offering congratulations and presenting him with an honorific decree. This he regarded as a servile gesture, and was disgusted rather than pleased.

Word of Alexander's feats quickly spread throughout the known world. A certain legend began to be attached to his name. People began to remember the tradition that he was descended from Heracles and Achilles, and that he was Greek by birthright, since the Macedonians came from the Dorian tribe.

A story also began to circulate that on the night of his birth (July 20, 356 BC) the Temple of Artemis at Ephesus burned to the ground. The priests bewailed this loss, and wondered aloud how the goddess could have permitted such a thing to happen. The explanation offered by a prophet called Hegesias, from Magnesia, was that she must have been otherwise occupied that evening, "bringing Alexander the Great into the world" — implying, in other words, that she was his mother.

— How did Philip happen to choose you to be Alexander's teacher? And where did you have your lessons, and what were they like?

THE CHOICE OF ARISTOTLE
AS ALEXANDER THE GREAT'S TEACHER

First of all, I was not his only teacher. Before me he had been tutored by a man from Epirus, called Leonidas; he had been chosen by Alexander's mother, Olympias, who as I have told you was a stern and autocratic princess of that land. And there were others as well, whose instruction had to do mainly with self-discipline and physical endurance.

Philip, however, believed that his son needed a different kind of schooling as well as hard physical training, an education that would equip him mentally for the future he envisioned for him. He needed a teacher who would broaden his mind and initiate him into the art of politics, rhetoric and persuasion, skills that were essential for a successful leader.

It happened that just around that time I found myself obliged to leave Athens and the Academy where I had been teaching. Plato was gone, and the climate in Athens was no longer friendly towards me. The Athenians didn't like Macedonians on principle, and I was Macedonian by birth. So I left and went to Assus, on the Trojan coast, opposite the island of Lesvos. There I met Hermias, who later became the tyrant of Atarnea. Hermias was on very good terms with Philip, and had often supported his policies. He recommended me to Philip, who invited me to his court (in 343 BC) and asked me to take over the education of his son, who was then thirteen years old. Of course, I was not a complete unknown. On the contrary, I was famous throughout the civilised world. Moreover, my father had been the court physician during the reign of Philip's father, Amyntas III. In the final analysis, though, I was a Macedonian with an Athenian education, and I think that both those things weighed in my favour when it came to choosing a teacher for his son.

And so I found myself engaged to teach the young Alexander and the sons of other Macedonian noblemen and neighbouring princelings. Those boys became Alexander's friends. Closest of all was Hephaestion, his alter ego, with whom he made plans for the future they both dreamed about. And they remained inseparable, until death finally parted them.

THE SCHOOL AT MIEZA

Following Philip's instructions, we took up residence in a country house in the Nymphs' Grove at Mieza, ten kilometres from Pella; for he wanted to remove his son from the pernicious influence of the boy's autocratic mother.

We read a lot of Homer. This was in part because I was engaged with my own studies of his work at that time, for that was when I wrote my Homeric Questions, of which only fragments now survive. Mainly, however, it was because the Iliad and the Odyssey are incomparable works; more than that, they are eternal, enduring, ageless, points of reference standing outside time.

I tried to give my select band of pupils a good general education, emphasising politics and civics rather than philosophy. For I disagree with my own teacher, Plato, who said that unless we are governed by philosophers or by rulers with a philosophical education there will always be unhappiness in our cities and our world. In my view, it is neither necessary nor wise to have a king whose main study is philosophy. A king should, rather, have counsellors who are philosophers, to whom he should listen and whose opinion he should always be ready to seek.

I also instilled into Alexander the need for virtue, practical wisdom and moderation, with particular emphasis on moderation, since his mother, Olympias, had such entirely different views. Those were the qualities I considered indispensable for a ruler.

These lessons, which I later incorporated into my *Nicomachean Ethics*, really touched a chord with my illustrious pupil. They were of immense help to him, and perhaps inspired him to make his Asian expedition a civilising mission. He always carried with him his copy of the *Iliad*, with my handwritten commentaries. Alexander also studied the works of Thucydides, Herodotus and Xenophon — in fact, the *Anabasis* can be considered a foretaste of his own expedition.

Much of what he knew about the art of war he learned, of course, at his father's side. You may remember that at the Battle of Chaeronea Philip had given him the command of a select corps of two thousand cavalry, and that with them he defeated the Sacred Band of Thebes. In the Grove of the Nymphs I also instructed Alexander in the natural sciences: physics, geography, botany, medicine, and so on. His mysticism and impetuousness were inherited from his mother.

—*How much do you think Alexander the Great was influenced by your teaching?*

I think, a great deal. This is apparent not only from his deeds and actions, but also from his confession that he loved me more than his father because, as he said, he was indebted to his father for living but to his teacher for living well —that is, for his intellectual life.

A CULTURED COMMANDER

Alexander has been described as a cultured commander, and I think that is justified, if only for his action at Thebes; you will remember that he ordered the whole city destroyed, except for the temples and the house of Pindar, the poet revered throughout Greece. He also rebuilt my home town of Stagira, which his father had levelled.

I am of the opinion that his thinking was substantially influenced by my lessons on kingship, which is the subject of one of my books. Indeed, they say that if a day passed in which he had not done someone a good deed he lamented that "today I have not acted like a king".

His favourite reading was the *Iliad* and his favourite hero, Achilles. He was particularly struck by Homer's praise of Agamemnon as "a good king and a doughty warrior, too". I instilled a love of reading in him, and while on his campaign he had me send him the tragedies of Aeschylus, Sophocles and Euripides.

He took an active interest in an extraordinary number of things for a military commander. He drew up a plan for draining Lake Copais, something that was eventually done roughly twenty-five hundred years later. He sought ways to exploit the mineral wealth of the Indies. He was interested in designing and building cities, shipyards and temples.

The education he received from me is also reflected in the fact that his campaign staff included experts in many scientific and technical fields, including engineers, architects, town planners and bridge-builders, as well as a team of famous physicians, for Alexander attached great importance to providing medical care for his soldiers. There were also naturalists, to study and describe the plants, animals and products of each country they passed through, who had orders were to send accounts of their observations and conclusions to me. I have calculated that his dedication to my research must have cost him, directly and indirectly, about eight hundred talents.

—*That is an enormous amount. Do you think Alexander's support for your research in biology was money well spent?*

I shall tell you what was accomplished with that money, and you can judge for yourself.

ARISTOTLE'S RESEARCH IN BIOLOGY

From the material that he had arranged to have sent to me, I wrote much of *Parts of animals, Progression of animals, Movement of animals,* and some of the *Parva Naturalia.*

I grew up in a medical family, which may explain my keen interest in biology. My contribution to that science is generally agreed to have been significant, a claim I cannot make for mathematics.

Many of your contemporary biologists consider my work groundbreaking —at least for my day[30]. In my work I describe five hundred species of animals, a remarkable number for the time. Of course, my treatment of them varies from case to case, from a simple mention of the creature to a detailed description derived from personal observation and from dissections I performed myself. It was my father who taught me the art of dissection, and I dissected at least fifty different species of animal, as well as the human embryo. I also drew material for the books I mentioned from shepherds, hunters and fishermen, particularly in Macedonia and Thrace. People I could meet and talk to in person.

I proved that whales are mammals[31], which the experts hesitated to accept until the 16th century of your era. I was the first to distinguish between bony and soft-bodied fishes[32]. I noted the appearance of the heart in the embryonic chick on the fourth day of incubation of the egg[33], and the existence of four chambers in the stomach of ruminants. I also recorded important characteristics of the fertilisation of cephalopods[34], and made observations on the development of the bee that still continue to astonish. Finally, my studies of the mammalian circulatory system are considered quite remarkable[35].

I was the first to attempt a systematic classification of animals, using a system of my own devising which, if I may say so, has proved very successful since, with minor modifications, it is still in use today.

First of all I distinguished two main categories of animals, vertebrates and invertebrates, which I described as animals with blood (the vertebrates) and animals without blood (the invertebrates); these initial groups have, of course, further subdivisions. I also distinguished a special category of creatures that seemed to me to be half animal, half plant: for example, the sponges. Finally, I ordered the classes of animals according to a natural scale based on how well developed their young are at birth.

One key factor in my classification system was body temperature, which is higher in red-blooded animals than in those with some other fluid in their veins.

I classified animals as oviparous (those that lay eggs, e.g. birds and reptiles) or viviparous (those that produce living young).

I also observed a peculiarity in the manner in which fishes lay their eggs; these do not have a hard shell, but are incubated within the fish's body and —for protection— remain there until the young have formed[36]. I was also the first to recognise the correspondence between the wings of birds and the fins of fishes, and similarly between feathers and scales[37].

I also noted that it is rare for an organ to serve more than one purpose[38], and that each animal has a single main organ of defence[39].

I further observed that there are living creatures that are bridges between one species and another, as is the case with certain tetrapods intermediate between animals and men[40].

Man I did not assign to any class of animal, for I consider human beings as something separate.

I observed that animals have two sorts of characteristics: the essential features that characterise a particular species, and the secondary characteristics that can vary from individual to individual of the same kind. The primary characteristics of the species are predetermined, and are not accidental but perform some basic function: for example, when we say that animals have eyes, that is an essential feature, because sight is indispensable to their survival, a *sine qua non*. What colour those eyes are is a secondary characteristic.

I observed that the life of living creatures has five aspects: reproduction, nutrition, development, and the capacities of sense and motion. I was particularly interested in the process and method of reproduction, although not to the exclusion of nutrition and development.

I came to the conclusion, which I explain in my writings, that in some creatures the reproductive process involves two parents and in others only one, as is the case with plants and certain animals. Plants, of course, have neither motor nor sensory capability[41], while animals have both.

In the case of reproduction involving two parents, I was curious to know what part each one played. After a series of observations I decided that the contribution of the male parent is not material, but that his seed[42] determines and transmits to the generative substance of the female certain characteristics that subsequently appear in their offspring. The female body in which the seed is housed has the same function as clothing: just as your body remains the same regardless of what you clothe it in, so the characteristics of a man's seed remain the same regardless of the woman he couples with. The value of a work of art depends chiefly on the creator, rather than on the various materials he uses[43]. The seed is the beginning and the creator of the offspring, the alpha and the omega of reproduction.

Although the seed is not the same as flesh and blood, it is from the seed that flesh and blood are formed[44]. The reverse also occurs: excess blood is converted into seed in the male, while the female, lacking sufficient heat for this process, retains it as blood and excretes it every month in menstruation. At least, so I thought.

Every part of the body is contained potentially in the seed: for example, the arm and the face of the new creature exist undifferentiated in the seed[45]. The male seed, in other words, is a very highly evolved product, and for that reason the male plays a more determinant role than the female in reproduction. The seed acts on the female fluids the way rennet curdles milk.

The seed ejaculated by the male is not incorporated into the resulting embryo[46], does not become part of the foetus thus generated, but is the spark that kindles its development.

Another question that intrigued me was whether all the parts of the animal to be born are present, preformed, in the embryo or whether some of them develop progressively, one after another –somewhat as a fishing net grows from an initial cluster of knots by the gradual addition of others.

From my observations I concluded that the organs do not exist preformed in the embryo, but exist potentially in some imperceptible sign. Nor do I agree that an embryonic organ can produce another, even in the most rudimentary form. If that were so, the second organ would have to be the same as the first, which is patently not the case. As you know, the different organs and tissues that are produced are very different from one another. Each organ is created integrally.

The first part of the body to be formed in the embryo is the heart, because that is what pumps the blood that sustains the animal through the blood vessels. The next part to be created is the alimentary system, which is needed as soon as the infant is separated from its mother[47]. Then come the sensory organs, and last of all the mind, the capacity for reasoning[48], which is what distinguishes man from the animals. Reason alone is not the result of a sequence of physiological processes. Reason, as I see it, is divinely imparted[49]; you will remember that in Ancient Greece the word *logos* meant both speech and reason.

I also observed that the generative organs appear later than the rest.

The question of heredity was another subject that fascinated me[50]. How are the characteristics of the parents passed on to their offspring? The characteristics of the offspring depend on the *impetus* furnished by each parent —this is what today you call chromosomes. The child will resemble the parent whose impetus is strongest. A child can, however, also resemble a grandparent or a more distant ancestor. If the impetus from each parent is of equal force, then the child will resemble neither of them. It is also possible for these driving forces to be so disordered and disturbed that the resulting child lacks some of the characteristics of the human species. Such progeny are described as monstrosities.

Nature always acts towards some end, and when I say nature in these cases I do not mean the whole set of natural beings that exist but the vital force, the generative force that exists in all living beings. Generally, I believe that nature does not endow an animal with any organ that is useless to that particular creature. For God and nature do nothing without purpose[51]. Of course, as a perfect and immutable being God does not intervene in nature out of some personal need, but out of immediate interest.

I admit that there are imperfections in nature. And one might well ask why, if nature can produce perfect beings, not all are perfectly made. Is it that somewhere the wrong orders are given? My opinion is that the orders given, whether by what we call nature or by what we call God, are always correct, but the result is sometimes flawed because the material is not quite right, so that certain organs are not perfectly formed[52].

Nature operates like a doctor or an engineer, who first shapes a mental image of what he wants to create or construct in its final, ideal form, and from there on all his actions are directed towards the realisation of that final object[53].

In biology, research does not progress from the formation of the embryo to the animal in its final form, but assumes the existing final characteristics and tries to explain how they came to be[54]. That is why I classify the natural sciences as practical and not theoretical, because in the theoretical sciences, such as mathematics, one works from a starting-point towards an unknown final result[55].

I totally disagree with Empedocles, who held that the backbone is made up of vertebrae because it broke into pieces under pressure from the position of the foetus in the womb[56]. I think, rather, that the vertebrae exist for a purpose: to provide flexibility.

Every part of the animal is designed to serve that animal. It is very rare for some feature of an animal not to have a purpose useful to the particular creature. Take, for instance, the shark, whose mouth is on the underside of its body, near the stomach. This makes it harder for the shark to catch its prey, because it must twist itself around. One might suggest that the purpose of this unusual arrangement is to protect the other species of fish from extermination. But is it not possible that nature designed the shark this way for its own sake, to prevent it from eating too much? [57]

I see a grimace on your face. Is your leg hurting? This accident will have shown you how valuable our legs are. And just think: they are neither our most useful part nor a distinctive human feature. Most animals have legs.

The hands are a far more peculiarly human feature. The hands are not merely tools, they are multi-purpose tools. Man uses his hands, in conjunction with his brain, most adroitly, and they give him an advantage over all the other animals.

There are some who think that certain animals have been more greatly favoured by nature than man, because they have been given coats of fur to keep them warm, teeth and nails for attack and defence, and hard hooves to protect their feet, whereas man needs clothes, weapons and shoes. I say, though, that because man has hands and a brain, he can make clothes for himself, and shoes, and weapons and tools for every purpose. What is more, he can change them for others, and is not obliged to sleep in them but can remove them whenever he wishes.

Nature gave man hands because he is able to make use of them. As I have often said, you don't give a flute to just anyone, but to a man who knows how to play it, for he can make proper use of it.

I admit that as far as biology goes I got a lot of things wrong. That may be due to the deficiencies of the means of observation at our disposal. We had no microscopes, no diagnostic tools. The fact remains, however, that my observations were new, original and groundbreaking, not only for the period but for centuries afterwards. All these things, as I said in the beginning, are contained in my books. So, what do you think? Was that money well spent?

—Every penny, I would say. You did such amazing work, and so much.

45

Let's get back, then, to Alexander and his expedition. As I told you, he took with him a large non-military staff, including poets and artists for the entertainment of his companions and the troops. There were also philosophers in the company, the best known being Callisthenes.

It was, in other words, perfectly clear that the point of this expedition was not glory, or prestige, or even vengeance, but that Alexander had higher objectives in mind when he planned this campaign.

—*What were his aims, in your view?*

ALEXANDER THE GREAT'S CULTURAL ASPIRATIONS

Close contact with the various peoples the Greek army encountered as it advanced through Asia made Alexander have second thoughts about some of Plato's opinions. These views, which to some extent at least I shared and which we had often discussed in Mieza, can be summed up in one short sentence: everyone who is not a Greek is a barbarian.

Over the course of this expedition, however, Alexander came to be of the opinion that what —if anything— distinguished the Greeks was their virtue, while what distinguished the "barbarians" was injustice. This opinion, which he did not conceal, helped temper the complacency of the Greeks in his army and keep in check their tendency to act on Plato's dictum.

In the final analysis, I think that what Alexander was trying to do was to bring all the nations of the lands he conquered into a single social, political and economic system. He wanted all people to feel themselves to be citizens of the world, a world without conflicting interests, in which social justice could exist. He believed in universality, not ethnic communities. His goal, in other words, was what you would call globalisation, but in its ideal form, in which all the peoples of the world would be partners rather than subjects. And he thought that he could achieve this by melding the mores and customs of the peoples through mixed marriages.

He encouraged his men to marry local women. During the course of the expedition more than ten thousand such intermarriages were made, and he himself married twice, both times choosing a noble bride. One of these was the daughter of Darius (Hephaestion married her sister). In all, eighty Macedonian officers married daughters of influential local noblemen. These weddings were celebrated with great pomp and ceremony, both to honour the event as conspicuously as possible but also as a way for Alexander to demonstrate his approval of such actions, which would lead to the homogenisation of the nations.

His efforts to globalise his empire were further aided by the common laws he instituted and the cities he founded along the great trade routes. There were more than seventy of these (according to Plutarch), and while their original purpose was to keep an eye on the conquered regions and facilitate communication, they developed into important commercial centres. Further steps towards globalisation were achieved with the introduction of a common currency and the incorporation of thirty thousand local youths into the Greek army, on the same terms as everyone else once they had been trained by Macedonian officers.

Although he respected the will of the peoples, as I have said, he regarded the Greek language, Greek customs and Greek law as the glue that would bind the peoples together, for he firmly believed in the superiority of Greek civilisation. That is why he kept his council of artists, poets, historians and philosophers with him throughout the campaign. The one area in which he refused to intervene was religion: let every nation worship its own gods.

His dream of universality, of globalisation if you like, was to be achieved through persuasion. Those whom he could not persuade, however, were left free to go their own way, to adhere to their own national customs. And while he believed that only a minority would ever be persuaded, he persisted, because he wanted to create at least a nucleus of the new way of life.

Alexander's attitude in this matter was highly approved by a number of writers. Plutarch, for example, said that the sight of those mixed marriages would have made him shout for joy and apostrophise Xerxes as a blockhead, a madman, an idiot, for having wasted so much time and energy on bridging the Hellespont. "This is how wise kings unite Europe and Asia! Not with beams, or pontoons, or soulless, unfeeling ties, but with the bonds of honest love, marriage, physical union and the mutual desire for children. That is what binds nations together".

— *Alexander the Great really had great ambitions, didn't he? I have read that throughout the expedition he never lost an opportunity to sacrifice to the gods, whether of the Greeks, the Egyptians or the Asians. Did he believe in all those gods, or was it just a matter of expediency? What did you teach him about religion?*

I will tell you what I believe about God, for that, naturally, formed the basis for our lessons on religion.

ARISTOTLE'S VIEWS ON GOD

I believe that the religious feeling that exists in man is the result of internal (mental) processes and external stimuli. That is, man's perception of the gods comes from a combination of the workings of his mind and his observation of natural phenomena.

When I say internal processes, I mean some chain of thought, something along the lines of: Where there is good, there is also better and where there is better there is also the best. That is true of all living creatures, including man. There are men who are very bad, bad, good, and very good. If we extend the scale, we reach the best, the perfect man, the deified man. That is, the proof of the existence of God is confirmed by logical reasoning[58].

Careful observation and study of natural phenomena, however, also lead to something metaphysical, to an immaterial being, to a spirit, to God. For example, observation of the movement of the stars or the sun can create religious sentiments, because spontaneously we ask ourselves, "Who has set them in their courses?"[59] What sets things in motion and keeps them in motion is the "unmoving mover", and that is what we call God. And since the movement of the planets is eternal, the cause that initiated that movement must also be eternal. Because, if we do not accept that there is something that sets everything in motion, then we have reached an impasse.

Some think that every planet has its own "unmoving mover", its own god, which keeps it in motion. But they are all coordinated by the prime mover, which is God[60]. The rest are secondary divinities, hierarchically inferior to God. Mind you, now, the existence of a lot of minor deities does not deny the singleness of the one God[61]. It is true that this is a question that I have often wrestled with: one God or many gods? I think that is obvious to anyone who reads my books. But when it comes right down to it, I believe that there is just one God. How can there be many gods, since God, as we have said, is not material and multiplicity is a material condition? My words are often misinterpreted, so I will say it again: I believe in the existence of one God[62]. I could see no point in denouncing the polytheistic beliefs of my fellow-countrymen, in undermining their religious sentiments. I respected their form of worship, just as I respected their mores and customs.

Worship is a spiritual necessity; in it we find happiness. When we enter a temple, we turn our thoughts inwards and are filled with reverence.

Mythology tells us that the ancient Greeks worshipped the twelve gods of Olympus. The father of all the gods was Zeus, who ran the whole show. The other gods each had their own particular mission: Demeter was the goddess of agriculture, Hephaestus the patron of craftsmen, Hermes of trade, and so on.

Mythology also tells us that the ancient Greeks gave their gods human form and human weaknesses, to make them less remote.

—That is something like what we believe in Greece today. We believe in one God, the Father Almighty, and in the saints, who we think of as having special duties: for example, St Nicholas is the patron and protector of sailors, and St Paraskevi protects our eyesight.

It is not at all the same thing! Your saints were human beings, ordinary mortals, who were sanctified by their exemplary lives and in many cases their martyrdom. They are in some sort an example for the rest of us. They have nothing in common with the gods of Olympus and their goings-on. Just bracketing them together is sacrilege, since the Greek gods made a habit of coming down to earth, in all sorts of strange disguises, to engage in most improper behaviour with mortal men and women.

WHAT IS GOD LIKE?

God, in my view, is unseen, a spirit. He is pure intellect. He is faceless, and we cannot depict him; we can only symbolise him. Far less can he be portrayed in human form and ascribed ordinary human actions[63].

I believe that God is entirely separate from anything material. God is self-sufficient, lacking nothing. If we conceive of God as lacking something, then he is dependent on that something, and therefore is not God. Nor has he any desires. He does not need our friendliness. He is blessed and happy. I do not think that we can feel friendship for God[64].

God is the creator of the world, and that is why he looks after it. Divine providence exists. God and the world are linked. And because God has absolute knowledge of himself, it goes without saying that he has absolute knowledge of the world. The creator of the world provides for his creation, but does not act.

God's relation with the world is like that of a general with his army. The most valuable quality in an army is discipline. Without discipline there is no army, but discipline exists because there is a general[65].

God is a sovereign power, but he does not use his power

arbitrarily; rather, he expresses the part of wisdom, which is the measure of our actions and our desires for the acquisition of goods. Excess and lack of measure are both impediments to the worship and understanding of God.

God tries to perfect his human creation, to make man as like him as possible. Of course, if that ever happened, if man ever reached his ideal state and became like God, then God would thereby have abolished himself. Like medicine, for example, which tries to improve people's health and eradicate illness. But if it achieved that goal, then it would no longer have any reason for existing. To simplify things, let us just say that God lays down the general lines. The details, the individual actions, belong to the human sphere and are man's responsibility.

I believe that we should never pay excessive reverence to any mortal, for reverence belongs to the gods alone[66]. Of course, it did happen to Alexander a few times. Some of the peoples he conquered treated him like a god.

As Plutarch says, although Alexander accepted the opinion of the Egyptian philosopher Psammon that there is only one king and that is God, who treats all mortals alike, deep down he believed that God looked with particular favour on the noblest and best of men, regarding them as peculiarly his own.

Alexander had strong religious feelings. He offered to rebuild, at his own expense, the Temple of Artemis in Ephesus, which had burned down on the day of his birth. All he asked in return was that his name be on the dedicatory plaque. The Ephesians refused. A similar offer made to the city of Priene, for the Temple of Athena Polias, was on the contrary accepted. Shortly before his death, he was making plans to build splendid new temples in Delos, Delphi, Dodoni and Dion.

—*Could you describe some incidents from his expedition that illustrate his character, his intentions and his beliefs?*

* * *

THE BEGINNING OF ALEXANDER
THE GREAT'S ASIAN EXPEDITION

The expedition set off in the spring of 334 BC, despite certain signs that were taken as bad omens: for example, the wooden statue of Orpheus began, they say, to sweat. While this was initially considered a negative sign, the seer Aristander of Telmessus had a different interpretation, namely that the expedition would be so glorious that the poets and musicians would have to labour greatly to do it justice in their songs and verses. The statue, I might add, was made of pine, and the resin in the wood softened with the warmth of spring, producing droplets that looked like beads of sweat.

Is that a smile I see on your face? Well, things haven't changed so much, have they? You still hear reports of statues and icons that shed tears and the people say it is a miracle and portends some catastrophe.

Orpheus was a legendary hero from Thrace, a poet with superhuman musical skills, whose name is associated with a number of sacred rites, the Orphic Mysteries.

Despite Orpheus' apparent distress, Alexander set off, at the age of twenty-two, to campaign against the Persians, leaving Antipater as regent in Macedonia, and charging him particularly to keep a sharp eye on his allies in other Greek cities. Antipater was a friend of mine, a follower and patron of the Peripatetics.

Alexander's army was made up of thirty thousand foot-soldiers and five thousand cavalry. It was impeccably organised, despite the limited resources available for such an enterprise. The initial purpose of the expedition, you will remember, was to punish the Persians for the destruction they wreaked during their invasions of Greece.

This was reason enough for the Greeks, who first acquiesced in his plans and in the end were persuaded to unite under his leadership. One of his objectives was to liberate the Greek cities of Asia Minor, which had been forced to pay heavy taxes to the Persians.

Wanting to stress the panhellenic character of the expedition and establish a parallel with the Trojan War, in which all the Greeks were united against the Asian foe, upon reaching Asia Minor Alexander made a detour to Troy where, in his dual capacity of generalissimo of the Greeks and king of Macedonia, he paid tribute to the memory of his favourite hero, Achilles, and the other champions of the *Iliad*.

This expedition against the Persians would eventually take him to the Nile, in Egypt, and deep into Asia, where he reached the banks of the Indus. And I can tell you now that it was the most glorious expedition in the history of the world. He marched with his incomparable army from victory to victory. And they were not easy victories: the armies he fought against were well-disciplined, battle-hardened troops, and what is more, they were far superior in number. He also had to deal with semi-savage tribes who fought in various unconventional ways. But as he advanced from triumph to triumph he was at the same time implementing his great vision of spreading the Greek spirit and Greek culture and creating a universal empire, thus laying the foundations for a whole new era.

— *How did Alexander the Great behave towards the peoples he conquered?*

In the Greek cities he freed, he re-established democracy, restored the economy, set in train a series of public works, and re-organised their administrations. Then he enrolled them in the League. He did not demand troops of them, and he lightened their tax burden. Their only obligation was to furnish a number of ships.

In the other cities he maintained the Persian satrap system, but installed Macedonian generals as satraps (local governors) and usually separated political, economic and military power. In the Greek cities that surrendered without giving battle, he left their old governor in place but replaced the military governor with a Macedonian officer. In everything he did, however, he held to the precept of *ne quid nimis*, nothing in excess.

In the barbarian city of Caria, which surrendered at his approach, he left the aging Queen Ada on the throne. She was so taken with the young Alexander that she offered to adopt him as her son. He willingly agreed, for this was another way of showing that he had not come to Asia Minor as a conqueror.

Darius was aware that Alexander had reached Asia, but was not particularly concerned. He left his satraps to deal with him, with their large and well-equipped armies.

THE FIRST GREAT BATTLES

Alexander's first great battle against the Persians was fought at the Granicus River, where he found an army four times the size of his own arrayed against him. Among them were five thousand Greek mercenaries led by Memnon, a clever and highly capable professional commander from Rhodes. Against all odds, Alexander won the battle, after a fierce fight in which he himself was saved from death by the timely intervention of his cavalry commander, Cleitus.

After this victory, he liberated many of the coastal cities of Asia Minor, including Miletus and Halicarnassus.

The most exciting battle of the campaign, however, and Alexander's real moment of triumph, came a few months later, when he found himself face to face with Darius himself. When the great king of Persia heard that Alexander was marching on his kingdom, he sent thousands of cavalry to the bank of the river Pinarus, in the narrow Issus plain, to stop him. Alexander, however, with a clever manoeuvre, managed to cross the river and confront the Persian troops directly. The army he faced was six times the size of his own, but the plain was small and Darius could make no effective use of his numerical advantage.

Before the battle, Alexander galloped his great horse Bucephalus up and down the Greek lines, encouraging his men. When the two armies were within bowshot of one another, he charged the splendid chariot carrying the Persian king,

The entire Persian royal guard rushed to protect him, but the furious Macedonian onrush overwhelmed them, and within minutes Darius was left surrounded by the bodies of dozens of his highest-ranking officers. The Greeks suffered losses as well, of course, and Alexander himself was wounded by a sword cut to the right thigh.

The Persian front collapsed. Afraid of being taken hostage, Darius turned away and galloped for the Euphrates, to put that great natural barrier between himself and Alexander. His chariot, left behind on the battlefield, was seized by the Greeks.

The spoils from this battle were enormous, and of colossal value. Darius' tent was huge, beautifully decorated and exquisitely perfumed. The tubs, basins and other utensils in his bathroom were made of gold, ornately worked. When Alexander saw all this opulence, he turned sadly to his companions and said, "This is how kings live." He must often have compared his own life with that of other kings, and would surely sometimes have felt envious.

After that great victory, the cities he came to as he continued towards the Phoenician coast surrendered to him one after the other. When he camped outside the great seaport of Tyre, a delegation arrived to declare its submission.

Alexander thanked them, and announced that he wished to enter the city to sacrifice to Heracles, from whom he was supposedly descended. Fearing that this was a pretext to occupy the city, the Tyrians refused and withdrew within the city walls.

Tyre was built on an island about six hundred metres from the shore and protected by strong stone walls of great height, and the Tyrians were confident that the Greeks could never take it. After all, had they not held out for thirteen years against the siege laid by Nebuchadnezzar, the king of Babylon?.

* * *

THE SIEGE OF TYRE

When the Macedonian generals saw Tyre, they realised that it must indeed be an impregnable fortress. They were greatly disappointed, but thought it useless to attempt a siege. Their spirits were raised, however, by two dreams that Alexander saw in his sleep. In one, he was visited by Heracles, who took him by the hand and led him into Tyre[67]. In the other, a satyr was mocking him from afar, and eluding him each time he tried to catch hold of him; in the end, however, after much chasing, the satyr yielded to his coaxing. The seers pounced on the word satyr (*satyros*) and interpreted it as meaning that "Tyre [*tyros*] will be yours [*sa*]"!

These dreams, coupled with his conviction that he should not simply bypass Tyre and advance into the Asian interior, leaving it like a thorn in the side of his expedition, persuaded him to give the signal for attack. In this battle the organisation and the sheer potential of his army came into full play. Beneath the storm of arrows and the hail of stones and burning sand that the Tyrians rained down on them from the walls, the Greeks built a pier from which their siege engines could approach the fortress wall.

The Tyrians, however, filled a boat with wood, pitch and sulphur, hung pots of flammable material from the spars, set it alight and launched it towards the wooden pier, which caught fire and burned, along with the siege engines.

A new order was given, this time to build a causeway to the island, seventy metres wide and six hundred metres long, along which the huge, six-storey siege towers could be trundled. The towers were covered with skins, to protect them from the arrows, stones and burning sand that the Tyrians continued to hurl from the battlements. Crane-ships were also deployed to clear away large boulders, approach the walls from another point, and throw across landing ramps. Alexander's famous striking force, the Agrianian javelin men, managed to scale the wall at one point and reach the battlements, where they engaged fiercely with the Tyrian guard. This secondary action relieved the pressure on the main body of attackers, who were pounding the walls with their siege engines.

Finally a section of the wall gave way and the Macedonians poured into Tyre, with Alexander among the first in. Thus Tyre was taken, in July 332 BC, after a siege of seven months. Not seven months of simply waiting for the Tyrians to surrender, but seven months of hard and continuous fighting in every way the Macedonians could think of.

THE DETOUR TO EGYPT

After Tyre Alexander moved southwest towards Egypt, which was under Persian rule. As he advanced, the people welcomed him as a liberator, for there were strong ties binding the Greeks and the Egyptians.

Accomplished diplomat that he was, Alexander sacrificed not only to the Greek gods, but also to those of the Egyptian pantheon. He also paid honour to the Egyptians' Sacred Bull, in stark contrast to the Persian king Cambyses, who had had it killed.

Alexander also made a pilgrimage to the shrine of Zeus Ammon at Siwah in the Western Desert. This was a long and dangerous journey, across miles of burning sand with few oases. The oracle of Zeus Ammon was the most famous in the world in those days. Alexander undertook this journey to show that he had come to Egypt as a friend. He also wanted to see for himself whether it was in fact at the edge of the Libyan Desert, which would be a natural frontier for his empire. He made a substantial gift of money to the priests, for he knew how influential they were in the region and wanted to make sure of their allegiance.

Delighted by this behaviour, the Egyptian priests proclaimed him Pharaoh and gave him the titles and privileges that were traditionally reserved for their own kings.

—*Why, though, did Alexander turn aside to Egypt, allowing Darius to regroup?*

Alexander thought it wise to break up Darius' empire from the east coast of the Mediterranean and Egypt, before taking on what remained of the Persian army, which was still a formidable body. Of course, his ultimate aim was to capture Darius and place himself on the throne of the Achaemenid kings. To make himself the Great King of Persia and achieve the goal of the expedition, to make the Greeks' dream come true.

Thus, after a long march from Egypt he crossed the Tigris, and the two opposing armies met at Gaugamela, where they engaged in the most decisive battle of the campaign, which spelled the end of the Persian Empire.

THE BATTLE OF GAUGAMELA

It was clear from the beginning that this was not going to be an easy victory. When Alexander and his staff saw the plain with its encircling mountains, where the Persians had encamped, they were struck dumb. The Persian forces greatly outnumbered theirs and, as the Greeks well knew, they were experienced soldiers and superbly equipped. Their trump card was a chariot with scythe blades attached to each side, which could literally mow down the Greek warriors. Moreover, the Persians had cleared and levelled the ground so that these chariots could operate with maximum effectiveness. The Persian army also had a troop of elephants, which the Greeks had never seen before. Alexander began to worry about how his cavalrymen's horses would react when confronted with these strange beasts.

He succeeded, however, in forcing a gap in the solid Persian line, through which the serried ranks of the Macedonian phalanx advanced in good order. Darius lost his nerve, retreated, and took flight. Alexander pursued him for a fair distance, and while unable to overtake him he did capture his chariot, his arms, and all the baggage that Darius had brought with him to the battle.

This splendid victory may not have delivered Darius into

Alexander's hands, but it did leave him master of the great capitals of the East: Babylon, Susa and Persepolis.

The celebrated and fabulously wealthy city of Persepolis was looted. Alexander deliberately burned down the palace of Xerxes to emphasise the fact that his place had been taken by another. He then entered Darius' palace in Persepolis and sat on the royal throne, which was placed under a golden dome. But his mission was not complete as long as Darius was living freely in the Median capital of Ecbatana.

—*What was it that enabled Alexander's army to stand up against much larger, well-equipped and highly experienced forces?*

ALEXANDER'S INVINCIBLE ARMY

What made Alexander's army invincible —apart from the genius of its leader— was its versatility, the tight-knit co-operation between the foot-soldiers and the cavalry, and his use of the cavalry as shock troops. Alexander usually commanded the first squadron of cavalry, but would readily take charge of any unit if he thought it necessary, even the famous phalanx. In general, his army was remarkably flexible, both in composition and in tactics, and could adapt on the instant to whatever the enemy's weaponry and the lie of the land required.

A key role in the victorious outcomes of his battles was played by the famous *Macedonian phalanx*. The men of the Macedonian phalanx wore helmet, cuirass and greaves, carried a shield, and were equipped with a short sword and the famous *sarissa*, a spear nearly five metres long. The soldiers were arrayed in ranks, shoulder to shoulder. In some cases they would align their shields to form a solid wall. Those in the front rank held their spears low and parallel to the ground; the length of the sarissa meant that they could hit the advancing enemy before coming within reach of their swords or shorter spears. The phalanx advanced as a slow, solid mass, usually as a rectangular block, although they could also form a wedge or split in two for a pincer movement. They could form and reform very swiftly, even in the middle of a battle. Just seeing the phalanx move was often enough to strike terror and confusion into the opposing army.

Another important part of Alexander's army were the *hypaspists*, the royal battalions, formed of men from the Macedonian nobility. There were also several thousand soldiers sent by allies in the Greek league, as their contribution to the campaign against their common enemy, as well as five thousand Greek mercenaries.

Alexander's army also had its commando force, the Agrianians, who were famous fighters, and especially skilled at climbing sheer mountain faces. The Cretan archers, too, were fierce and determined warriors.

Another thing that made the army so effective was its use of various kinds of *siege weapons*. It had multi-storeyed siege towers, which could be as much as fifty metres tall, mounted on wheels, from which they could strike the enemy's walls at any height. Can you imagine what that looked like, those wooden towers the height of a five-storey building, trundling towards the walls of your city? Alexander was also the first general in history to use landing ramps. Both of these innovations, developed by his engineers, were, as we have seen, used in the siege of Tyre.

He also used *battering rams* to break down the enemy's walls. These were heavy timbers with a metal cap resembling a ram's head at the front, which were swung against a wall or gate to break it down. He also made use of mobile roofs, to shield the siege engines from enemy arrows.

The greatest military invention of antiquity, however, was the *catapult*, which could easily hurl great bolts and stones weighing up to fifty kilos over a distance of a hundred and fifty metres. They were used to attack enemy ships or troops drawn up on the far shore of a river.

The army was also capable of building ships. And their large ships could be dismantled and carried on carts to some other coast or shore and there be re-assembled. This was done with the ships they had on the Indus, which were taken apart and carried overland to the river Hydaspes, a hundred and fifty kilometres farther east.

Another remarkable feature of this army was the perfection of its ordnance, commissariat and communications network, and the smoothness with which reinforcements arrived from Greece: sixty thousand of them in the first eight years of the campaign. Obviously, the farther from Greece they got, the harder it was to maintain the lines of supply and communications. That is why Alexander conscripted local troops from the countries he conquered: in India, for example, he added five thousand Indians to his army. He had used barbarian troops before, without encountering any problems.

He often entrusted important administrative positions to former adversaries, many of whom had fought hard and bravely against him: Mazaeus, for example, who had commanded a Persian force at Gaugamela, was appointed satrap of Babylon. He did what was right and just, regardless of his own personal interest. Of course, he also meted out harsh punishment to those who abused their position or misused funds, and he showed no clemency to looters, grave robbers and the sacrilegious.

Upon his return from India he imposed severe sentences, sometimes even of death, on satraps, viceroys and nomarchs who had instigated revolts or acted unjustly towards their subjects. These were men whom he had appointed himself, and some of them had been friends. This he did as much as a warning to others as to punish the guilty.

—*How do we know all these details about Alexander's campaign?*

When Alexander set out on his expedition, he took with him a company of experts in various fields, including secretaries and official historians. One of these was my nephew, Callisthenes, a man of letters, very good at his job and of no little renown, who attached himself to Alexander uninvited. Alexander was happy to have him, though, for he thought that in Callisthenes he had found someone who could describe his feats and achievements as Homer had described those of his hero-ancestor Achilles in the *Iliad*.

Callisthenes, however, was entirely self-centred, and wrote selectively about whatever he considered noteworthy. In his view Alexander was lucky to have him there: Alexander would be famous because of Callisthenes, not Callisthenes because of Alexander.

He had a more reliable historian in Aristobulus, but the man who really chronicled the expedition was Alexander's secretary, Eumenes of Cardia. Most of our information about the expedition, however, comes from the memoirs of the Macedonian general Ptolemy, who after Alexander's death became king of Egypt. Arrian based his history of Alexander's campaigns largely on Ptolemy's account, and that work is the best surviving history of Alexander that we have.

What kind of a man was Alexander the Great? Did you see any change in him over the course of his expedition?

Alexander may have been ambitious, egotistic and quick-tempered, but he was also a man of great nobility, sensitivity and magnanimity. I will relate a few incidents from his life so that you can judge for yourself what sort of man he was.

ALEXANDER THE GREAT'S CHARACTER

Immediately after the League of Corinth had recognised him as its head and confirmed him as generalissimo of the Greek expedition against the Persians, many well-known philosophers and politicians went to meet him. The exception was Diogenes, the Cynic, who lived in a barrel. Alexander, as I am in a position to know, did not share the views of the Cynics, and particularly their indifference to society and their country. Nonetheless, in order to do honour to Diogenes, he went himself to pay him a visit.

When he found him, he greeted him, introduced himself, and asked what he could do for him. Diogenes replied, "You can get step aside, for you are blocking the sunlight." Alexander was greatly struck by this unexpected answer, and by the philosopher's self-sufficiency, and uttered the famous words, "Were I not Alexander, I would fain be Diogenes". As we have said, for the Cynics virtue was the only good, and vice the only evil. Country, social position, glory and wealth counted for nothing.

Here is another story that you may find enlightening. In the citadel of Gordium, a very ancient city on the river Sangarius, there stood the chariot of the father of the legendary King Midas, which had been dedicated to Zeus. The yoke was lashed to the pole by means of a rope of dogwood bark tied in an intricate knot. There was a tradition that whoever could untie that knot, the Gordian knot, would conquer Asia.

The knot, however, was very curiously tied, with neither end visible, and no one had ever been able to unfasten it. To one of Alexander's character this was a challenge. He was advised not to make the attempt, since he would surely fail, but he went to the citadel, studied the knot carefully, and realised that it could not be simply untied in the usual way. But, being Alexander, he found a solution. Some say that he pulled out the pole to get at the interior of the knot, others —and this is the most prevalent opinion— that he sliced clean through it with his sword. Whichever it was, this action was intended to demonstrate that he was destined by fate to conquer Asia by whatever manner or means and that he was not going to let anything stand in his way.

After this his morale soared, although if you want my opinion it had never sagged.

Alexander wanted to win his battles at all costs and whatever it took. But at the same time he was always careful to treat his men with kindness and decency. He wanted them to be in good health and good spirits. He visited the wounded and saw that they were well cared for. He talked to them, asked how they had come by their wounds, and discussed their personal problems with them. He paid a pension to the families of those killed in battle, and exempted them from paying taxes. He also allowed the newly wed to spend the winter, the first winter of the campaign, at home in Macedonia with their wives.

When he decided to discharge ten thousand Macedonians on account of age and length of service, he not only paid them the full amount of their agreed salary but gave them the same amount in addition for travel expenses to see them home. Moreover, he asked Antipater, whom he had left as regent in Macedonia, to pay them the honours given to victors at the Olympic Games: places of honour and wreaths to wear at any games they wished to attend.

The honours paid to victors at Olympic Games in ancient Greece were remarkable. They were seated with the authorities at public events, and were considered the happiest of men. When Diagoras watched both his sons win prizes at the Olympic Games, the whole crowd of spectators was unanimous in wishing him the good fortune to die then and there, for there could be no greater happiness in his life.

Alexander also took charge of the children born to Macedonians who had married Asian wives. He promised that he would see that they were brought up as Greeks, and would be sent to their fathers when they were old enough. He would also provide for their mothers, who remained in Asia.

While Alexander was hastening with his army towards Persepolis, which was Darius' capital, he met a group of about eight hundred men, most of them elderly and all of them maimed. Some were missing an arm, some a leg, some their nose or ears. They had been left only those parts that were necessary for them to ply their trade, so that they could be of service. These men were Greeks, who had been taken prisoner in earlier battles. Despite his haste to reach Persepolis before Darius, he stopped, wept, and promised that he would see that they got home to Greece. But they would not go, they said, for they did not want their compatriots to see them in this sorry state. Whereupon he gave them each a full purse, and animals and other goods, so that they might live comfortably. He exempted them from all taxes and ordered the overseers to look after them and see that no one took advantage of them.

—*How did Alexander behave towards Darius and his family?*

Beautifully, as you will see from the following incident.

After the Battle of Issus, when Alexander sat down to eat, someone told him that Darius' mother, wife and two daughters were among the prisoners that had been taken, and that his wife and mother had broken into lamentation because they had seen the empty chariot and thought that Darius was dead. Upon hearing this Alexander immediately sent one of his guard, Leonnatus, to tell them that Darius was alive, and not to worry about their own fate because he would see that they continued to live in the style to which they were accustomed. He also promised to bring up Darius' six-year-old son as if he were his own, with all princely honours.

But there is more to the story. The next day Alexander and Hephaestion went to the tent where Darius' family were lodged. Unsure which of the two was the king, for they were both dressed in the same fashion, Darius' mother bowed deeply to Hephaestion, because he was the taller of the two. But when he drew back and one of her courtiers pointed to Alexander, saying that he was the king, she was embarrassed at her mistake and sought to retire. But Alexander assured her that no mistake had been made, for there was nothing to choose between them.

He also paid a visit to the tomb of Cyrus, the great general and founder of the Achaemenid dynasty, to which Darius belonged. While there, he gave orders that the tomb should be restored at his expense, as a mark of respect and admiration from one who, as a boy, had studied Xenophon's *Anabasis*.

—*What finally happened to Darius?*

He met an inglorious end. Let me tell you exactly how things transpired.

THE DEATH OF DARIUS

When Alexander, in pursuit of Darius, passed through the Caspian Gates, a Babylonian officer called Bagistanes entered the camp and told him that Bessus and two other Persian generals had seized Darius in a coup and were about to murder him. Alexander immediately left his army and with a few chosen men raced off to save the hapless Darius, for he wanted to return him alive to his mother, who was already under his protection along with the rest of his family.

In one night they covered eighty kilometres. When the conspirators realised that he was so near, they left Darius half-dead in his chariot and fled, abandoning soldiers, women and children, and much treasure. Alexander sped past the king's chariot without realising what it was or who was in it. When he later discovered what had happened, he turned back.

But it was too late. Darius was dead, and in a manner unbefitting a king. This caused Alexander great sorrow. He covered him with his mantle of royal purple and gave orders for the body to be prepared and adorned with royal pomp and buried in the royal tombs at Persepolis.

Bessus, who had behaved so ignobly, for he was a kinsman of Darius and had been highly favoured by him, was sentenced to be whipped and executed.

—*I can see from these episodes that Alexander the Great was indeed a man of great sensitivity. But on the other hand, he is also said to have destroyed certain cities and enslaved many of their citizens.*

That is true, as far as it goes, but wherever it happened there was a particular reason for it.

ALEXANDER THE RULER

Alexander destroyed Tyre, yes, but not because he was exasperated by the long siege and the spirited defence put up by its citizens. No, it was because of their barbarity towards their Greek prisoners, whom they brought to a place on the ramparts in full view of the Greeks outside the walls and there killed them and fed their bodies to the fish. In other words, he repaid them in their own coin.

Alexander was not a man who decided things lightly. While the siege was still in progress, he received a delegation from Darius with an enticing offer: friendship, alliance, ten thousand talents, all the Persian territory west of the Euphrates, and marriage with whichever of his two daughters Alexander preferred.

Most democratically, Alexander discussed the matter with his council. At some point Parmenio, his close friend and right hand, stood up and said, "If I were Alexander, I would accept the terms and end the war". To which Alexander replied, "So would I, were I Parmenio". Alexander may have been a romantic in many things, but where it counted he was a realist. He knew that an accommodation with Darius would leave a powerful empire on his eastern frontier, which could prolong the war and thus undermine his whole enterprise. In the end, he refused the offer, for he wanted to defeat Darius by strength, to show the Greeks that he had successfully completed the mission they had charged him with.

As for what Alexander did in Persepolis, there are a lot of stories, and they all illustrate some part of his character. Walking through the palace, for example, he saw the statue of Xerxes lying on the floor. Alexander stopped in front of it and spoke as if to Xerxes himself, saying, "Shall I leave you lying here because you made war on the Greeks, or shall I restore you to your pedestal for your magnanimity and the virtue you displayed in other things?".

One thing that people find hard to understand is why he ordered that the palace in Persepolis be put to the torch. But this was meant to be read as a message, addressed to the whole world but particularly the Greeks, that the reign of Darius was over and the Greek war of revenge at an end.

As we mentioned earlier, the non-Greek cities that put up no resistance were granted a sort of autonomy, and Alexander respected their customs and religion. The degree of liberty and the details of their administration varied, of course, from country to country, depending on how civilised they were. In Babylon, where he was received with great pomp and circumstance, he honoured their gods, ordered the temples that Xerxes had destroyed to be rebuilt, and sacrificed to the local god Bel. He also observed the annual tradition of the kings of Babylon of touching the hands of the city's own special god, Marduk.

After the famous battle of Gaugamela he sent money from Asia to rebuild Plataea and advised the Greek cities of the League of Corinth to conduct their own affairs independently. This he did to counteract some of the activities of his regent in Greece, Antipater, who had helped certain tyrants rise to power.

For humanitarian reasons, and possibly also out of expediency, he sent word from Persia to the Greek cities of the League to lift the ban on the political exiles who had opposed it, and consequently him. These people and their families —there were about ten thousand of them— had been wandering from place to place in Greece, looking for work. This decree, though, was beyond his competence as head of the League, and was badly received by the cities in question, which saw it as unwarranted interference in their affairs. So why did he do it? Because he thought that it would solve a very serious problem and ensure peace and harmony in Greece.

For the Greek cities under his protection Alexander was a much less oppressive ruler than Athens, Sparta and Thebes had been in similar circumstances. He never imposed or favoured tyrants or despotic regimes.

Alexander also shared all the hardships of his soldiers. In a reprimand to a group of disgruntled Macedonians he asked, rhetorically, "Who among you thinks he has been in greater danger or suffered more than I on this campaign?" And once, on a desert march in blistering heat some of his soldiers found a little water. When they had drunk, they brought the rest in a helmet to Alexander, who despite his raging thirst found the courage to pour those drops on the ground, for he would not drink when the rest of his men could not.

His mother, with whom he corresponded, advised him not to be too generous with his friends and companions.

Not to distribute money and titles profusely, because, she said, this tactic would equate them with kings and weaken his position. And it is true that some of his companions did not use their wealth wisely. Agnon, for example, is said to have decorated his sandals with silver ornaments after the treasury of Persepolis had been emptied.

Alexander loved and honoured his friends and companions. He paid his soldiers' debts and gave gifts and honours to those who had acted bravely. When Hephaestion died, after a short illness, he shut himself away for three days and touched no food. He believed in friendship.

HIS FRIENDSHIP WITH NEARCHUS

Alexander entrusted his boyhood friend Nearchus, who was the commander of his fleet, with a very important and very dangerous mission: to sail around the coast from the mouth of the Indus to the Persian Gulf. A long, long journey through unknown seas. He worried about Nearchus, his men and his ships, especially when no word came from them for a long time. Eventually the fleet limped into a small port, where Nearchus learned that Alexander was up-country and not very far away. Immediately, he took six men and set off to find him.

When Alexander saw him in his rags and tatters, and realised that there were just six men with him, he exclaimed that his joy at seeing him alive was quenched by his great sorrow at the loss of thousands of men and the ships they sailed in. And when Nearchus assured him that the fleet still existed and the mission was accomplished, he swore by the gods that this news —that his men were alive— pleased him more than his conquest of Asia, and he immediately ordered games and festivities to be held.

—You said that Alexander the Great believed in friendship, but from what I have read he killed his friend Cleitus with his own hands. How does that chime with what you are telling me? When you say 'friendship', what do you mean?

FRIENDSHIP ACCORDING TO ARISTOTLE

I have though a great deal about the concept and the meaning of friendship. In my time, the word —that is, the Ancient Greek word *philia*— meant any mutual attraction between two people, regardless of sex.

True friendship is a very important thing, and it requires mutual understanding and much time for it to develop between two people. They must eat bread and salt together[68], as we say.

Friendship is reciprocal; each must desire good for the other and implement this desire through action. Friendship is an example of virtue and is necessary in social life. Our friends enable us to achieve much. I believe that friendship and living in harmony bring happiness.

Have I not already said that one of the components of happiness is the existence of friends? We cannot feel happiness if we cannot share it with a friend. A friend is a person's alter ego[69], or a part of himself[70], in the same way as a mother feels her child's pain as if it were in her own body.

Now, what happened with Cleitus is something that I cannot explain in a word or two. Perhaps we will have another opportunity later to talk about the particular circumstances of the episode. *What I will tell you now*, though, is that there are some things that should not be oversimplified.

—*You said that friendship is one of the factors that bring about happiness. When should a person be considered happy?*

Before I try to answer that question, we need to consider whether a person is happy from birth or whether happiness is acquired later. There are some who believe that a person is born happy, just as he is born black or white, while others think that happiness comes to a person after a series of chance happenings[71].

HAPPINESS ACCORDING TO ARISTOTLE

I could tell you that happiness is subjective. Everyone has

their own idea of what it is. One person thinks he is happy when he is virtuous, another when he has moral wisdom, and another when he can enjoy sensual pleasures. Some think that a person is happy when he has a satisfactory amount of all those things.

This means that each one of us has to think about it seriously and decide for himself what he wants out of life - education, honour, glory, money, pleasure - to be happy, and, when he makes up his mind which thing he wants most of all, he must pursue it with constancy. The worst thing, in this case, is not to know what you want.

When I was young I thought (influenced by my teacher, Plato) that happiness comes only through the practice of philosophy. Nothing else was important. Because I had been taught, and was persuaded, that philosophy springs from truth and has virtue as its constant aim. Later I realised that virtue alone cannot ensure happiness; health and a certain amount of money are also necessary. In general we must not underestimate the contribution of earthly goods and pleasures to the whole question of happiness. How can a mere mortal, lacking the basic material goods, be happy, since his every action will be directed towards keeping himself alive? The absence of children, noble descent, and beauty also lessens happiness[72].

On the other hand, we must not expend all our energy on acquiring material goods. Observing the sky and the heavenly bodies or studying nature or seeking truth may not earn you money to buy things with, but they make your soul rejoice. Besides which, we willingly do many things from which we not only gain monetary benefit but which on the contrary we have to pay to enjoy[73]. When we attend the games at Olympia or the plays at the Great Dionysia, do we not spend our money gladly?

Also, if a person could see the grandeur hidden in eternal things, he would understand that earthly honours and glories are trifles and of no account, so that zealously chasing after them is foolishness and stupidity.

Mental activities are the most important a man can engage in, and they bring pleasure. I am telling you now that the pleasure of thinking is the greatest of pleasures. If it could last forever, we would always be happy. So do not let anyone tell you that we are but mortals and therefore must be contented with material goods. No, we must try to make good use of our mind and soul, to improve our intellectual condition, to approach God. We must do everything we can to activate the best that is within us. Stretch our minds and step up our intellectual activities. That, after all, is what differentiates us from the animals. For my own part, I might add that happiness is also a question of education.

You must never forget, young fellow, that life is not all smooth going. A man may well live happily for years, and then in the twilight of his life be afflicted with calamities. As happened to Priam, the legendary king of Troy, who in his old age lost his children, one after the other, and witnessed the destruction of his powerful kingdom[74].

—Very true, but let's get back to Alexander the Great. Was the way of governing the states he conquered something he had decided on beforehand? Had you discussed the matter with him?

THE GOVERNANCE OF CONQUERED PEOPLES

The problem of how the peoples in his vast empire ought to be governed, and especially whether he should follow Greek or Asian models or whether a mixed system would be better, was one to which Alexander gave considerable thought. He believed that the different peoples should not all be governed in the same way, since they had different experiences, different constitutions and different beliefs. His guiding principle in the matter was that whatever kind of administration they had, he should not interfere with the local mores and customs and the religious beliefs of the people. He also firmly believed that he should not radically change a place's political system, but bring it into harmony with his own standards. Finally, he believed that he should

persuade each people that he was their ruler, not their conqueror. This he did largely through such actions as sacrific-
ing to local gods, encouraging intermarriage, and inviting
local leaders to banquets. In pursuit of this goal he even
adopted local dress and accepted such customs as prostra-
tion before the king, an ancient traditional element of Asian
court ceremonial. All these things were grist to the mill of
those of his fellow Greeks who accused him of abandoning
Greek ways and being too pleased with the opulent luxury
of the life of the Asian kings.

All this, as we have said, was part of his general plan to
make the conquered peoples feel that he was their own
king; but he also wanted to send a message to the Greeks,
that they should stop taking certain of their privileges for
granted just because they were Greeks. This was all part of
his plan for a universal empire.

What were the Greek systems of government?

Now, that is another big question, but I will try to answer
it as succinctly as possible. In Ancient Greece there were a
great variety of political systems, running the gamut from
democracy to oligarchy.

What do you mean by 'democracy' and by ' oligarchy'?

DEMOCRACY AND OLIGARCHY

Democracy, one might say, is that system of government
in which the views of the majority prevail. But things are
not that simple. We will not dispose of democracy as easily as that.

Let me ask you a question: would it not be wrong to describe as a democracy the admittedly unlikely case of a state
governed by the majority, where that majority was of wealthy
people which acted in its own interest and prevented the
poor from sharing in the government? Usually, of course,
it is the poor who form the majority. The rule of the many
should not be the sole distinguishing feature of a democracy; it must also offer equal possibilities for all its citizens

to exercise power[75]. And its citizens must enjoy equality and freedom. But who defines the equality and freedom of the citizens?[76]

The limits of equality and freedom are defined by the laws. The citizens must act within the limits of the laws. Because absolute equality and unlimited freedom cannot exist. We cannot all be equal in everything. A lazy man cannot expect to earn as much as a diligent one, an unlettered man as an educated one, a fool as a clever man.

Freedom, too, has its limits, and when we overstep them we are moving towards corruption. No person can do just what he wants and live just as he pleases, because the excessive freedom of the one is an impediment to the freedom of his neighbour, and that is wrong[77]. To live as you please means that you must live alone, and then you will not have the advantages of organised society. Ideas such as these are a distortion of democracy.

Democracy is the most stable of all political systems[78]. It assures the greatest social equilibrium and is the most harmless regime[79], because it is difficult to corrupt or deceive an entire people[80]. Democracy is also the system in which it is easiest to change those in power[81].

A democracy is a community of individuals who act as a group. Their collective decisions are more correct than those of even the wisest or greatest of their number. With two qualifications: democracy cannot be suitable for all peoples, and there must be caution regarding the extent of popular power[82]. A democratic regime can have many different forms, or, to put it another way, there are many kinds of democracy. The best case is when all citizens participate freely and equally, on condition that the laws are applied. And the worst case is when all the citizens participate equally but the laws are not applied[83].

The decrees of the popular assemblies are a case in point, for they are set above the laws, and in that they are no different from those of despotic regimes. In these cases power is exercised autocratically, demagoguery flourishes and it is the demagogues who shape public opinion and steer the people where they want them, for their own personal benefit and not in the interests of the body politic.

The demagogues in a democracy play the role of the flatterers who surround a monarch. They make suggestions and toss out slogans that please the crowd and tickle the ears of the populace. They say things like, "Power to the people!" and, "Let the people decide!" It all sounds good, the people lap it up, and the demagogues always manage to present things as the will of the people. In the end, democracy is corroded from within, by disorder and anarchy, since in this case the laws are circumvented[84]. For, as I have said, in a true democracy it is not enough to have good laws, before which all citizens are equal, but these laws must be respected and observed. And here we see the value of a statesman: it is the ability to strike at the root of the evil. That is, when he sees that the demagogues are beginning to be dangerous, he must step in and thwart their plans. *I don't need to tell you*, of course, that this intervention must be made within the framework of the law and not by military coup.

The biggest threat to democracy is the infringement of the laws, by the people, of course, but more especially by the politicians, who are responsible for defending the laws against infraction[85] and educating the people to obey the laws.

Democracy is not a simple matter. For it to function properly requires great care, on the part of both the people and the politicians. These are the two pillars of democracy, and of the two it is the politicians who must be most careful in preserving it, because they are the likelier to slip into demagoguery, which —I repeat— is the worst enemy of democracy. In general, the obligations of the politicians in a democracy are greater than those of the citizens[86].

I believed, and I still believe, that there is no system of government that suits every people: one size does not fit all. That means that the politicians and legislators must choose the laws and the regime best befitting their people, depending on its readiness and temperament. But their aim must always be the public interest, because the interest of the whole is superior to that of the individual[87]. Such a regime must fall somewhere between democracy and oligarchy.

The basic criterion for the choice of regime must be the possibility that it will be able to function. For we have to be realistic, not utopians; feet-on-the-ground, and not head-in-the clouds. We should not be aiming for the theoretically ideal system, but for one that works. How viable a democratic system is depends on the quality of both the governors and the governed. Because the citizens, too, have serious responsibilities in a democratic regime[88].

– *What are the qualities that citizens and politicians in a democratic regime must have, and what are their obligations?*

As we have said, the politicians, those who govern, must undeniably be good men. But since every citizen also exercises power, indirectly, it follows that the citizens must also be good men[89], must have a sense of their responsibilities, and must elect the most worthy and honourable politicians.

THE OBLIGATIONS OF THE CITIZEN

But what are the qualities that make a good citizen? What does he expect of the state, and what are his obligations towards it?

The answers to those questions vary depending on the system. In a democracy, for example, the citizen has to be able to govern and be governed. He must have virtue (that is, moral excellence), knowledge, and sound judgement[90]. Certainly, we must not expect all the people to have those qualities, but it is necessary that the majority have them to a satisfactory degree.

A man who is accustomed to be virtuous is considered to be a good citizen[91]. But much of the responsibility for training citizens to be virtuous lies with the politicians[92], who have a duty to see that the citizens acquire virtue[93], and not only by exhorting them to do so but by example, especially when addressing people who are not so inclined, although this can be achieved by systematic teaching. Those citizens who are so inclined[94] must also be taught virtue, and must perform good (virtuous) deeds every day so that virtue, character, becomes a habit and a lifestyle[95].

The citizen must not consider it degrading to obey the laws, and less still as servile, but must feel it to be a duty and a precondition for the preservation of the democratic regime, because any citizen who is active in the collective bodies and who has the required qualities will sooner or later stand out from the mass, be recognised by the people and *de facto* become a prospective leader.

—*What qualities should a politician have?*

THE QUALITIES OF A POLITICIAN

First of all, I think that the qualities necessary for a politician also vary depending on the system. The qualities needed by a democratic leader are not the same as those required by a dictator. However, whatever the system, I cannot conceive that a man without character and prudence can be a political leader. Character is what differentiates the statesman from the petty politician[96].

Unfortunately, however, character is not something that graces many politicians. As I have told you, character and virtue are not innate in man, they are acquired. Because if they were part of human nature, they would be unable to change. I think that man has the ability to practice virtue and become virtuous[97], because he learns to act virtuously. Indeed, this happens with everything: when a person does something continuously, and particularly if he has done it from his youth, it becomes habitual — a second nature, you might say[98]. This is very clear in our Greek language, where the very word for 'character' (*ethos*) is a lengthened form of the word for habit (*ethos*). Virtue and character require constant care and attention[99].

Another quality that is indispensable for politicians is the practical wisdom that permits the politician to distinguish what is good and what is bad. This is an acquired quality, not a moral virtue, and it presupposes a combination of right thinking and experience.

Prudence means mindful practical wisdom[100]. We say that a politician acts with prudence when his acts are aimed at the good of the whole body of citizens. That is what makes prudence essential in a politician.

And because — as I keep telling you — a thing is judged by its essential purpose, the end for which it was intended, the politician, whose reason for existence is to serve the business of government, is in the final analysis assessed on what he was able to do for the state and how far he was able to defend it. That is, the politician must be a sensible realist and not cling to ideologies and types. As I've said, politicians are judged in the end not on their words but on their acts, on what they have actually done, how they used their power.

Just as ethics is not pure theory but also correct praxis[101], so politics is not disconnected from life but operates in reference to the everyday life of the communal body.

Politics is not unrelated to ethics as regards ends and means, for both have human good as their ultimate object. They overlap, but they are inherently different in scope. Ethics is for the most part quite separate from politics, being the more theoretical approach to moral living, just as politics has its own sphere, quite separate from ethics.

Most politicians are not worthy of the name, for they choose that vocation out of cupidity and not as a means of being of service to the body politic through correct deeds and actions without ulterior motive[102].

The politician must exhort the people to respect and obey the laws[103]. In order to do so effectively he must be familiar with the psychology and the mentality of the people. This is only possible if he remains in constant direct contact with them, not remote or isolated in his own world[104].

Politicians have a duty to teach the people where the limits of their civic freedom and equality lie, and what dangers the abuse of freedom creates for the state[105]. They also have a duty to be perceptive, to sense when something is going wrong with the state and understand what it is, and take immediate action to set it right[106].

The politician has to keep faith with the system he serves. He must respect its laws and have the skills to perform his duties[107]. He must not mask the true state of affairs; knowledge of how things really stand is always in the best interests of the state and the individuals comprising it. The common advantage is always weightier than individual gain[108].

Thucydides used Pericles as an example of what a politician should be like[109]. Pericles, he says, could sway the people because he was universally respected for his wisdom and abilities. He was not interested in money. You couldn't bribe him. He held the reins of government firmly. He was not led by the people, but on the contrary he led them. And having come to power honestly, legitimately, through his own merit, he told the people the truth, however unpleasant it was. He was able to do this because the people held him in great esteem.

What I am telling you is that good politicians can achieve wonders. In Pericles' day (490-429 BC) Athens reached unsurpassed heights. That was when the Parthenon, the Propylaia and the port of Piraeus were built. Arts and letters flourished as never before, and democracy attained its perfect form.

The things that Thucydides so admired caused British philosopher Bertrand Russell to describe the age of Pericles as one of the few moments in the history of mankind when a man could be both happy and a genius[110].

Plato[111] said that politicians must have reverence for the gods; they must be just, and they must have a sense of duty and self-sacrifice. They must also have the gift of being able to govern and to persuade[112]. He though that the ideal politician would be a philosopher[113], because philosophers know most about things and can thus guide human action correctly.

Where I differ from Plato on this subject is that in my view the ideal governor needs more than wisdom: he also needs experience. Ideally, that is, a politician's knowledge should come not only from direct master-to-disciple instruction, but from actual practice: in a word, from experience. For this, I think, brings him closer to reality. In politics there has to be a realistic assessment of the day-to-day situation, which serves as the basis for planning political action and instituting the appropriate laws. Of course, if you are going to have correct laws you must have virtuous lawgivers[114].

—*You spoke earlier of politicians' obligations. Which of them did Alexander the Great meet?*

Let me tell you that I paid particular attention to giving Alexander a good grounding in the science of politics. We also had lessons on the constitution and structure of society and the state, and on the elements of political economy. I also taught him something about the organisation of a city, a subject I discuss in my book On kingship, which unfortunately was lost before it could reach your Western scholars.

I also have a lot to say about political science in the *Politics* and the *Nicomachean Ethics*.

POLITICAL SCIENCE AND THE STATE

Political science deals with the principles governing political life, and its aim and object is achieving justice for the general advantage of the citizen. As Plato said, politics is concerned with the highest and most important interests of the individual.

As I explain in my treatise on *Politics*, political science is related to many other sciences, from pure philosophy and sociology to economics and history. My views on politics have been discussed by many historians and political philosophers, including Montesquieu, Rousseau, Marx and Machiavelli.

Marx, for example, refers to me in the first volume of *Das Kapital* as a great thinker and hails me as the first to analyse the concept of the value of social life and other topics of vital importance to human existence. Some have said that it was Book V of my *Politics* that inspired Machiavelli to write *The Prince*. I cannot agree with that, and in any case I think that the term 'Machiavellianism', which is synonymous with the pursuit of some goal without scruple or moral qualm, is unfair to Machiavelli, who in his other books extols democracy[115].

But how many politicians have actually studied political science?

Usually, those who are masters of political science are not themselves politicians and therefore cannot apply what they teach, while the professional politicians are generally not interested in political science or in a position to pass their accumulated experience on to their political successors[116]. I would go so far as to say that political activity does not make a man a real politician[117]. Political science explores and proposes what is good for the functioning of the state, the polity, and, as I have said elsewhere, the whole structure of the state helps the individual to lead a moral life, because the laws oblige people to master their desires and not do wrong to others[118].

Wrongdoing in Attic legal parlance meant breaking the law. In that sense justice could be said to be concerned with observance of the laws and its sphere is thus that of communal living and the functioning of the state[119].

In Ancient Greece the citizen saw himself as a participant in the state rather than a taxpayer. Because the state, strange as this may seem to you, distributed wealth to its citizens. It was common for land in the colonies to be given out to citizens, and assistance was provided to the poorest members of society[120]. There was even some justice in the distribution of honorary offices. This reciprocity was something that the citizens expected, and it underlay the stability and cohesion of the state.

In organised states transactions were either lawful or otherwise. Lawful transactions were those assented to by both parties; the others were the product of blackmail or bodily harm. The latter type included breach of contract and criminal activity. A transaction that initially complied with the principles of legality but was later found to be unjust to one of the two parties concerned was also held to be unlawful and the judge would order the wrong to be redressed. In such cases particular attention was paid to the nature of the act, the damage caused and whether or not the injustice was deliberate.

The court would take into account not only the material loss to the victim, but also the mental and moral injury suffered[121]. Mental distress, as your civil law calls it.

For the politician and the judge justice was an obligation; for the merchant, it was a necessity, to keep prices stable and the system running smoothly.

—*You spoke earlier of experience. Experience is a word we use all the time, and we have a pretty good idea of what it means. I'd like to know, though, what ' experience' means to you.*

I think that when you say 'experience' you mean the same thing we do. That, at least, is my experience (pun intended). But I am happy to give you a quick analysis, if that is what you want.

WHAT IS 'EXPERIENCE'?

The things we learn through our sensory organs are the first building blocks of knowledge[122]. But sometimes, for whatever reason, our sensory perception of physical things may be wrong. For that reason we must check the representations we have formed by commenting on and explaining them. This elaboration of representations received is, of course, what differentiates man from the animals[123], for as far as the senses are concerned they are often more acute in animals than in man. Man has the capacity (as do some animals) to mentally retrieve those representations, to recall things that happened in the past, to use his memory. For while sensory perception operates in the present, the mental representation of events is a question of memory, and memory is the basis of 'experience'.

Experience is acquired through memory, for it is an accumulation of memories of the same thing. That is what makes empirical knowledge so important. Lack of experience nurtures faith in chance.

Experience is acquired; it cannot be taught. Or, as the proverb says, experience is the best teacher. (Proverbs, one might say, are knowledge distilled by time, and they survive because they are both apt and concise.)

Theoretical knowledge is the net result of systematising the empirical knowledge of many people on a particular subject.

Empirical knowledge concerns specific cases, whereas theoretical knowledge considers its subjects globally. Consequently, if you know only the theory, you will be unable to address the individual situations that, taken together, constitute the theoretical knowledge. You may, for example, know a great deal about human health in general but still be unable deal with a particular illness, because you lack specific experience of it[124].

We tend to consider those with theoretical knowledge as wiser than those with hands-on training, because they are better able to explain the general problems with which their science is concerned. But in everyday life the practitioners get along better, because they are dealing with specific problems.

—You often use the word 'virtue'. Can you explain exactly what that means?

WHAT IS 'VIRTUE'

Virtue could be said to be a quality that elicits praise. Virtue —and by this I mean moral virtue— has to aim at moderation, at the mean, as nature does; nature follows the moderate and the harmonious[125]. Virtue, that is, must aim at evaluating our good and bad actions. Our actions are assumed to be the product of our free will; but since it is not always easy to be clear, in any given situation, about the lesser or the greater evil or the lesser or the greater good, we must always choose the least harmful action so as to achieve a balance[126].

We must also be wary of the attraction of what is pleasurable, because it tends to corrupt our judgement. And we must take note of which immoral actions we find most tempting, which ones we seem most inclined to, and how we can avoid them[127]. Because it is up to us whether we are good or bad, and whether we become important or remain insignificant[128]. For most of our actions are voluntary; we do them of our own will. We are responsible for them, because we know from the outset what the outcome is likely to be.

Our habits are a different matter. We are responsible only for developing them, for after we have acquired them they get out of hand and often lead to unpleasant results, just as an illness, once it has taken hold, may develop rapidly and uncontrollably. But since in the beginning at least our habits should be within our control, they too can to some degree be considered wilful[129]. A virtuous man must be moderate in his words, his acts and his desires.

In my opinion it is more important to know how to become virtuous than simply to know what virtue is. I do not want a soldier simply to know what courage is; I want him to act courageously. I do not want a citizen merely to know what is just but to act justly, or a man only to know what health is but to be healthy. It is better to be well intentioned than to know what it means to be well intentioned[130].

—Can you tell me a bit about how democracy worked in Ancient Greece?

I will be delighted to do so.

DEMOCRACY IN ANCIENT GREECE

In a democracy it is the people who rule. In modern democracies the people elect representatives to a parliament, which takes decisions on matters concerning public affairs; in Ancient Greece, the citizens took part personally in the assemblies and decisions were taken collectively. Only free citizens voted; slaves and women were excluded.

Our democracy is more democratic, then, since we allow all adults to vote.

I wouldn't be quite so ready to jump to conclusions. You don't have slaves, of course, so I can see that you might find the idea shocking. But what about the economic migrants that have flooded into your country? How would you react to seeing them given the right to vote? As for women, don't forget that in Greece women have only had the vote since 1954.

One disadvantage of your democracy compared to ours is that the person you elect to parliament for a four-year term may change his views during that time and go over to another party, while your views remain the same. In such a case, how can you say that he represents you?

—That reminds me of a story about the former Soviet Union. A Russian and an American were talking about which country's citizens lived better, and presenting arguments to support their case. At one point the Russian said, "In your country only those who can afford it drink champagne, while most of the people, who have little money, don't spend it on champagne. But in our country everyone drinks champagne through our deputies in the Duma." In the same way we think that we exercise power through our representatives.

I will take that as a joke —but I admit it was clever.

THE DISTRIBUTION OF POWER

One thing that puzzled me about our democracy was whether all the powers can properly be assigned to the people, and if not, which ones can and which cannot. In the end, I came to the conclusion that political and judicial power can be exercised collectively to good effect, but not administrative authority in areas like health and military preparedness. In those cases the decisions must be taken by those with specialised knowledge. A judicial decision, on the other hand, may be more correct if it is a synthesis of many opinions than if it is the decision of a single individual, however wise he may be. And it is better that power be shared by all the citizens rather than being in the hands of one or another social group[131]. Of course, going by what is to the common advantage, it would be fairest for all who have the same qualities to share power equally[132]. By qualities in these cases I mean those that are socially useful[133]. I think, however, that no quality is sufficient of itself to entitle its possessor to exercise authority over others[134] in some government position. For, as I have said, the qualities of a public figure are demonstrated in action, in how justly and correctly he wields power.

What, then, is the fairest way to distribute power within the community of citizens? One reasonable answer is, proportionally. To each in due proportion, according to what he contributes to the city, and to his qualities. For example, a rich man pays more tax, and a nobleman has more knowledge of public affairs through his family's generations of public service. But this view is not, it seems to me, absolutely correct. Because power is not a good that is given in exchange for the qualities a man offers, but a tool in the service of the whole. It would be correct if the city were a business, where it is only right that the person who has invested the most capital has the greatest share of power. Another logical answer is that certain powers should be given to the best people. Unfortunately, though, in our day as well as in yours, those elected to office were more likely to be the most popular rather than the best.

How the powers are structured and operate is also extremely important, and particularly the most sovereign of them all, namely the power that decides how the executive bodies operate. How the powers are structured is a function of what we call the system of government[135].

—*What do you think is the best system of government?*

Since I suppose that you do not want a one-word answer, I cannot tell you what the best system is without first giving you a brief description of the commonest types of regime. If we do not describe, we cannot specify.

THE BEST REGIME

In order to describe the kind of regime, we have to know who rules. Is it an individual, a minority or a majority? The kind of regime is defined by the kind of government[136].

Power can be in the hands of an individual, in which case we have a *monarchy*, or of a few persons, the best people, in which case we have an *aristocracy*, or of the people as a whole, in which case we speak of a *democracy*. If these regimes aim at serving the common advantage, then they are acceptable. But if they aim at serving only the interests of those who govern, then they are vicious and corrupt[137]. A *monarchy* is a system in which a single person rules. If the monarchy is corrupt, then it is described as a *tyranny*. The tyrant keeps himself in power through violence and force. That is the worst system of government. When power is in the hands of a few, if those few look solely to their own interests then the system is described as an *oligarchy*.

A democracy can be described as vicious if the governing majority has its own motives, which aim at reducing the advantages of the minority: for example, if the majority is one of poor men who act unjustly to diminish beyond reason the wealth of the prosperous.

In my view, any system that serves the common advantage is acceptable. But the best system, I think, despite its faults, is democracy.

Some people argue that in a democracy there is a danger that it is the mediocre who will govern, since they are usually the majority. While this idea is not illogical, I think that the majority will always contain enough experienced and competent people to influence the opinion of the many in the right way. In any case, the decision of a collective body is in my opinion generally more correct than that of a few individuals.

Others think that it is better for the decision-makers to be experts and people of experience, arguing that if you want a fine suit you go to a good tailor, not to a collection of people who know nothing of that art.

My response to remarks of that sort would be that politics is an art whose products are judged by their intended users, that is, by the people, and not by the politician[138], in the same way as the final opinion on the functionality of a house belongs to the man who lives in it rather than the architect who designed it.

—*I guess that means we rule out monarchy.*

On the whole, yes; and I will tell you why. Let us imagine a city where the laws are perfect and the monarch devotes himself zealously to his subjects' affairs. But a monarch, no matter how well disposed, is still a man and has passions. And the law, no matter how perfect, has weaknesses, for it cannot foresee the particularities that appear in each separate case. Let us now imagine another city, where it is the people who deliberate and who judge: here the decisions and judgements will be more correct, provided that the intellectual level of the citizens is satisfactory and that the population contains some enlightened minds. In this case, for this particular city[139], a monarchy is not the best regime.

When this is not the case, however, or when the population of a city is not sufficiently mature because it is too accustomed to a monarchy, democracy will not be able to function properly and there will be problems. In such cases a good king is preferable[140]. You have seen for yourself the initial chaos caused in your neighbour states by the abrupt transition to democracy from the totalitarian regime of existing socialism.

—*What were the economic systems in Greece at that time? And which economic system do you think was the best?*

It would be easier and less complicated to describe how goods were traded in Ancient Greece, which is after all the basis of the economic system. If it's all right with you, I will take agricultural products as my example.

That's fine by me.

* * *

ECONOMIC SYSTEMS IN ANCIENT GREECE

On that basis, then, we can distinguish three types of economic system:

- Private ownership of all farmland, with each farmer cultivating his own fields and marketing his own produce. That is, everything in private hands. What you would call a *liberal economy*.
- Common ownership of farms and their products, with all farmers participating equally in the cultivation, while the state handles the marketing and distribution. That is, *real socialism*, not an ersatz variety.
- Private ownership and cultivation of the land, with marketing and distribution handled by the state but with the goods distributed according to each one's input. A *mixed system*.

Personally, I have reservations about how well a system of common ownership and distribution can function, especially when the land is worked by the communal owners, for inevitably there will be disputes over who worked more or less than another.

Of course, things were simpler in Ancient Greece because the land was worked by slaves. But the slaves had masters, so the dispute would be about whose slaves had worked the most[141].

The advantage that some see in the communal system is that it reduces the incentives for crime, since all citizens are fed and clothed, for cold and hunger drive people to theft and other offences. Also, a communal system helps prevent social conflict[142]. Because people are naturally greedy, when everything is privately owned they are not satisfied with what they have, no matter how much that is, but always want more. And to get more they commit crimes, which leads to social conflict and uprisings. For these systems to survive, they have to ensure that everyone has a basic stable income from some steady work. But the desire to own property is part of human nature, and that is something that should not be forgotten.

In the end, I think that the best economic system is a blend of private and communal ownership. On condition that there are good laws and the citizens are educated and well intentioned. Because it is education that brings magnanimity and tolerance, which are essential if a socialised (even partially) economic system is to function properly.

In this system, the farms would be privately owned and worked by their owners, so there would be no friction over who worked and who shirked. And the farmers would have a financial incentive to do their job well, because the property would be theirs and the produce would be distributed proportionally to each one's input in land and labour, with part going to feed the city. This, I think, is the fairest system, as long as the laws are sound and the citizens have the proper moral character. And it has in fact been successfully applied, in Sparta, for instance[143].

I think it is a good rule to attempt what is feasible, not what is most desirable.

In choosing a system one must also consider how to provide the resources necessary to feed and defend the city. The wealth of the state must not be excessive, however, lest it entice its more powerful neighbours to make war on it[144].

I am also of the opinion that there should not be great inequalities of fortune among the citizens, for that creates social problems. In some cities there are limits to the amount of land a man may own, and care is taken to preserve the original size of each plot of land. That is a wise measure, as long as the number of family members working the plot does not increase. For when a piece of land has to support more people than was originally intended, because in the meantime more children have been born, the economic equilibrium is upset and insurrectionary movements develop[145]. Unless of course a limit to the number of children per family is set, so that the land does not have to be carved up into smaller and smaller pieces. But many children make a happy household.

Curbing the appetites of the citizens, though, is a far better solution than restricting inequalities of landholdings. The people should be modest in their demands. Their requirements should be reasonable. Mastering one's desires is a matter of education. It is, therefore, very important that everyone should have access to the same quality of education. Then people will not be greedy, for money or glory or both, for such desires foster revolt.

It is my belief that any system requires education to be effective, not just an economic system. The strange thing is that while a man is willing to go to the ends of the earth to make a profit, he in unlikely to bestir himself to gain wisdom, let alone spend any money to do so[146]. The roots of wisdom are bitter, but the fruit is sweet.

As I like to say: "Learning is an ornament in prosperity and a refuge in adversity."

—*What else do you think is important for the smooth functioning of society?*

Money. And more specifically, a common coinage.

THE USEFULNESS OF MONEY IN SOCIETIES

Products that are exchanged through a barter system have to be comparable. For example, if one man is a shoemaker and another a builder, and the shoemaker needs some work done on his house, then he must give the builder in exchange a quantity of shoes of equivalent value. In the same way, with the farmer he will exchange shoes for food. Already the system is complicated, and it gets worse when you extend it to other occupations: how many baskets, for example, would it take to pay for a doctor's services?[147]

There are needs that cannot be met by an exchange of products, and for that reason organised societies introduced money as a medium of economic exchange, a commodity with a nominal agreed value, in terms of which all prices and values are expressed. The builder's work is valued in coin, as are the shoemaker's shoes and the farmer's produce. Coinage facilitates trade, and without it there can be no organised society.

The value of the currency is agreed by common consent, but it can happen that a man who has a certain amount of money and can thus buy a certain quantity of goods finds himself essentially poorer if the price of those items increases[148].

The price of a slave is also calculated as an amount of money.

—You have mentioned slaves and slavery a number of times. What is your opinion on the subject? It really troubles me that enlightened minds like you and Plato should have been in favour of slavery.

SLAVERY IN GREECE

Slaves did different jobs, some of them requiring great skill. They were not just what you would call unskilled labour, but were often craftsmen and technicians. They lived in the same house as their master and his family, and were entirely dependent on him. Legally, they were excluded from active participation in the affairs of the city. In our day those who performed manual labour were not considered apt for education, because all their energy was expended on labour and they had neither the time nor the inclination to learn. In other words, education and nobility of spirit were the prerogative of the prosperous, leisured class[149].

The slave system was neither as arbitrary nor as repugnant as it appears today. Just as the male is fitted by nature to fertilise and dominate the female, so the free citizen is mentally cultivated and therefore more suited to intellectual activities. He therefore legitimately rules over the slave, who is intended for manual labour. But they are interdependent. The citizen plans the work that has to be done to meet his family's needs, and the slave furnishes the labour to accomplish it; and the whole system benefits both of them.

In my view slaves were intellectually inferior to free citizens, because most of them came from other peoples or less highly developed societies/ Without the education of a free man, their rightful place was in the service of the practicalities of life[150]. I compared the difference between master and slave to that between soul and body.

Slavery was an institution in Ancient Greece, and thus to some extent I took it for granted. Later, when I began to study nature, I noticed the inequalities in the natural world and was not perturbed by the existence of slaves. Nature taught me, or rather familiarised me with the idea of the supremacy of the strongest.

Let me tell you, though, that my views on slavery were opposed by many in my day, because I did not exclude the possibility that the mind of a slave could some day be set free.

The prisoners of war and hostages that were taken from captured cities and sold as slaves, did you consider them as intellectually inferior as well?

No, that to me was unacceptable. You will be happy to know that Alexander very rarely used prisoners of war as slaves.

—*The picture you have painted of Alexander the Great portrays a man of great courage, noble spirit, magnanimous and altruistic, who respected the culture of his adversaries. But this same man allowed Persepolis to be destroyed, murdered Philotas and Cleitus, and permitted the philosopher Callisthenes to be condemned to death.*

Alexander was hot-tempered and egotistical, and had been since his childhood. I was always afraid that he would do something really bad in one of his rages, and lost no occasion to remind him that anger is a bad counsellor for anyone, let alone a prince and a general. I used to tell him that, just as smoke gets in our eyes and we cannot see what is in front of us, so anger clouds the mind and stops us from seeing the evil that will follow, and that reason flies out the window when anger comes in at the door[151].

THE DESTRUCTION OF PERSEPOLIS

The case of Persepolis was different, for it was not the result of a fit of anger but the product of sober determination. The

Persians had to be punished for the devastation Xerxes had wrought in Greece. This was part of the Greek revenge. We must not forget that it was in the name of vengeance that the Greeks rallied to Alexander's summons and made the Asian expedition possible. Alexander considered the destruction of Persepolis as a consequence and a duty, which marked the culmination and completion of his mission.

The following anecdote illustrates the general feeling. In Persepolis, Alexander seated himself on the throne of Darius, a gesture he had not made anywhere else. All those who saw it wept, and his friend Demaratus of Corinth exclaimed that the Greeks who were present should bless their good fortune at having seen Alexander seated on the throne of Darius.

With the fall of Darius and the destruction of Persepolis, the Greeks had achieved their revenge. Alexander was now king of Macedonia, leader of the Greeks and king of Asia. And all before his twenty-sixth birthday.

THE EXECUTION OF PHILOTAS

As for the execution of Philotas, there were many who admitted that there were extenuating circumstances for this otherwise reprehensible act.

Let me tell you how it all happened.

To start with, the army was exhausted by the endless marches in adverse conditions over harsh terrain and the successive battles. Even among Alexander's close companions there were many who wanted to stop a while and enjoy the spoils of their labours and sacrifices. The result was a conspiracy against his life involving some young nobles whose training officer Philotas was.

Philotas was the leader of the cavalry corps, a man famous for his courage and a member of Alexander's inner circle of Companions. For some reason, though, when he drank he spoke disparagingly of Alexander. He was often heard to say that whatever Alexander was he owed to Philotas and his family. All these things came to Alexander's ears and of course they bothered him enormously. But he let it go, for he knew that malice and envy are part of human nature, and he was fond of both Philotas and his father Parmenio. Parmenio and his family had indeed served the throne of Macedonia faithfully, and nowhere more than on this expedition, where two of Parmenio's sons, Hector and Nicanor, had fallen in battle.

But when Alexander learned that one of this group was planning to kill him and that Philotas knew about it, he was furious, for Philotas had said nothing to him although they were together every day. This made him suspect Philotas of being part of the conspiracy, a thought that some of his courtiers were quick to encourage. He therefore had him arrested and brought before the military council, a sort of court martial. Philotas was found guilty, sentenced to death and executed. They say that at some point he admitted his intentions, but nothing was ever proved.

—*And what about Callisthenes?*

I'm coming to that.

THE FALL AND DISGRACE OF CALLISTHENES

The strenuous operations and colossal responsibilities, aggravated by wounds and sheer bodily weariness, had left Alexander physically and mentally drained. In addition, his close political collaboration with the defeated peoples and their leaders, and the oriental mentality of his sycophantic hangers-on, were beginning to have their effect on his character. Willy-nilly he acquired some of the customs and attitudes of the local lords and became increasingly autocratic. Remember, he was still very young.

What the Greeks found intolerable, however, was being asked to make obeisance to him in the Asian manner. His reason for this was so that the Persians should not feel humiliated by offering this token of submission, which to them was the normal and natural thing to do.

This famous obeisance was a deep, deferential bow, accompanied by a semicircular downward sweep of the right arm.

Alexander wanted the conquered peoples to forget their defeat and regard him as their own king. He also did not want the Asians to feel different, or if you will inferior, to the Greeks. For the Greeks, however, this was the sort of reverence paid to a god.

What disappointed and displeased me in Alexander was the way he treated my nephew Callisthenes, out of pure spite. Although he would not let himself show it, Callisthenes had an enormous admiration for Alexander. He followed him everywhere, and served as the official historian of the expedition for most of the campaign in Asia.

Callisthenes was annoyed by the obeisance and by the sycophants who surrounded Alexander, and began to react. He said more than once that while others had come on the expedition to appropriate a share of Alexander's glory, he himself was there to give glory to his enterprises. This attitude of his was no secret, and it disturbed Alexander. Callisthenes wanted to see Europe and Asia joined in a great Hellenic empire and was afraid this was not Alexander's intention. But he underestimated Alexander, who was as brilliant a politician as he was a general. He may have respected Asia, but he did not succumb to the culture of the Asians. Unlike the Romans, who conquered Greece but were culturally absorbed by the Greeks.

Greek was the official language of all the countries Alexander conquered. He appointed tutors to teach Darius' children Greek.

And then at some banquet attended by Greek and Asian officials, one by one the guests drank from the king's cup and performed the deep Persian obeisance, and Alexander kissed them as a sign of friendship. When it was Callisthenes' turn, he drank from the cup but did not bow, and received no kiss from Alexander. Callisthenes then left the hall saying "I depart the poorer for one kiss". Alexander was galled by this, because he had become accustomed to the flattery of the Persians, who were always very deferential to him and praised him continually, but it was not the cause of my nephew's fall from grace. That was a conspiracy among the royal pages to kill Alexander, for which Callisthenes was held responsible because he was in charge of their training and education. After that nothing more was ever heard of Callisthenes. They say that he followed the expedition in chains, until he died. His treatment of Callisthenes left an ugly stain on Alexander's subsequent fame.

THE MURDER OF CLEITUS

The murder of Cleitus was an even blacker mark against Alexander, and I cannot condone it. This is how it came about.

Alexander, Cleitus and some others of the king's circle were at a feast in Maracanda, in company with some of the local (Sogdianan) nobility. This was nothing unusual, nor was the fact that they had all been drinking heavily. At some point in the festivities one of the company began reciting a satire about a Macedonian defeat, a battle in which Cleitus had taken part.

Alexander and many others paid no attention, but Cleitus, who was a hot-tempered man, jumped up and shouted that it was shameful, in front of the barbarians, to mock the Macedonians for a setback. Whereupon Alexander also rose to his feet and said that it was shameful to call cowardice a setback.

Cleitus could not let the slight go unanswered. Pointing to himself he said to the king: "This coward saved you from the sword of Spithridates, and the blood of the Macedonians made you what you are, and now you deny even your father Philip by claiming to be the son of Zeus Ammon". His next words caused great consternation and uproar: "Why, we cannot even speak to our king without demanding an audience through these barbarians!" More insults flew between them, until Cleitus finally said: "If you don't want to hear the truth then don't invite proud, gallant men to your table. Eat with barbarians and slaves, so you will hear only flattery".

At that Alexander lost all self-control, drew his sword and lunged at Cleitus. One guard seized the sword, others tried to calm him. Cleitus was hurried out of the room. But just when everything seemed to be under control, Cleitus came in by another door and started reciting verses from Euripides, with sly jabs at Alexander, whereupon the king seized the sword from the hand of a guard and plunged it into Cleitus' breast.

When he realised that Cleitus was dead, Alexander tried to turn the sword on himself, but was prevented by his bodyguard, who disarmed him and led him to his quarters. All through the next day he wept, and for three days he ate nothing. Many of his friends came to try to console him, even Callisthenes; and in some measure they succeeded.

Although Alexander has been accused of adopting the Asian lifestyle, he never felt himself to be anything but Greek. He wanted to spread the Greek way of thinking, but this was no easy task, since the Asians were accustomed to regarding their kings as unapproachable beings while the Greeks saw them as *primi inter pares*, first among equals.

It must be acknowledged that although Alexander was showered with flattery every day, it did not go to his head nearly as much as with many other Macedonian officers. Nor did his great victories, the almost divine honours paid him, and the high offices bestowed upon him by the conquered peoples ever make him forget who he was: a Greek, and proud of his heritage.

This is confirmed by two things. One is the way he sought to have himself admitted to the Greek pantheon in the year before he died. The other is a speech berating a group of Macedonian officers who were complaining that the Asians were being shown greater favour, a speech that he began by speaking of Philip and in which he spoke continually of "my father Philip".

—*It seems to me, though, that from constantly being treated like a god Alexander the Great came to believe that he was one. What do you think?*

I don't know whether he really believed that he was a god, or the son of a god. In any case, the opinions about such beliefs in those days, that is, who can be recognised as a god or the son of a god, were far from clear. Quite the opposite, in fact. You must not forget that mythology was part of everyday life then, and many elements of it reflect real historical events.

Traditionally, the gods were regarded as having produced many mortal offspring. Also there were cases of people who were honoured during their lifetime as gods: Lysander, for example, who in 404 BC won the final victory for Sparta in the Peloponnesian War and installed his thirty tyrants in Athens, was revered as a god in several cities in Ionia. In Alexander's case, things are less straightforward.

DID ALEXANDER THE GREAT BELIEVE HE WAS A GOD?

First of all, it is a fact that the Medes and the Persians regarded their kings as gods and revered them as such. Then, too, Alexander was held to be a descendant of Heracles, and through him of Zeus, since Heracles was the son of Zeus and Alcmene.

Another story, recorded by Plutarch, says that he was fathered by Zeus Ammon, who lay with his mother Olympias in the guise of a snake; she apparently revealed this secret to him when he bade her goodbye before setting off on his great expedition.

Arrian says that when Alexander the Great reached the shrine of Zeus Ammon in the Western Desert and asked the oracle to tell him whether those who had killed his father, meaning Philip, had all been punished, he received the reply that his father was immortal. For him to ask such a question, he cannot have believed that he was the son of a god. This is confirmed, as Plutarch says, by Alexander's remark concerning a wound he had received, namely that his blood was mortal. Several historians also recount the following anecdote. Once, while Alexander was talking with some friends, there was a terrifying clap of thunder. When the philosopher Anaxarchus of Abdera, who was one of the group, asked Alexander if he, the son of Zeus, could thunder like that, Alexander replied with a laugh that he would not wish to frighten his friends so.

So the answer is that we do not know what he believed himself to be —a god, the son of a god, or a mere mortal. According to Plutarch, he cultivated the idea of his divinity out of political expediency, thinking that it would help him impose his will more easily and more effectively. This was something that Callisthenes had encouraged him to do.

—*I'm curious to know when and why Alexander decided to stop pushing farther east.*

Alexander was determined to get as far as India. It was a fabled land, and one that had fascinated him since he was a child. Moreover, both Heracles and Dionysus were said to have travelled there.

When he reached the Indus river he was received by Prince Taxilas, the ruler of those parts, who concluded an alliance with him and showered him with gifts; gifts were also given to the Greek officers travelling with him. They all wondered at civilisation of the Indies, the way of life, the customs so different from their own —not to mention the elephants.

He did not intend to go much farther east than that. His plan was to reach the river Hydaspes (which flows into the Indus) and follow it south to the Indian Ocean, which was believed to be the southern boundary of the world.

It was his intention to build a number of great cities and ports on the Indian Ocean coast, to stimulate the economy of this eastern part of his empire. But his army rebelled. Not because they doubted him. On the contrary, they all agreed that he was a supremely competent leader, and the only person who could get them safely back home —if that was ever going to happen.

For they were tired. They had been campaigning for eleven years, and had covered more than fifteen thousand kilometres. They were weary and sated. They had won battles, garnered booty, earned prize money, seen new places and different peoples, other cultures, and so much more.

Alexander did his best to persuade his companions to push onwards. Seeing that it was useless, however, he gave in.

He realised that his army was indeed exhausted. He discussed the matter with his staff, and it was agreed that there was really no point in moving on, farther and farther away from Greece. And so the eastward march was halted, and the army began to make its way home.

THE JOURNEY HOME

Plans for the return journey had been made long before. A fleet of eight hundred ships had been built to carry part of the army by sea; this fleet was placed under the command of Alexander's friend Nearchus, of whom we have already spoken. The rest of the army would march overland, following the course of the river, to meet them at the mouth of the Indus. This march was as challenging as anything that had gone before, for they encountered savage tribes and fought fierce battles, in one of which Alexander was yet again seriously wounded.

As Arrian tells us, Alexander wanted the main body of the army to continue along the coast from the mouth of the Indus river to the mouth of the Tigris river and from there to the Persian Gulf, where they would be joined by Nearchus and his ships, who was going to hug the coast to maintain communications with Alexander.

They knew that this would be a long and difficult journey and that the army would face serious problems in keeping itself fed and watered, for no one had ever heard of there being any villages along the coast. The historians assured him that this journey had never been made before, although several people said that Scylax of Caryanda had done so. Perhaps his historians had never heard of Scylax and his voyage. In any case, Alexander liked the idea of being the first, and cultivated it. I sometimes wonder, could something similar not have happened with the discovery of America? The Vikings got there first, but Christopher Columbus gets all the credit.

Alexander was not merely out for glory, though. He was eager to make this voyage for commercial, cultural and scientific reasons. He sent Nearchus by sea to explore the possibility of maritime communications between India and the Persian Gulf, via the Gulf of Oman. He also planned to explore the coast between the Persian Gulf and Egypt, for he was anxious to find a passage from the Arabian coast to the Mediterranean.

At first, at least, everything went as planned. Towards the end of 325 BC Alexander, with the bulk of his army, headed for home along the coast, so that they could maintain contact with Nearchus and be able to provision him. Unfortunately, however, they encountered some great mountains and were obliged to abandon the coast and find another road. The difficulties were almost insuperable.

The journey was brutal. The searing heat by day in the vast deserts they had to cross, when men, horses and carts sank deeply into the burning sand, meant that they had to travel by night. Their food and water supplies ran low, and it was difficult to replenish them, for the region was uninhabited. They became so hungry that they were obliged to eat their horses and mules.

Nearchus and his men fared no better.

On the shore they met semi-savage tribes who ate only fish. But Nearchus had been ordered to record everything of interest that he saw on his journey, and this he did. He gave detailed descriptions of the coasts, gathered information about the topography, marked the places where ports and naval yards could be built or colonies established. In other words, he mapped the coast completely. This was part of Alexander's plan to develop a sea route between Persia and India.

Alexander had also asked Nearchus to find out if there

were any natives living near the coast, and if so how they lived, what their habits and customs were. Another of his tasks was to collect information about the local flora and fauna of the regions he sailed past. In other words, he wanted information pertaining to geography, folk life and the natural sciences. Truly, this was a scheme of tremendous scale, undertaken in large part for purely scientific reasons.

Despite the difficulties, Nearchus' voyage produced a rich harvest. He recorded the morphology of the coast, including a natural harbour that he named Port Alexander; this must have been the site of the present-day Karachi, the old capital of West Pakistan. While sailing along the coast, Nearchus' sailors were startled to see water spouting up from the sea like a fountain. When they realised that this water was being spouted by great sea creatures, they were so petrified that their oars dropped from their hands. What they had seen, of course, were whales.

On the shores of Arabia they found and described, among others, the plants that yielded myrrh, incense, cinnamon and nard (valerian).

Nearchus presented him with a remarkable body of information, but it barely dented Alexander's scientific curiosity. He wanted to send out teams to see where the great rivers of Asia emptied their waters, to explore the coast of North Africa and build naval yards there, to sail to Carthage and the Pillars of Hercules, which you call Gibraltar. He wanted to conquer the world. These plans came to nothing, for they were ended by his death.

—How did Alexander the Great die, and where?

THE DEATH OF ALEXANDER THE GREAT

As I may have mentioned, his constant and unflagging mental and physical activity had exhausted him and, coupled with the burden of his tremendous responsibilities and the effects of the serious wounds he had suffered in various battles, had so worn him down that when he was stricken by a high fever he was unable to recover. He died in Babylon on June 13, 323 BC, at the age of thirty-three.

At the time there were rumours that he had been poisoned, in revenge for the death of Callisthenes. Some even said that I was the one who furnished the poison. I can assure you that there is no truth in those stories.

Because he was still such a young man, and because he was stricken down so suddenly, Alexander had made no provision for a successor. When asked to whom he would leave his kingdom, he answered "the best".

—*What happened after Alexander's death? What impact did it have on the army? I imagine that it must have thrown everything into confusion. And the men? How did they feel?*

When the soldiers heard that Alexander was dying, they all wanted to bid him farewell. Many did manage to visit him, and even at death's door he was able to thank them for their devotion.

THE IMPACT OF THE DEATH OF ALEXANDER

When the news of Alexander's death reached the royal court, Greek and barbarian alike bewailed him. The mother of Darius declared that she would neither eat nor see the light of the sun again. She kept her vow, and five days later was dead. She who had survived the defeat and death of her own son was unable to endure the death of his generous and endearing conqueror.

The news of his death reached Greece a few days later. At first the Greeks did not dare to believe it. Admirers and enemies alike were taken by surprise, and hesitated to react in any way. His enemies were especially cautious, for they had not forgotten what had happened twelve years previously, when word had spread that he had been killed in a battle on the Danube and the Thebans began to celebrate. You will remember what happened next, that just two weeks later he appeared before the Seven Gates of Troy and reduced the city to a smouldering ruin.

In Babylon, a pall of silence lay over the city for four days, but slowly the inevitable quarrels over the succession began. In Macedonia Alexander's half-witted half-brother Philip Arrhidaeus was named king, with Perdiccas as regent, with the proviso that if the child Alexander's wife Roxana was carrying should be a son then he would eventually be proclaimed king. Twelve years later both she and her son were executed, while Olympias put Arrhidaeus to death and was herself eventually killed by relatives of her many victims.

One year later Alexander's body was carried from Babylon to Alexandria, and is most probably buried there.

Already, Alexander the Great was becoming a legend.

RECOGNITION OF WHAT
ALEXANDER THE GREAT ACHIEVED

After the death of Alexander the Great countless works were written about him —his personality, his life, and his achievements. There were eighty versions of just the history ascribed to Callisthenes! Many of these had little to do with reality. The most accurate works were those that appeared in mediaeval Europe and in the East. And interest in him is still as keen as ever, I see. Books about Alexander have been translated into twenty-four languages in countries from Iceland to Malaysia.

In Asia he is venerated as Iskandar.

Numerous Turkistani princes have claimed him as an ancestor, and in many parts of Asia the people still say that they are descended from his soldiers; the Kalash people of south Afghanistan are one example. Alexander the Great is also mentioned in the Koran.

The Egyptians considered him the son of their last Pharaoh, and the first Christians portrayed Christ with the features of Alexander the Great.

In his short life he created a new age for mankind. He abolished the city-states, and expanded the horizons of Greek culture, which had been limited to the Aegean basin.

He created, albeit incompletely, a global state that later facilitated the spread of Christianity.

His achievements still stand as a shining example for mankind. His own behaviour was an object lesson in encouraging solidarity in place of pettiness and dissension.

—*Did he ever tell you that he wanted to rule the whole world?*

Not directly, but from the things I taught him I can see that he may have had some such idea in mind.

THE IDEA OF WORLD IMPERIUM

I believe — and I said this to him many times — that the peoples who live in Europe, and in general in cold regions where life is difficult, need to be tough and courageous in order to survive. And they are, but they have no social life and are deficient in intellectual and artistic abilities. The Asiatic peoples, on the other hand, who live in warm climates, have an easier life and are thus softer. But although they are clever, and their societies abound in intellectual and artistic activity, they live in a state of subjection and slavery.

The people of Greece, though, who live between Europe and Asia, in a moderate climate, have the qualities of both the Europeans and the Asians, ruggedness and courage combined with great intellectual and artistic abilities. With these qualities the Greeks could rule the world, provided that all her cities were united.

I think that these words of mine had a great impact on the young Alexander, and may have inspired the idea of a world imperium and globalisation.

—*I would like you to give me a summary account of precisely what Alexander the Great achieved.*

In a very short space of time, and despite being constantly engaged in gruelling battles and unending warfare, Alexander managed to accomplish an extraordinary feat of civilisation.

I think I told you that he founded more than seventy cities in key locations. Few of them were really cities, of course.

Most were just settlements, although many did, later, develop into cities. Several of them he called Alexandria, after himself. Historically, we know of sixteen such Alexandrias, six of which still exist, although all but one now have different names. The one that survived and became a great metropolis is, of course, the one in Egypt, which was and still is one of the great port cities of the Mediterranean.

THE CITY OF ALEXANDRIA

After the destruction of Tyre, a new seaport was needed in the Eastern Mediterranean. Alexander envisaged it as a great new centre that would be the perfect link between East and West, not only for trade, but also for culture.

He chose the site himself — a natural harbour surrounded by hills at the western edge of the Nile delta. The new city was laid out to his instructions by the Rhodian architect Deinocrates, and he kept a sharp eye on the process. He specified where the agora was to be, and the sanctuaries of the Greek and Egyptian gods. He was present when the line of the city walls was marked out. He even asked to see the preliminary models for the main streets, the agora and the temples. And he supplied the funds necessary to fuel its initial operation and growth. The city of Alexandria was founded towards the end of 332 BC, when Alexander conquered Egypt — or rather when he liberated it from the Persians, whom the Egyptians hated.

Alexander's vision proved to be very astute. The city of Alexandria was and still is one of the most famous and most important cities on the Mediterranean.

When it was founded Alexandria was an intellectual centre on a par with Athens. It was the link between the civilisations of Greece and Egypt. You will perhaps remember that one of the Seven Wonders of the ancient world was the great Library at Alexandria, which contained seven hundred thousand books. It was burned to the ground in 47 BC, in one of the greatest losses to mankind of all time.

—Recently I read something in a magazine about a book called 'Black Athena'. The author, Martin Bernal, says among other things that the intellectual achievements of the Ancient Greeks were more or less borrowed from, or at best based on, the culture of Ancient Egypt and Africa in general. And he also says that you raided the Library in Alexandria and that everything you wrote was in fact taken from there. George James' book 'Stolen Legacy', which unfortunately is still widely read, says much the same thing.

Let me remind you of just one thing to show how unsubstantiated these books are: I was dead before the Library of Alexandria was even built. But let us return to Alexander.

Alexander founded cities all across Asia to support his sovereignty over the conquered territories. He chose their sites carefully, building them at strategic locations to ensure commercial and political communication. He filled them with Greek settlers, so that from the beginning they would have a mixed population of Greeks and local people. He encouraged nomadic peoples to become farmers, which boosted the development of those regions.

A new idea began to emerge from the new landscape he created: that all people, whatever race they belong to, whatever language they speak, have the same rights and must be co-equal partners in the polity. He made every effort to ensure that there would be no discrimination between citizens anywhere in his vast domains, but all would live together peacefully.

One aspect of his plans for the blending of peoples was intermarriage on a grand scale and in accordance with local custom, with Greek men taking Asian brides. During his years of campaigning some ten thousand such marriages took place, and he always bestowed rich gifts on the new couples. This trend was reinforced by his own decision to marry Roxana. According to Arrian, Alexander captured a fortress in Sogdiana and took prisoner the family of the Bactrian chief who was defending it, whose name was Oxyartes. His daughter Roxana was reputedly the most beautiful woman in Asia (after the wife of Darius), and Alexander fell in love with her and married her.

There was obviously a political dimension to this marriage, in that it strengthened the bonds between the conqueror and the conquered people. Alexander was not a man who loved easily.

—*In the end, what is your overall opinion about Alexander the Great's contribution to the world?*

I think that it was extremely important, in many different areas.

ALEXANDER THE GREAT'S CROWNING ACHIEVEMENT

As we have said, in one way or another he united the Greeks, who may have worshipped the same gods and spoken the same language but were attached to the institution of the city-state. From citizens of different cities, he made them feel that they all belonged to the same nation. It helped that they were all eager to punish the Persians, and saw that Alexander could help them achieve this. In the end, from a punitive campaign the expedition to Asia became a civilising mission. This was, I think, inevitable, given Alexander's education and culture. Did I mention that he kept Homer's epics under his pillow all those years?

He firmly believed in the uniqueness and the grandeur of the Greek spirit, and he carried it to every place he went. Without Alexander the world might never have known Greek civilisation, and without Greek civilisation it would have been difficult for the Roman Empire to acquire, along with the military, the cultural substance upon which European civilisation rests. The Romans, remember, embraced Greek culture and became Hellenised.

Without Alexander, the language of the Gospel might not have been Greek.

Alexander's rule was so firmly established in the minds of the conquered peoples that even after his death no real change occurred.

The cities he founded and peopled mainly with Greeks

became cultural beacons of the spirit of Hellenism and connecting links between the Greek, Asian and Chinese civilisations. That was a world-changing development, with implications that endure to this day. It was a contribution of inestimable value to the global history of civilisation.

Another thing that Alexander did was to establish a single currency. From end to end of his vast dominions the Greek drachma was used. This facilitated trade and boosted the economy, just as you in modern Europe have attempted to do with the euro.

The drachma in Ancient Greece was equivalent to six obols, a small silver coin, the number one could comfortably hold in one's hand. The word drachma comes from a verb meaning to grasp, and thus literally meant a fistful. The duodecimal system was abandoned in favour of the decimal system.

Alexander has been criticised for not having made proper arrangements for his succession, since he had no natural or legal heir (his half-brother Philip Arrhidaeus was mentally incompetent), in order to ensure that his empire would live on.

But his empire did not break up after his death: it was merely divided into four kingdoms, ruled by four of his friends and Companions whom he had from time to time singled out.

Many people compare the pacifying and civilising work of Alexander to that of the Roman Empire. But while some degree of comparison is possible from the point of view of outcome, it must be remembered that the Roman Empire and its achievements were the work of numerous emperors over a much longer period of time. Not of one man in the space of ten years. No other achievement of such magnitude has ever borne the personal stamp of a single man.

—*Do you think that he deserves to be called "Great"?*

Unquestionably. Because anyone who considers himself able to do great things and believes he has what it takes to achieve them is worthy of honour and respect and may become great[152]. And Alexander showed that he was capable of great feats and could carry out great missions.

When someone is aware of his limitations and therefore does not attempt great deeds, he is following the admonition to "know thyself" in not seeking to become great. But if he knows that his abilities are limited and yet ventures beyond them, then he is a fool or deluded and far from becoming great.

If, however, he has the capacity to achieve great things but thinks himself capable only of small-scale endeavours and humble deeds, then at best he merits the label "modest", and can no more than the others become great.

By the way, do you know who the first person to call Alexander "great" was? Darius.

Alexander knew his abilities and dared to use them.

He was also gallant and dauntless. He spoke his thoughts and showed his feelings. He was interested in truth and indifferent to the opinion of others. Like all men of spirit, he condescended little and his friends were those of his own choosing.

You are looking troubled. I suspect that what is bothering you with regard to his greatness is the revels he organised and shared in and especially the regrettable outcome of some of them. Let me explain.

I believe that amusement is part of life, as long as it is enjoyed decently and with moderation in word and deed. When a person makes a joke in a modest and decent manner, he is described as witty and everyone enjoys his company, But when his jokes are hurtful, then he causes displeasure and is described as sarcastic[153].

Nor is there anything discreditable in the kinds of pleasure to be obtained from banquets. All men love pleasure. This is justified by the fact that pleasure is inseparable from the act that perpetuates the human race. One might therefore say that men love pleasure because they love life itself.

But is that true? Or do they love life for its pleasures? Which is the primary incentive? [154]

There are, of course, other acts that procure pleasure in life apart from sex. For example, enjoying a piece of music or a work of art, or solving a problem after long, hard thought —these induce feelings of exquisite pleasure and delight. In general, mental activity is one of the most important human occupations and gives great pleasure. In fact, the greatest pleasure of all is the pleasure of thinking.

—*Since the subject came up, what did Alexander the Great think of sex?*

Alexander was passionate and impetuous in a great many things, but very sober when it came to sex. In general, physical pleasures carried very little weight with him, and he was moderate in his pursuit of them. He believed that a king ought to be able rule himself first of all if he was to rule others. He rarely drank, and when he did it was usually deliberate, because it helped him mix more easily with others.

ALEXANDER THE GREAT'S RELATIONS WITH WOMEN

Alexander was very guarded with women. The beauty and nobility of many of the women who were essentially his prisoners was often a temptation, but one which he resisted. But it is a matter of record that he once described Persian women as being tantalising.

He married twice, both times for political reasons. His first wife was the daughter of Darius, and the second Roxana, of whom we have spoken. And between ourselves, neither marriage can have been much of a hardship, for they were both beautiful women.

—*Are you telling me that he liked beautiful women? How does that square with the insinuations that Alexander the Great was a homosexual?*

That, I can assure you, he was not. He married two wives, he had affairs with a number of women, some of whose names we know, some we do not. One that I know of was Barsine, the widow of Memnon, who was the commander of the Persian forces at the Battle of the Granicus A rare beauty. The question of homosexuality in ancient Greece is misunderstood and needs much fuller discussion.

—*That's true, I've read a bit about how widespread homosexuality was in Ancient Greece and I'd like to hear what you have to say about it.*

HOMOSEXUALITY IN ANCIENT GREECE

When Alexander and his companions were about fourteen, and at school with me in Mieza, I explained to them why it was necessary, for all living creatures that could not ensure the survival of their species by any other means, for the male to mate with the female for the purpose of procreation[155].

For man, this co-habitation is not only essential for the perpetuation of the species but is also pleasurable. It improves the quality of life, makes life more beautiful.

In other words, human beings live in pairs not only in order to procreate, but for mutual support and the achievement of shared goals[156]. The love between men and women is a bond of mind and soul, it combats loneliness, and it fosters noble creativity. As I say in my book On the Soul, all living creatures —including man— have a natural inclination to leave another similar being behind them. Plato also said something of the sort.

This natural inclination towards physical union between man and woman was powerful among the ancient Greeks. Any other sort of sexual intercourse, between men, for example, or between women, was deemed unnatural, abnormal, a perversion. An abnormality of the flesh becomes a vice, a disease, and a vicious, diseased society cannot live and thrive for any length of time. Do not forget that the watchword of my day was "a healthy mind in a healthy body".

In my opinion, the modern view that homosexuality was rife in ancient Greece is due to the misinterpretation of the words *eromenos* and *erastes*, both meaning 'lover', which occur frequently in literary texts. Open a dictionary of Ancient Greek and you will see that the word *erastes* also signifies admirer, follower, adorer, and the word *eromenos* means both one's love and one's bosom friend.

If homosexuality was accepted in Ancient Greece, then

why were there laws against it? A number of historians mention the case of a man called Timarchus, who was brought before the judges because he was a homosexual. This shows that they were not accepted, an din fact were social outcasts, and referred to as "loose-arses". There were also laws against pederasty: in Sparta, for example, such a law was instituted by the famous lawgiver Lycurgus[157].

As in all societies, so too in Ancient Greece there were those who performed unnatural acts. There were certainly homosexuals, but they were the exception that proves the rule. Like illnesses, abnormalities are part of human nature, part of life.

Also, the way of life then was different from what it is today, and can easily be misinterpreted. Boys spent a lot of time in the gymnasium, and they did many things in pairs, which bound them together in close friendships. Such friends had common goals and common aspirations.

In Ancient Greece the sons of free citizens had to be properly educated, so that they would be able to take part in public affairs, serve as judges and make laws. Who would see to their education? Their fathers? They were not, in my view, the most suitable persons, for between their public duties, which for a free citizen were numerous and important, and their household affairs they had little time to spare. They therefore had to engage tutors for their sons. The more they were able to pay, the better the teacher they could hire.

A tutor would necessarily be older than his pupil. Usually the age difference was about half a generation, so that they would understand one another better and would be more likely to become friends. These were lifetime friendships, the result of daily intimate contact over a number of years. And by intimate I simply mean marked by very close association and familiarity: it was a mental and spiritual intimacy, not a physical one. The teacher was a sort of spiritual father to the boy; he wanted to turn out into the world sons of his own spiritual fashioning, children of his soul. This tutorial relationship was much the same as that of a guru and his pupil in Asia.

In your day such intimate friendships are unlikely to be misinterpreted. But when a father caresses his son and demonstrates his love for him, do you immediately think that this is unnatural? That it is pederasty? So why is there this misunderstanding in the similar case of the spiritual parent and child, between whom similar feelings have grown up over their years together?

In the final analysis, the teacher, the spiritual father, is largely the personal choice of the pupil, while the natural father is not the choice of the son.

Teacher and pupil are bound by ties of mind and spirit, not body. They become the closest of friends.

Ancient literature offers many examples of famous pairs of friends: Socrates and Alcibiades, Achilles and Patroclus, Alexander and Hephaestion. Their love for and devotion to one another was misunderstood by some, who accused them of homosexuality.

Such friendships were cited by various mischief-makers as proof that homosexuality was a common practice in Ancient Greece. The delusion still persists, and this canard is trotted out occasionally when someone wants his few minutes in the limelight.

Take, for example, Socrates and Alcibiades. Socrates may have admired Alcibiades' beauty, but there was no sexual desire there. If you have read the *Symposium*, you may remember that Plato has Alcibiades declare that he spent what was left of a night after some banquet in Socrates' room without any of the traffic that takes place between lovers. Besides which, we know that, although he was an ugly man, Socrates had love affairs with women, one of them the niece of Aristides the Just.

The other celebrated and similarly misunderstood pair, Achilles and Patroclus, are heroes in the *Iliad* and, however persuaded some may be of the contrary, they were not lovers. People cite Achilles' lament for the death of Patroclus as evidence of homosexual love. Achilles was not grieving for the loss of a lover, but for the loss of his inseparable companion. At some point in the *Iliad* Homer says that the lovely Briseis slept in Achilles' tent, and elsewhere describes how she lamented the death of Patroclus. Would she have mourned him so if he had been her darling Achilles' lover? She would have rejoiced, instead.

Alexander, too, mourned and would eat nothing for three days after the death of Hephaestion, his friend and companion since childhood.

Even Epaminondas, who before he died uttered the famous words "Fight for your country — that is the best and only omen", was accused of being a homosexual.

But anyone with a bit of common sense could come to the right conclusion simply by reading Aristophanes' comedy *Lysistrata*, where the Athenian women send word to their menfolk at the front declaring a sex strike until they make peace and end the war. Now a war is not lightly abandoned. The women knew perfectly well what this threat would mean to their husbands. If the men were able to satisfy themselves sexually among themselves, especially those in the army's camps where some maintain that homosexuality runs rampant, would the women's strike have goaded them to end the war?

One last word before we leave this subject. You are still very young, and so I want to impress on you that friendship is a very precious thing. It must be cherished like fine crystal. Friendship demands sacrifice, has in fact been called the daughter of sacrifice. A man without a friend is a beast. The only poem I ever wrote was in memory of my friend Hermias of Atarneus, who was assassinated as the result of a conspiracy within his own circle.

—*You only ever wrote one poem? But I know that you were interested in poetry, and wrote two books about it. What are they about?*

They are about poetry as an art form.

THE ART OF POETRY

Poetry is a form of literature. It is also a creative process, in the sense of making, of creating, something entirely new, which as I mention in the Physics is something that man is able to do.

The difference between prose and poetry is the same as that between the poet and the historian[158]. The historian sets down the facts as they happened, the poet as they might have happened. That is why I think that poetry is more akin to philosophy and more important than history.

In my books I often quote from Homer's epics. I also used them to arouse and sustain Alexander's interest and indeed his enthusiasm. Epics, as you know, are poems that recount the deeds of heroes.

My first book on the art of poetry deals with tragedy and epic poetry. I wrote about comedy in my second book, which unfortunately has been lost. But I can tell you that of all the dramatic arts I have the least regard for comedy. It merely imitates vulgar actions for the sake of laughter, whereas tragedy imitates serious actions of great magnitude, which are narrated in appropriate and pleasurable language, and its heroes are serious figures[159].

But we have got a long way from your namesake, Alexander, which is where our conversation began. Have I told you enough about him? Have you learned what you wanted to know?

Yes, I think I have.

I have the feeling that there is something you want to say.

You're right, but before I ask my next question I want to tell you a story I heard from one of my professors at the University. He was standing for election to Parliament and he found himself having a meal in a taverna one day in some less rarefied company. There was some serious talk, but also a lot of jokes, and what with the food and the retsina a good time was being had by all. After a couple of hours of this the professor stood up to leave. They exchanged mutual good wishes all round, and one fellow, a man of about forty, got up and clapped him on the shoulder and said "You've got my vote for sure, mate, because besides being a university professor you seem like an educated man!"

I saw you smiling while you were telling that story, Alexander. The joke was that a university professor was not automatically assumed to be an educated man. Your shoulder-clapper was right to be confused, though, and I will tell you why.

WHO IS TO BE THOUGHT AN EDUCATED MAN

It is very difficult in the age you are living in to say who should be considered educated. Things were much simpler in my day. A philosopher was considered educated, because he had some general knowledge about all the sciences of the time. This was of course easier than it is now, since the body of knowledge was so much smaller, in every domain. When the ancient philosophers tackled a specific subject, they did so because they want to verify a theory, to formulate a general principle or a general law.

A philosopher nowadays cannot be said to be an educated man in the same way. For philosophers today, those who have really studied philosophy, deal mainly with the so-called humanities. Their knowledge is of history, sociology, education, theology and other related domains, but not the natural sciences.

So let me ask you this: can a man, however deeply he has studied the humanities, be considered educated if he is ignorant of the basic principles of how his own body works and has no idea of how or why the various natural phenomena in the world around him occur? In my view, no. An educated man must be well informed —knowledgeable, that is, not learned— in all the subjects that concern mankind. And so your shoulder-clapper was right. Too often the so-called educated know too much about too little. But your professor, he saw, was knowledgeable about many things outside his own science, in which he might be presumed to be an expert. To top it off, he was also good company.

—*You have taught me a lot about Alexander tonight, and about a great many other things as well. But your own contribution to humanity is immeasurable. I would like you to tell me something more about yourself and your work.*

Well, then, since you ask, here is my story.

THE LIFE OF ARISTOTLE

I was born in the little town of Stagira in northeast Chalki-diki in 384 BC. We spoke a variant of the Ionian dialect there, because the city had been founded by colonists from Andros and Chalcis. Perhaps you have been to Stagira? It's only a hundred kilometres from your own city of Thessaloniki.

—*Yes, I've been there. The folk there are immensely proud of you, and have erected a fine, imposing marble statue of you.*

Yes, it is indeed a grand one. But it makes me think of what your Kolokotronis said during the 1821 War of Independence when someone asked him why he didn't go and visit other regions where he was admired as a fighter and commander, to rally support for the cause. Kolokotronis, who was short and slight, simply said "Better they listen to me than look at me". It's the same with me: they have put up a fine, great statue because they have only heard of me, they've never seen me. For I have to admit that I wasn't much to look at either. Short and scrawny, with very thin legs. So I always took care to wear good clothes and be well turned-out. And just for the record, my birthplace, Ancient Stagira, was a little to the west of the present village.

My father's name was Nicomachus. He was a doctor, a member of the guild of the Asclepiads, and the personal physician (and friend) of Alexander's grandfather, King Amyntas III. I may have told you that already. My mother was called Phaestis, and she came from Chalcis.

My father often took me with him when he visited patients, and I learned a lot about medicine from him that way. He insisted particularly on teaching me anatomy, and he showed me how to perform various surgical operations.

I never practised medicine myself, but that experience left me with a lifelong interest in the subject, and in biology. That is why I often use medical examples in my texts. My knowledge of anatomy proved very useful later for my work in zoology.

Both my parents died while I was still a child. A kinsman

of mine called Proxenus took me into his household and gave me an education, for both of which I am very grateful. I was able to repay some of what I owed to him later, for when he died I adopted his son, Nicanor.

When I was eighteen he sent me to the best school in Greece, Plato's Academy in Athens. I went there not to become a philosopher, but to acquire the finest possible education. But spending my days studying with the other students there gave me a great love of philosophy, and I decided that I too would become a philosopher.

When I first came to the Academy, Plato was in Sicily and the school was being run by Eudoxus, a brilliant man, a mathematician, astronomer and geographer.

—*When you say that you wanted to become a philosopher, what exactly do you mean? How would you define philosophy, and, since 'philosophy' means 'love of wisdom', who would you describe as wise?*

Be patient and I will tell you.

WHAT IS PHILOSOPHY?

Philosophy is the science that seeks the truth without aiming at any practical benefit. That is why I consider it superior to all the other sciences, for they are expected to have some utilitarian outcome, to be of some practical use, while philosophy pursues knowledge for its own sake. Philosophy is the supreme science. It is more fit to be served than to serve. Philosophy is the science that tells us the ultimate purpose of everything we do.

Those who serve the science of philosophy are the happiest of men, and indeed the only truly happy men. It is a favourite saying of mine that philosophy is an ornament in prosperity and a refuge in adversity. The same is true of learning, as I have already told you.

As for the second part of your question, who can be described as wise —well, wise is a word that is very hard to define. Your contemporaries might describe as wise someone who can understand and find solutions to problems, in his own domain or elsewhere, which his colleagues struggle to grapple with. For although many may perceive the existence of the problem, the wise man is the one who lays it bare and then lays bare its cause. A wise man must also, in my opinion, be able to set forth his knowledge with clarity and precision.

But let us return to me.

ARISTOTLE'S LIFE AT PLATO'S ACADEMY

At the Academy Plato's personality and philosophy were a formative influence in my life. And I think that in my books, the different opinions I have heard notwithstanding, I almost always begin by stating Plato's opinion and commenting on it, and only then formulate my own theories. With the exception, perhaps, of the works on the natural sciences.

Obviously, I disagreed with Plato on a number of subjects, and some people thought this was disrespectful. Plato may have been irritated by my disagreement, but he still called me "the mind of the School", and as long as he lived I remained a faithful member of his Academy. I believed, however, that an intelligent man should not hesitate to retract an earlier opinion when the truth was at stake[160].

I admired Plato. When I criticised his work, I have to admit that I was not happy about it. The members of the Academy enjoyed a certain freedom in the pursuit of their studies, and I was the only one who spent so much time on the natural sciences; in that area, therefore, I was under no form of direction. The only thing I taught at the school was rhetoric, the art of speech-making. But what I tried to teach my students was that rhetoric should not just aim at eliciting an emotional response in the hearer, at persuasion through polished expression alone, which was the practice of most rhetoricians, including Isocrates. I told them, rather, that reasoned argument was also important in a speech, that proof was also a mode of persuasion. Isocrates was a distinguished orator, a golden-tongued man of unparalleled eloquence, and I admired him for that. But he was no thinker. He was more interested in making an impression than in seeking the truth.

During my time in Athens I also wrote a number of works, many of which have been lost.

When Plato died, in 347 BC, I was not appointed head of the Academy, as I had secretly hoped. Instead, he was succeeded by his nephew Speusippus, who truth be told was closer to Plato in his views. After that, as you will understand, there was not much point in my remaining at the School.

In those days, too, anti-Macedonian feeling was running high in Athens, because Philip had sacked the city-state of Olynthus, which was an Athenian colony. I was looked at askance, because I was not only Macedonian by borth but had kept up my contacts with Macedonia. And so, after twenty-two years, and with great sadness, I said good-bye to the Academy. My years there had been very fruitful, and very pleasant. But since I had to leave, I was glad to be able to accept an invitation from my friend Hermias to come to Assus, in Asia Minor, on the coast opposite Lesbos.

ARISTOTLE IN ASSUS AND LESBOS

In Assus I set up a sort of school of my own. I also took a wife, Pythias, who was the niece and adopted daughter of Hermias. We had a daughter, but sadly she died, very young, in Athens; she was my first child. The mother of my second child, a son whom I named Nicomachus, was a fellow Macedonian called Herpyllis. Our liaison was never formalised, and after years in Assus I went to Lesbos. There I met Theophrastus, who became my closest associate. He followed me to Macedonia. Theophrastus was my name for him, because of his beautiful turn of expression. His real name was Tyrtamus.

Both in Lesbos and in Assus my chief interest was in biology, and I spent a good deal of time in observation and investigation.

ARISTOTLE'S LIFE AT PELLA

In 343 BC King Philip of Macedonia invited me, upon the recommendation of my friend Hermias, to undertake the education of his young son Alexander. I agreed most willingly, because Philip's power and prestige were rising steadily. Besides which, I was eager to teach a future monarch.

In Pella I had everything: prestige, authority, and money. I taught Alexander and his companions Homer and the tragic poets, which were the backbone of Greek education in those days. But we also spent hours discussing politics, political economy, rhetoric, and in general the qualities and duties of a leader. These discussions formed the basis for two new books, which I wrote at that time, *On kingship* and *In favour of colonies*, which contained material that was very useful and of direct interest to Alexander on his expedition. That was also when I had the idea of assembling all the material that I later published as *Politics*.

When Alexander came of age, I went home to Stagira.

THE FOUNDING OF THE LYCEUM

After Philip died I returned to Athens, with the idea of founding a school of my own. I had plenty of money, for Philip had paid me very well. Just northeast of Athens there was a grove dedicated to Apollo Lyceus and the Muses, where Socrates often used to take his pupils. Near the grove were some buildings, which I wanted to buy for my school, but as a foreigner in Athens I did not have the right to own property. In the end I leased them.

Every morning I would walk around the grove with my students, and we would discuss various subjects. My school derived its later name of Peripatetic from this habit of ours of walking around (=*peripatontas*). During these morning perambulations we discussed the easier subjects, such as rhetoric and politics. The subjects that required closer attention and more study, like logic, physics and metaphysics,

I lectured on in the afternoon, inside the school. I called the school my Lyceum, from the name of the grove, which, as I said, was dedicated to Apollo Lyceus. My closest associate in the school was Theophrastus.

In the Lyceum I created the first library that was more than a private collection. It contained hundreds of maps and manuscripts, and may have inspired the creation of the libraries at Alexandria and Pergamum.

I also set up a museum of natural history, with a remarkable collection of exhibits for the time, which I used to help my students understand my lectures in physics and biology. These collections were assembled with Alexander's help, both financial and through his order that hunters and fishermen in Macedonia and Thrace should send me, or at least inform me of, anything unusual they saw or heard. Today you would say that Alexander sponsored my research programme.

The students took it in turns to serve as president of the Lyceum, a position from which they could freely criticise anyone, inside or outside the school. This system was later adopted by a number of mediaeval European universities.

All the students ate together, and once a month we held a banquet.

—*Banquets in the Lyceum? Now, that is something I would not have expected.*

That is because your idea of a banquet in ancient times is conditioned by the cinema, with scenes of Roman banquets degenerating into orgies.

In Ancient Greece things were different.

BANQUETS IN ANCIENT GREECE

Banquets were an organised social institution, which followed certain rules and had their own etiquette161. They were a forum for the exchange of ideas and centres of intellectual ferment. Remember, there were very few books or libraries in those days. Knowledge was spread orally, by word of mouth.

The banquet in Ancient Greece had two parts, first the dinner and then the drinking-party. The dinner part was brief, and usually simple. The real work, the intellectual work, was done during the drinking-party, which followed the dinner and was introduced by the burning of incense, the singing of hymns and the offering of sacrifices to the gods. The wine they drank was mixed with water, and in fact the modern Greek word for wine, *krasi*, comes from the ancient word *krasis*, which means mixing.

When and how much they drank, and how much water was added, was decided by the banquet-master, who was elected at the beginning of the session. They then set about devising and playing word games, reciting poetry and singing songs. Some of these songs and poems were later published and became popular hits. After that, they chose a subject for general discussion. By the end of the evening, the guests would not only have enjoyed themselves but would also have learned a great deal.

The Greek word for this kind of drinking-party was *symposion*, which means 'drinking together'. Plato considered them great schools, when properly organised, and this sense is reflected in the modern sense of the word 'symposium'.

ARISTOTLE'S LIFE AT THE LYCEUM

The twelve years I spent at the Lyceum were my most productive, because I wrote down my lectures. Those written lectures form the bulk of my surviving works as you know them today. My years at the Lyceum, when I was preparing and recording my lectures, were a time of great intellectual ferment.

The practical orientation of my lectures at the Lyceum and the fact that the students did not live at the school, as they did in Plato's Academy, helped spread my opinions. And they did in fact have a real effect on the everyday life of the city. The Lyceum was no ivory tower, shut away from the real world and the life of society.

Alexander's death rekindled latent anti-Macedonian sentiment. The climate in Athens, for me, his teacher, was becoming oppressive. The Athenians were hostile towards me and they showed it, and I heard that they were preparing to bring charges against me of impiety and of denying the gods.

All the charges were based on the poem I had composed for my friend Hermias, who had been assassinated. They said that was written in the form of a paean, which was a traditional hymn to Apollo.

This threat of a trial for impiety reminded me, of course, of what had happened to Socrates, which had so disillusioned and disgusted me. I contemplated leaving Athens again, although the thought of the journey and the upheaval at my age was daunting. But I preferred to go rather than to face the mental misery of a trial that would be the quintessence of hypocrisy. I knew I would not be able to stand that, not least because I was already so distressed by the death of Alexander. And so I went to Chalcis, which was under Macedonian control and where I had a house, which I had inherited from my mother.

In Athens in those days there were many conservative people who reacted strongly not only to any contrary opinion but even to any discussion about religious matters. And two insignificant Athenians, Eurymedon and Semophilus, were now accusing me of impiety and atheism.

All this trouble, and my great frustration at being deprived of the possibility of teaching, which was my life and my living, affected my health, worsened the stomach condition from which I had been suffering, and in the end led to my death.

How could they have accused you of atheism? You, who taught that "God is the cause and the beginning of all things."

Those words are not the only proof that I am anything but an atheist. My work is full of statements attesting to the contrary. Here are just a few:

- It is reasonable to suppose that happiness is divinely given[162].
- God is the Good-itself[163].

- God is always in that good state in which we sometimes are.
- The gods see everything.

They cannot have been unaware of these things. The formal charges were that I believed in and proclaimed my thoughts about different gods from the ones they believed in.

A man who was truly an atheist could never have been honoured, as I am, by the Christian Church[164].

My portrait appears in both Catholic and Orthodox churches. In Greece, for example, I am depicted in St George's in Negades Zagoraiou as Aristotle the Wise, in Late Byzantine dress and holding a long strip of parchment (1792). There is also a picture of me in the church of the Prophet Elijah in Siatista, with the legend "Here too is Aristotle the Wise" (1744). I appear with Solon in a fresco (1560) in the Philanthropenon Monastery on the island in Lake Ioannina and in the Great Lavra on Mount Athos.

In Italy, I stand in conversation with Plato on the bell-tower of the Cathedral in Florence, and we are, of course, the central figures in Raphael's famous painting of "The School of Athens" in the Vatican.

—*You must have felt bitter about having to withdraw from the world. Do you think that your work was, and perhaps is, not appreciated as much as it deserves?*

No, I cannot say that. Most of Athens was with me. You know, I always liked to talk to ordinary people, farmers, fishermen, artisans. I used to have long discussions with them, and they, I promise you, were interested in my work. And after my death, many of them sang my praises and talked of my contribution to philosophy.

My friend Theophrastus, who succeeded me as head of the Lyceum, erected a statue to me there. At Stagira they honoured me as a hero and named a square and a festival after me. They erected an altar on my grave, called the place Aristoteleion and held their council meetings there. And I don't need to remind you that your own university, which is the largest in Greece, also bears my name: the Aristotle University of Thessaloniki.

RECOGNITION OF ARISTOTLE'S WORK

My work has been read, understood, admired and translated more than that of any other philosopher in history. Luther, who embraced many of my teachings, wanted to adapt some of my books, to make them easier to understand. I have also been called the father of modern science.

Some of my followers were so fanatical that they would not tolerate the slightest questioning of my opinions, even those that were demonstrably false. Galileo, who taught at the University of Pisa, was booed once for that very reason. And in France, a law was passed in 1626 making it illegal to disagree with me! Which is outrageous. That law was the product of the fanaticism that set Catholic against Protestant in the Wars of Religion. I still find it impossible to understand how it can be called a crime to question my opinions.

I am well aware that some of my opinions are not clearly enough expressed, or in the light of modern knowledge are now seen to be wrong. On the other hand, though, the Protestants misinterpreted my ideas, often wilfully, based on very poor translations, and waged war on me quite unjustly.

In the years that followed, my works became known throughout Europe and were studied by eminent scientists in various fields, including Newton and Keppler.

After the 19th century, no scientist considered his work complete unless it contained some reference to me.

—*I'm wondering, now, where did we get our information about your life? And how did your books make their way into our libraries?*

The main source for my life is Diogenes Laertius, who lived in the 3rd. century. The other ancient *Lives* were written by neo-Platonists and Arab and Byzantine scholars.

WHERE DID ARISTOTLE'S MANUSCRIPTS GO?

Theophrastus kept all the manuscripts that were at the Lyceum. After him they were passed on to Neleus of Scepsis, from the school in Assus. His heirs hid them in a cellar, to keep them out of the hands of the rulers of Pergamum, who wanted them for their new library, which was one of the finest in the ancient world. They mouldered in that cellar for a century or so, until in about 100 BC they were bought by a wealthy bibliophile named Apellicon and taken back to Athens.

Fourteen years later they were seized as spoils of war by the Roman general Sulla and carried off to Rome. There they were acquired by Andronicus of Rhodes, a man truly interested in my philosophy, who systematised, edited and published them. That was around the middle of the 1st century BC. Some of my works, however, remained hidden for much longer: the *Constitution of Athens*, you may remember, was not discovered until the end of the 19th century.

— *How many books did you actually write, and how many have survived?*

My estimate is that there were about four hundred altogether, of which one hundred and forty-three are extant. Several of those, however, are to varying degrees incomplete. In general, the ancient world has come down to you in fragments.

THE WORKS OF ARISTOTLE

The list of my works that you have today was established by Immanuel Bekker in 1831 and published by the Berlin Academy. Bekker based his work mainly on the list compiled by Diogenes Laertius in the 3rd century; he mentions three hundred titles, which is certainly not all there were.

The form in which my texts have come down to you is not always authentic. That is understandable, for even in your day mistakes slip in between the author's manuscript and the printed product. So it is perfectly natural that changes should have crept into my works over the centuries, since they were copied and re-copied so many times. Sometimes, too, if a word or brief passage was missing, someone along the way would complete it as he thought best.

The real works are —according to Cicero— a 'flowing river of gold'. I should point out that the works that you have today were not actually written as books, complete in themselves. They are collections of treatises on similar subjects. I did some of the arranging, but most of it was done by my subsequent "editors".

The texts that have survived may not give a complete picture of the magnitude of my work, but they do give you an idea of the variety of subjects I explored.

Most of the works of mine that survive date from my years at the Lyceum. Some were merely lecture notes, which is why the text is incomplete, sometimes repetitious, and expressed in language that is not as polished as it might have been. Some of them contain two or three different opinions about the same thing; that is because they were, as I said, merely notes for use with my students. But because of those 'inconsistencies' famous thinkers, among them Molière, Gassendi and Voltaire, have from time to time tried to have my philosophy dropped from university programmes as incomprehensible.

Here is the list of my books as it was published by the Berlin Academy in 1831. You can print it out, if you like, just to have it.

THE CORPUS ARISTOTELICUM
(BEKKER 1831)

- The Organon: Categories, On Interpretation, Prior Analytics, Posterior Analytics, Topics, Sophistical Refutations
- Physics
- On the Heavens
- On Generation and Corruption
- Meteorology
- On the Universe
- On the Soul
- Parva Naturalia: On the Senses and their Objects, On Memory and Recollection, On Sleep and Waking, On Dreams, On Divination

in Sleep, On Length and Shortness of Life, On Youth, Old Age, Life and Death, and Respiration

- On Breath
- History of Animals
- Parts of Animals
- Movement of Animals
- Progression of Animals
- Generation of Animals
- On Colours
- On Things Heard
- Physiognomonics
- On Plants
- On Marvellous Things Heard
- Mechanics
- Problems
- On Indivisible Lines
- The Situations and Names of Winds
- On Melissus, Xenophanes,Gorgias
- Metaphysics
- Nicomachean Ethics
- Magna Moralia
- Eudemian Ethics
- On Virtues and Vices
- Politics
- Economics
- Rhetoric
- Rhetoric to Alexander
- Poetics

The Constitution of Athens was only discovered, as I said, in 1891, which is why it is not in Bekker's catalogue.

—Looking at that list of titles I can see that you took an interest in just about everything imaginable. I have heard your work called an encyclopaedia of antiquity, which pretty well sums it up.

That I wrote about almost everything is a fact, but so did many other ancient philosophers to a greater or lesser degree. Calling my work an encyclopaedia, though, does not do me justice, because encyclopaedias simply present knowledge without commentary and without the writer's personal experience and opinion. In my works, I present the existing knowledge together with other philosophers' views, but more importantly I set down and expound on my own personal experiences and my own beliefs. This I did religiously. I was also always very careful to review the earlier history of the subject I was dealing with, not only for the sake of objectivity, but also as a source of ideas and knowledge about the particular topic.

Which of the works that have survived do you think are most characteristic of you? And what are they about? Because the titles don't really tell me much.

Some of them we have already touched on the course of our conversation. I will try to give you a 'broad outline', as you say, of the ones we have said less about, stressing the most important points. I think my works on rhetoric are important.

RHETORIC

You may remember that I taught rhetoric at the Academy for years, and with considerable success. It was an art that was very popular with the ancient Greeks, because they loved politics and legal battles, and in those arenas rhetoric is held in high esteem.

I was, of course, not the first to write about rhetoric and the other arts of speech; many others had done so before me. But for them the sole aim of rhetoric is to elicit an emotional response from the listener. I do not disagree that an orator's words have to stir his audience, but in my opinion they should do so through reason and not through artifice, such as bringing widows into court to weep and wail, or wretched-looking children, to arouse pity.

The Sophists practised rhetoric in a similar manner. They would try to bewilder the ordinary man by seemingly disproving what he believed was true[165].

In my opinion it is more important to use proper arguments, and that I believe was my personal contribution to rhetoric.

The arguments used should not require expert knowledge, but be readily understandable to the average thinking man. They should be based on examples and be reasonably persuasive. What will win most applause is a clever syllogism, neatly placed.

Nor should an advocate be unconditional in his arguments. A politician, for example, may allow that that what he is proposing may be unfair, but he must never say that it is unprofitable. Or an advocate may admit that his client has caused injury, but he must never say that he has broken the law. A good orator must be able to discern and employ all possible means of persuading anyone of anything.

I think that an orator must take into account the age and level of education of his listeners, and adapt his speech accordingly. This also applies to his manner of speaking and his tone of voice.

Borrowing phrases from the poets is foolish, for poetry is a different art entirely. The words an orator uses must be carefully chosen: neither colourless, so that they pass unnoticed, nor pompous, which irritates people.

An orator who chooses the proper words to express his thoughts will always be clear. That does not mean that he cannot use elegant language, however, which creates a good impression. For people admire what is elegant and love what is pleasing[166]. I repeat, however, that prose does not admit of as much ornamentation as poetry. Ornate language shocks when it is used by a young person or a slave. An orator's speech should be natural, and for this he needs to be something of an actor. He should use the words and expressions of the ordinary people, but be careful to avoid cliché and dullness.

His words must always be seemly, and his sentences properly constructed and flowing. They must also be lively: a sentence like "he was in the flower of his youth" is much more effective than "he was a young man".

—I must admit that I was expecting you to begin with your works on logic. Because we learned at school that you raised logic to a science. Not that I understood much in our logic classes.

You are not wrong about my contribution to the science of logic. The great German philosopher Kant said that logic had been unable to take a single step forward since my time.

LOGIC

Logic is part of, or rather a tool of, philosophy and it has to do with syllogisms, deductive arguments that lead to useful (or possibly not) conclusions. I will give you an example from everyday life.

I think you will agree that a football fan is not objective when it comes to his team, and when you know that journalist X is a PAOK fan you conclude that his commentary on last Sunday's PAOK-ARES match was not objective. That is an example of logical reasoning.

I chose an example using football teams because you're a young man, and as I said earlier, one of the key things a speaker has to pay attention to is the age and general situation of his audience. But let us consider, now, the science of logic.

First of all, logic is not a self-contained science[167], but is useful in every branch of knowledge. Because logic is what helps show us where and what kind of proofs are needed[168]. Logic is, therefore, a tool for the scientist.

Actually, the word 'logic' (the word, not the concept) was unknown in my day. It was first used in its present sense by one of my successors at the Lyceum, Alexander of Aphrodisias.

The books of mine that deal primarily with logic are the *Prior Analytics*, where I describe different kinds of thought, the *Posterior Analytics*, where I describe scientific reasoning, and the *Topics*, where I describe dialectical reasoning.

But I will continue now with the notion of reasoning, because on the one hand I consider it more or less an invention of my own and on the other it is something that you are certainly familiar with.

REASONING

Reasoning for me is a sequence of thoughts that is set in motion when some question is raised. Once a subject has been introduced, it is immediately followed by some thought bearing upon the truth of the matter under consideration, and this train of thought continues under its own steam, so to speak[169].

I am sure you are not much the wiser for my explanation. But here is an example, of deductive reasoning, from the geometry you learned at school, that may help: "Things equal to the same thing are also equal to one another."

That is, if it is shown that two angles, A and B, are each equal to a third angle, C, then angles A and B will also be equal to one another. Another phrase that is probably familiar to you is reduction to the absurd[170]. It means taking a proposition and applying to it a logical sequence of statements that are each indisputably correct, which in the end show the original proposition to be impossible.

Another kind of reasoning is *inductive*. I will start with an example here, so that you can see straight away what I am talking about.

In order to reach the conclusion that vipers are poisonous, you do not have to confirm that this is true of each and every individual viper, which in any case is in practice impossible. What you can do in this case is observe that a sufficient number of vipers are poisonous, and infer from that fact that the rest probably are as well. That is, inductive reasoning leads from particular instances to a generalised conclusion, from partial knowledge to a universal truth. For when the mind perceives a truth in a sufficient number of cases, it can accept the possibility that this truth will apply in all similar cases.

Proof is also scientific reasoning, which always leads to

true conclusions. It is impossible for there to be direct proof of everything. There would be no end to it, for every new thing that emerged would have to be proven.

The *axioms* that are used in mathematics are accepted only if they can be demonstrated in practice. A characteristic example is Euclid's proposition that "If equals are subtracted from equals, then the remainders are equal". That is, if you have a pair of scales nicely balanced and you remove an equal amount of whatever is in the pans from each, the scales will continue to be in balance.

Another rule of logic is that two contradictory statements about the same thing cannot both be true. That is, it is impossible simultaneously to affirm and deny a fact and still be telling the truth. Necessarily, only one part of the contradiction will be true[171].

—That is only common sense. It reminds me of the story about the headman of a village who was hearing a dispute between two neighbours. When he had heard the first man's argument, he said "You are perfectly right". And when he heard the second man, he said "You are perfectly right". His wife, who happened to be present, exclaimed "But surely they can't both be right!" To which her husband replied, "You are perfectly right, too, my dear!"

But I think that's enough about logic. I remember that another of the human values you mentioned as emerging from communal living is morality. Can you tell me something about that?

Of course I can.

ON ETHICS

My best-known works on ethics are the *Nicomachean Ethics* and the *Eudemean Ethics*, which covered two sets of lectures at the Academy. The first was published by my son Nicomachus, and the other by my student Eudemus.

These works were strongly influenced by Plato's teachings on ethics, which dealt with the moral rules that govern human life, but they also had a religious aspect.

For me, ethics is the study of character, the moral character of men who live in society[172]. A man who lives alone cannot be said to be either moral or immoral. Therefore, ethics is part of sociology, of what I call political science.

I have told you something of my thoughts on ethics, on morality, earlier in our conversation, but it would not hurt to go over them again, from a different point of view.

When I speak of morality I mean the mental virtue that adorns and characterises the virtuous man and that can be summarised in the following observations:

- The virtuous man is a right-thinking man[173].
- The virtues concern emotions and actions.
- Virtuous activities are generally pleasurable only insofar as they have their achieved their purpose.
- The immoral man has no shame[174].
- The immoral man passively obeys his natural instincts, which in most cases are what urge him to perform immoral acts.

Prudence presupposes the total absence of vicious desires and is characterised by right thinking. That is, the prudent man must know what is good for man in general. The virtuous life is a very important thing, but it is undermined by pleasure, regret and evil, which prevent us from recognising what is truly valuable in life. Prudence in a man also has to do with his degree of self-mastery in the face of pleasure. And when I say pleasure here I do not mean intellectual satisfaction, or the delights of sight, sound and smell, but those sensual pleasures that gratify both man and beast, such as those that come from food, wine and sex[175].

The only regret that can result from prudence is an unfulfilled desire for the licit pleasures I mentioned earlier[176].

Pleasure is not related only to the act itself, but is in far larger proportion an outcome of the act. The tendency to derive pleasure from certain things is innate.

Pleasure and regret should not be avoided; rather, we must take care that they exist in proper measure at the proper time[177]. As you would say, timing is all.

Shunning pleasure is difficult, even more difficult than

shunning anger. The pleasures that derive from thinking help our spiritual growth.

That pleasures, including bodily pleasures, are an acceptable good is apparent from the fact that they soften regret, which is undeniably harmful. Physical, sensual pleasures are very powerful, and even alleviate pain. Pleasure is part and parcel of life. We also derive pleasure from perfection[178].

Speusippus thinks that no pleasure is good, while Plato is of the opinion that all pleasures are good. In no case, however, does he consider them a supreme good.

As for me, I think that some ordinary pleasures can be considered good for certain people and for a certain period of time. Pleasure is an element of happiness, or, if you prefer, happiness is accompanied by pleasure; when I say pleasure, I mean some form of gratification.

Happy is the man whose acts are guided by a good spirit, and happiness is for some pleasure and for others honourable living. Honourable living can, however, co-exist with inactivity and unhappiness.

Some think that wealth is happiness. But wealth is a means, not an end. People say that money does not bring happiness, and that is true as far as it goes; but it does not mean that money is not useful in the attaining of happiness. As I say in the *Nicomachean Ethics*, it seems that happiness requires material as well as moral resources, because it is very difficult to do what is noble if one has not the means. These are primarily money, political power and friends. Nor can one be absolutely happy who is ugly, or of humble birth, or childless, or has bad children or bad 'friends' or whose children or friends have died.

Enjoyment cannot be the purpose of life, but it is desirable and useful, to give us strength for serious activities.

Never forget that we are both mind and body.

I disagree with those who say that, being men, we should have a care only for our natural needs and physical gratification. I believe, rather, that our aim should be to live a life adorned with moral virtue and practical wisdom. Only then will we enjoy supreme happiness[179]. Happiness is inherent in virtue.

Human acts are the product of the union of mind and desire. Men are praised or condemned for the acts they perform consciously, for voluntary acts, not for involuntary ones. Acts are described as involuntary when they are the result of coercion or ignorance. Some involuntary evil acts can be forgiven because they are the result of intolerable pain. Others cannot be justified even under threat of death. Those committed out of ignorance can be justified only in the case where the offender has repented, when he has realised that what he did was wrong. Otherwise, if there is no repentance, the act cannot be considered involuntary.

The man who acts under the influence of drink or rage can be considered as acting involuntarily, that is, he is considered to be acting in ignorance due to the specific circumstances[180].

The intemperate man acts from passion although he knows that his action is wrong, while the temperate man does not give in to his desires when he knows that these are not right. Intemperance is due to weakness of will and not to absence of knowledge. Temperate men are admired for their logic and their strength of mind[181].

Unhealthy desires, such as pederasty, are due to illness[182]. Let those who say that homosexuality was normal in Ancient Greece take note.

Depravity is ingrained in human nature and it leads men away from the path of virtuous action, which ought to be the object of their life.

Avoidance of regret and the seeking of pleasure are the sources from which evil actions spring.

A personal criterion for self-knowledge is the pleasure or regret we feel when we do something good or bad.

In the end, I think that there is no general rule to tell us beforehand what we should do; we have to find ourselves in the particular situation in order to decide[183]. If we fear everything, we become cowards; if we fear nothing, we become reckless or insolent.

Indifference to reputation, yours or your family's, is not bravery. To be unafraid of death or poverty is not courage. But to be unafraid of death when it serves a purpose, for example death on the battlefield, that is courage. It is only human for the brave man to feel some fear, but he suppresses it for the sake of the object to be achieved[184]. One can also be brave out of over-optimism or ignorance, but courage, naivety and overconfidence are three different things. A soldier should not be carried away either by enthusiasm or by fear, but must always be guided by reason. A man's character appears in adversity[185]. Pride is not a bad trait; it is not the same as haughtiness or disdain. A proud man is one who is ready to do good but does not like to be the recipient of another's benevolence, and while not attracted to risk is willing to sacrifice his life for his good name. Towards the strong, he behaves pridefully; towards the rest, courteously. He does not rush to seek honours, nor shoulder others aside to be first. His love and hate are equally pure. He does not occupy himself with trifles. His speech is sober[186]. All in all, a proud man has many fine qualities.

ON THE SOUL

Another of my books that I hold to be very important is On the Soul, which is a treatise on psychology. Psychology is the study that explores the soul[187].

   –When you say ' soul', what precisely do you mean?

It is hard to give a give a general definition of the soul, because not all souls are the same. There is the kind of soul that exists in the different animals; there is the higher soul that exists in mankind, and perhaps the even higher soul that is God. All these kinds of soul share a common characteristic[188]: as the hand activates the different tools, so the soul activates the different mental processes[189].

The first question that interested me was whether the soul is independent of the body. If this is so, I wondered, then why do most mental phenomena have a direct impact on the body? Do we not say, I had a headache from worrying so much, or I was so afraid I couldn't move a muscle? The same thing happens in reverse, too: a physical irritation can provoke rage or fear, which are purely mental sensations.

I think, therefore, that the soul and the body must be connected in the same way that form and matter are. When matter acquires soul a living organism is created[190]. When that organism dies, the matter of which it is made will continue to exist, albeit in another form. The soul, however, departs from it.

Think of a wax figure in the image of, say, a philosopher. When the figure melts, the wax (the matter) remains, but the form, which we likened to the soul, is gone. That form can, however, be recreated in some other material-plaster, for example. Something similar occurs with reincarnation. From one creature the soul goes to a different one, although I do not accept that a human soul can go to an animal[191].

The soul is what instructs the body in its different faculties, for example, nutrition and reproduction. It is thanks to the soul that the eye can see, the tongue can taste, the nose can smell and the ear can hear[192]. In other words, without the soul, without the mind, there can be no perception.

MIND AND IMAGINATION

Thought comes from the activation of the mind. It is, therefore, something separate from the body. Thought is not images, but without images we would not be able to think. The mind cannot think, cannot perceive, without images. When the body is gone, the mind neither remembers nor loves, because these faculties are not of the mind but of the body. But when it co-exists with the body, it has full awareness of all the body's faculties and actions. The mind lives on after the death of the body. The mind is not something perishable. It is something divine.

The intellect withers with age because something wears out in the body[193]. That is what causes disorders like senile dementia and Alzheimer's disease.

There are two intellects, two kinds of mind: the agent —what you would call active— and the patient. The agent mind creates in the patient mind the conditions necessary for understanding things, as the light of the sun activates the eye and so we see.

Like the soul, the agent mind is but one step below God on a scale that reaches from the lowest, most purely material, beings, to man, who is but a tsep away from God. As I say in the *Metaphysics*, God is a transcendental being, possessing all human knowledge.

Imagination is a by-product of sensation[194]. The sun, for example, appears to be small, but we imagine it, we believe it to be, bigger than the whole world[195]. Usually, however, imagination operates in the absence of the perceived object. Do we not close our eyes in order to picture something?

MEMORY, RECOLLECTION, DREAM

Memory is a function with which we bring back to our consciousness an event that we experienced in the past. When we see a painting, it is imprinted on our soul, like the shape of a ring on a wax tablet. In the same way, when we recall an image to our memory, we imagine the real image of the thing as we saw it in the past. This process we call memory, while *recollection* is the process of activation of memory.

Given that during sleep the senses remain inactive, we deduce that *dreams* are a product of the imagination[196], which means, since the imagination is a by-product of sensation, that we cannot see things in our sleep of which we have no direct or indirect knowledge. Since, however, the mind receives no external stimuli in our sleep, it has greater freedom to play with the images stored in it. Its critical capacity is disarmed during sleep. That is why in sleep we confuse images with sensible objects —which is, after all, what a dream is.

* * *

ON THE SENSES AND SENSIBLE OBJECTS

My book On the Senses and Their Objects contains, I think, some interesting observations on the senses, both my own and those of other philosophers.

Empedocles and Plato hold that sight has no external cause, but comes from within the eye, like the light from a lantern. But if that is the case, I wondered, why can we not see at night?. If sight is due to an emission of light from the eye, like a lantern, then why can the eye not see in the darkness?[197] As for Plato's explanation that the light is extinguished in the darkness as soon as it leaves the eye, well, that is just ridiculous.

I was also curious about how we discern or notice the existence of material bodies. With the mind or with the sensory organs?

Careful observation led me to the conclusion that discerning the existence of material bodies is not a purely mental operation, because the mind cannot perceive the things around us without the mediation of some sensation. An auditory message, for example, cannot reach the brain if the auditory nerve is not working properly. That is, the eardrum may vibrate with the sound, but the signal will not reach the brain where it can be used.

I cited the following evidence in support of my theory that messages are transmitted to the brain via what you call nerves: there are known cases, I said, of warriors who were struck on the temple so hard that their "visual pathways" (their optic nerves) were severed. Although their eyes were intact, they thought that darkness had fallen, as though a lamp had been blown out.

This bears out the ancient Greek saying that the mind sees and the mind hears, a notion that is reflected in expressions like "keep your mind on what I'm saying".

From what I remember from school, the sensory stimulus is transmitted via the nerves to the brain. Only when it gets there are we aware of the stimulus, do we see the image or hear the sound. That is not quite how you imagined the process.

I don't think that there is any real difference in our views; we are just using different words. If you replace your word 'brain' with the word 'soul' or 'mind', and your word 'nerve' with my word 'pathway', then there is no difference at all. The messages are transmitted along the pathways from the nerve endings on each organ (eye, ear. tongue) to the brain. For the organ to be able to perceive the existence of an object or a phenomenon, that object or phenomenon must be able to cause a change of a certain intensity in the specific organ. Otherwise the organ's inactivity prevents the creation of a stimulus. For example, for the eye to be able to discern an object, that object must be of at least a certain minimal size, because the eye's discerning power is limited. The same is true of the human ear, which can hear sounds at frequencies between 16 and 20,000 hertz. Sounds outside that range are inaudible to us.

Another factor that plays a role in sensory perception is the medium that exists between the object and the sense organ. In hearing, for example, there is air between the ear and the instrument producing the sound. The sound is transmitted by changes in the density of the air, which cause the eardrum to vibrate, and so we hear.

Sometimes a sense cannot function after a particularly strong stimulation[198]: we are temporarily deafened by an explosion, or blinded by a brilliant flash of light. The intensity of a stimulation can even cause death[199]. The opposite occurs with the mind (brain). When a person comes across something hard to comprehend, then his brain works harder in order to understand it.

That all the senses are inactive when we sleep is not accidental, but must be due to the inactivity of the centre of perception, where the signals from the sensory organs end up and are used[200].

THE SENSES

I rank the senses by order of increasing importance: touch, taste, smell, hearing, sight.

Hearing is valuable, because with it we perceive speech, which is a basic factor in teaching and learning. But sight is even more important, I think, because it allows us to perceive the size, shape, colour, movement and number of things[201]. The colour of things is directly related to sight. I argued that the same colour that exists on the surface also exists in the interior of a body. But bodies of undetermined shape (fluids, you would call them) can have a different colour if you see them from a different angle or from a different distance. Think of the atmosphere, or the sea, whose colour apparently changes depending on your distance or point of view.

I also expressed some ideas on where the variety of colours comes from. It is plain, I think, that when material bodies mingle their colours mingle too. That is the main reason why there are so many colours[202].

I went on to explain that mixing different colours in different proportions yielded new varieties of colour, and that the colours that can be expressed in arithmetical proportions, like scarlet and purple, appear to be "softer". Something similar occurs with sound frequencies, as well.

At the time no one was willing to entertain that idea. Everyone thought it very odd of me (to put it mildly) to draw a parallel between the mixing of colours and the harmonies of sounds. If I were to tell you, though, that this comparison was directed not towards the colours qua colours but to radiant waves, what would you say? Sunlight, as you know, is made up of a mixture of radiant light waves of different frequencies. That is why different colours appear when the light is broken up, as happens with the rainbow.

Often the variety of colours is due to the fact that what from close up is seen to be a mixture of colours appears from a distance to be a single hue. Take, for example, the cover of a book. It may appear to the eye to be a uniform single colour, but if you look at it through a strong magnifying glass you will see that it is actually made up of tiny dots of more than one colour. This is the basis of the four-colour printing system.

—Are sight and hearing the only senses you dealt with?

Oh, no, and I will share some of my observations on smell and taste with you. Most of what I had to say about smell is contained in my book *On the Senses and Their Objects*.

SMELL AND TASTE

Smell is the result of the olfactory organ, the nose, being able to perceive odours; the sense of smell is activated when the emanation from an odorous substance excites the nose.

Odour is a smoky exhalation that comes from fire[203]. Most of the ancient Greek philosophers, and Heracleitus especially, held similar views about odour. I observed in my book that some think when the smoky exhalation is the same in the earth and in the air it is what we call odour. All, however, agree that odour is due either to emanations or to exhalations or to both[204]. That is why Heracleitus said that it would be possible to identify everything with the nose if everything gave off emanations, which in fact is largely the case.

You may have learned how the process of smelling works. The air brings the particles of odorous substances to the part of our nose attuned to smells, where there is a concentration of nerve endings with their corresponding receptors. The receptors have a specific shape and specific dimensions. The particles that have the right shape and size can enter the receptors on the nerve endings and excite the nerve. This excitation is transmitted to the brain and we have the sensation of the corresponding odour.

This means that for a liquid or a solid substance to have an odour it must pass into the gaseous state. In liquids this is called *evaporation*, and in solids *sublimation*. Both evaporation and sublimation are achieved by heating. That is, odour is linked to fire, to heat. That is why all smells are so much stronger in the summer. You have probably noticed that yourself, on the bus or in a public washroom.

The sense of smell operates both in the air and in the water. Fish and shellfish appear to be able to smell in their natural environment. The odorous substance is transmitted to them through the water.

Taste, whose sensory organ is the tongue, I thought was directly related to touch[205]. The substances that have taste are formed primarily in plants[206]. I think that there are seven kinds of tastes, just as there are seven radiancies that make up white light.

So, what do you think? Are today's views of the senses much like mine?

I have to say, they are.

With your permission we will move on now to some of my thoughts on astronomy and cosmology, and specifically on the properties and movements of the heavenly bodies, which I describe in my book *On the heavens*. I think that you will find them very interesting.

ON HEAVEN AND EARTH

I believed that the earth is stationary, that it is in the centre of the universe[207], that the universe is made up of a number of concentric heavenly spheres, and that they all move at the same pace, tracing a great circle. All the concentric spheres are drawn into this movement by the first sphere, which moves by divine energy, because God is interested exclusively in his creation, the universe. For this reason the movement of the planets is eternal[208]. I called the first concentric circle 'heaven'.

The vault of each heaven is the firmament to which the stars are attached; they are drawn into the movement of the spheres as these circle around the earth. The sun is located in the first sphere.

At first there were thought to be five heavenly spheres, but since there are so many stars I came to believe that they must number fifty-five.

I believed that the heavenly bodies are made of some matter that does not decay, alter or change size[209]. Plato had the same idea, that the heavenly bodies are perfect from every point of view and that they are made of an indestructible matter called aether.

Anaxagoras was the first to say that the moon shines because it reflects the light of the sun. For expressing that opinion he was indicted for impiety and died in exile.

Eratosthenes (3rd c. BC) argued that the earth is not flat, but spherical, and he calculated its size. He was the Director of the famous Library in Alexandria, and he read somewhere that at noon on June 21 (the summer solstice) in the city of Syene, which you call Aswan, a vertical pole casts no shadow and the sun is reflected in the depths of a well; this meant, of course, that the sun was directly overhead. Eratosthenes wondered whether this was true at Alexandria as well, and found that it was not: at noon on June 21 in Alexandria an upright pole did cast a shadow. Surely, he thought, if the earth were flat, poles of the same length would cast shadows of the same length wherever they were. But the length of the shadows differed from place to place, which made him think —perfectly correctly— that the earth must be spherical. From the difference in the length of those shadows in Syene and Alexandria he was able, using simple mathematical principles, to calculate the radius of the earth. He also found that the difference in latitude between the two cities was seven degrees and the distance between them was roughly eight hundred kilometres. His calculation of the earth's circumference (40,000 kilometres) was wrong by just two percent. Eratosthenes was the first to provide information about the dimensions of the earth.

Aristarchus of Samos (320-250 BC) was the first to maintain, with scientific arguments, that the earth revolves around the sun. Although his treatise on the subject has been lost, it is known from the works of other ancient writers, among them Plutarch, who mentions it in his essay *On the opinions of the philosophers*.

Aristarchus' theory was not accepted because most of the great names of antiquity, including Ptolemy and Hipparchus as well as myself, believed the opposite. Does that strike you as odd? It shouldn't, for besides the fact that I never claimed to be infallible, it is truly difficult to realise, on the basis of everyday observation, that the earth revolves around the sun. Do we not still speak of the sun rising and setting, as if it were the sun that was moving?

Nearly two thousand years would pass before the heliocentric theory returned, with the work of the famous Polish astronomer Nicolaus Copernicus (1473-1543), who supported it with new elements. That is why the heliocentric system is called Copernican, although it was first formulated by Aristarchus.

— *Did Copernicus know of Aristarchus' theories?*

Most definitely, and there is documentary evidence to prove it. Preserved in the Library of the University of War-

Page of the original manuscript of Copernicus' treatise *De revolutionibus orbium coelestium* (1543), with the paragraph referring to Aristarchus scored out (by whose hand?).

saw is a fragment of the manuscript of Copernicus' treatise *De revolutionibus orbium coelestium*[209a] (see p. 176) where a clear reference to Aristarchus, saying that he believed that the earth revolves around the sun, has been crossed out. When the treatise was eventually published and thus became generally known to the scientific world, that paragraph was not included and thus all the credit went to Copernicus.

Copernicus hesitated to publish his manuscripts, fearing the reaction of the Roman Catholic Church. The text was eventually published by a friend, in 1543, and in 1616 was indeed proscribed by Rome. Copernicus thus escaped conviction for heresy, the fate that, as you know, befell Galileo a century later, when on June 22, 1633, he heard a sentence of life imprisonment pronounced upon him by the judges of the Inquisition. He was condemned for his ideas "on the motions of the earth" and forced to renounce them upon oath.

— But, wasn't that dishonest on Copernicus' part?

Maybe, maybe not. The treatise was not published until after his death, and it is perfectly possible that someone else removed the bit about Aristarchus.

While we are on the subject of heavenly bodies, I should tell you that the first person to say that the earth moves was neither Copernicus nor Galileo nor Aristarchus. It was the Pythagoreans who challenged the theory that the stars hang on a vault that turns about the earth, believing instead that it is the earth that revolves in the opposite direction, with a movement that we cannot perceive. Ecphantus and Heracleides maintained that the earth revolves around an axis through its centre. Since that did not conflict with either the heliocentric or the geocentric theory, they co-existed for some time. To be fair, I should say that other peoples, such as the Assyrians, the Babylonians, the Chaldeans, the Phoenicians and the Egyptians, had made a great many astronomical observations before the ancient Greeks. The observations of those ancient Eastern peoples were mainly directed towards describing heavenly phenomena, while in Ancient Greece investigation of the heavens was raised to a science.

The ancient Greeks realised that the universe was governed by some sort of order and obeyed certain natural laws. Because of this order, this sovereign harmony, they called the universe *cosmos*, a word that comes from a verb meaning to arrange or adorn (which is the root of your word 'cosmetic').

In their efforts to interpret their theoretical predictions, the ancient Greeks invented different instruments that would later be used for practical purposes. One of the most astonishing of these is the Antikythera mechanism, which was recovered from the sea floor near the island of Antikythera in 1900.

The Antikythera mechanism is a complex clockwork mechanism composed of at least thirty meshing gears forming an intricate system requiring imagination and sophisticated scientific thinking as well as a profound knowledge of geometry. It was used for astronomical and calendrical calculations and is considered the forerunner of modern clocks and computers.

METEOROLOGY

Meteorology is a work that deals mainly with the explanation of certain natural phenomena, meteorological and other, which you would classify under astronomy. These include the comets, the galaxies and the shooting stars[210].

As I used to tell my students, meteorology is the science that deals with the phenomena that take place beneath the starry vaults, up there, and I would point to the heavens.

Meteorological phenomena also obey the laws of nature, but not with the regularity and order that characterise the behaviour of the heavenly bodies.

By my day a great deal was already known about this subject. I describe a fair number of meteorological phenomena in my book, but I also endeavour to explain some of them. My first concern was to find out what substance, what material, exists in the space between the earth and the moon, where the atmospheric phenomena that we know as weather develop. I thought that this space was filled with exhalations, which are the result of the action of the sun's rays on the earth. When the rays fall on dry ground, they produce hot, dry exhalations; when they fall on water, the exhalations they produce are cold and wet. Both kinds of exhalation exist in the lower part of the atmosphere.

It is the interaction of these exhalations, under the influence of heat, cold and movement, that creates the meteorological phenomena.

Under the influence of cold, the wet exhalation —what you would call vapour— creates fog, clouds, rain, frost, hail and snow[211]. Thunder, lightning and the winds are due to dry exhalations, while wet exhalations under the influence of heat create the *rainbow*. Today, you ascribe the creation of the rainbow to the refraction of light through drops of water (wet exhalation), but the other meteorological phenomena are still explained in much the way I did.

When the wet exhalations return to earth in the form of rain, they create the rivers, springs and floods and end up in the sea[212]. When the dry exhalations return to earth, in the right conditions they create the minerals.

In other words, I knew that water evaporates when the temperature is increased, and that cooling condenses vapour into water. I also observed that, for a given temperature, the speed with which a liquid evaporates depends on its surface area. What I actually said was that the greater the surface of the liquid the faster it evaporates[213]. This is a phenomenon that you exploit for a variety of purposes, one of them being obtaining sea salt from saltpans. Saltpans are large and shallow, so that the seawater evaporates quickly, leaving the salt behind.

Nor did it escape my notice that evaporation is an *endothermic phenomenon*, that is, that it takes place with the absorption of thermal energy from the atmosphere. In other words, the evaporation of liquids has a cooling effect. This is something that you feel on your skin when you are wearing wet clothes and the wind is blowing. The rapid evaporation in a short space of time draws considerable heat from your body, so that you feel cooler or even chilled. I also observed that the temperature of boiling water remains constant, which is something that everyone now knows.

Another thing I observed was that the steam created by boiling water contains no salt[214], because the salts are left behind in the bottom of the pan. Like the salt from saltpans, these salt crystals are small, fine and hollow, because of the speed of evaporation. Another very important observation I made was that while in general bodies expand with heat, which I already knew, the opposite is true of water, which expands when it freezes. That, of course, is why ice floats. I was, in other words, familiar with this primordial anomaly, without which life on earth would not exist, or at least not in the form in which we know it.

—*I'm anxious to hear what you and others thought about matter and how it behaves. And I'd like you to give me as much detail as possible, because chemistry, which is my subject, is the science of matter.*

I'm afraid you'll get tired of listening to me, for your ancient ancestors did a lot of important work in that field. Unfortunately, and I don't know why this should be so, you modern Greeks have paid much less attention to the work of the ancient Greeks in the natural sciences than others have.

Listen to what two world-famous modern scientists had to say about the ancient Greeks.

The first is the German physicist and philosopher Werner Heisenberg[215], who taught theoretical physics at Leipzig University, and who had this to say about the ancient Greek philosophers:

Those who think differently and want to find the sources of knowledge in their branch, whether it be technology or medicine, sooner or later go back to the ancient sources, and their work will certainly benefit from that, provided that they have understood the way in which the ancient Greeks thought and expressed their thoughts.

The other is the Austrian theoretical physicist Erwin Schrödinger[216], (Nobel Prize-winner), who said that the reason why we are so strongly attracted to Greek philosophy is that nowhere in the world, either before or after the ancient Greeks, has there been such an advanced and well-articulated structure of knowledge and thought.

My own thoughts on matter and its properties are contained primarily in the Physics, the Metaphysics, the Meteorology and in On Generation and Corruption, where I mention a number of chemical reactions. There are also references to the subject in other works of mine, and some of my opinions are repeated in different places, sometimes somewhat modified.

This has led to my being accused of inconsistency, but it is perfectly understandable, I think, that my opinion may have changed between the writing of one work and another, for a dozen or more years might have gone by in the interval. I have also been criticised for repeating myself, for coming back to the same subject two or even three times, and not always with the same theories. But this, too, is understandable, when you remember that my writings were more lecture notes than books.

You must also remember that, as we have said before, the texts that you have today come from copies of copies and translations of translations. Along the way everyone added something of his own to the text, to fill in a gap or make it easier — he thought — to understand, while unintentional errors also crept in.

PHYSICS AND METAPHYSICS

In my Physics I deal with natural science, and comment on the immense body of work the pre-Socratic, and particularly the Ionian, philosophers did in this field. Like them, I deal with the primal, the elementary, part of matter, of which all material bodies are composed, and with the causes of the changes in material bodies.

My Metaphysics deals with the science of real entities considered with what I might call a philosophical gaze.

— *What do you mean by a philosophical gaze?*

I mean man's innate tendency and fierce desire to extend his thinking beyond his own experience. That is why I open the *Metaphysics* with the words: "All men by nature desire to know" [217].

This is clear from the delight we feel when, through our senses, we acquire knowledge, knowledge which stamps itself on our memory and creates the experience that leads to practical rules, which we can then use in the practice of various arts. That is, we use experience for practical purposes. The highest level of knowledge is science, which seeks knowledge exclusively for its own sake, while wisdom is the widest possible knowledge, the knowledge of the final cause of the creation of all things, the complete understanding of the world.

Another subject I deal with in the *Metaphysics* is whether, apart from what our senses can perceive, there are other entities that we cannot perceive. For, as I say, apart from the real *being* there also exists the immaterial being, the *not-being*.

The variable terrestrial world is only a small part of the natural universe. Beyond it there are things that do not change [218], such as the heavenly bodies, which are in perpetual motion. This perpetual motion presupposes the existence of an eternal entity that is able of itself to produce motion.

How can a being produce movement without moving itself? [219] Imagine a billiard ball: how can it move another if it remains stationary? Is it possible for something that produces motion not to move itself? In other words, can the mover remain unmoved? For me, this *unmoved mover* is a divine force. In the case of the heavenly bodies it is God himself.

God is an eternal being, whose influence pervades the universe in such a way that everything that takes place in it depends on him. He is the one who pulls all the strings, you might say.

Indeed, it is impossible, when you see for the first time the beauty of the earth and the sea and the majesty of the starry heavens, not to accept that these are divinely created.

Diogenes Laertius, who wrote a history of Greek philosophy entitled *Lives of Eminent Philosophers*, considered physics as part of philosophy. He called "natural philosophy" the part of philosophy that deals with the universe and all the things in it.

My physics deals with the natural processes and changes that physical things undergo. For the study of these things I use theoretical reasoning, whereas for biology I use experiential methods. That is why some of those who came after me accuse me of engaging in 'desktop physics'. What else could it be, though? In those days we were not able to carry out sophisticated experiments. There are others, however, who consider me the pre-eminent student of certain natural phenomena, such as motion and change in physical things. For if you do not understand those two characteristics of physical things, then you do not understand nature[220].

I have said that one of the basic properties of matter is motion. For something to move, however, there must be something that moves it, something that exerts a certain force upon it, something that has the ability to produce an effect upon it. This is power.

Power is the ability of a body to bring about some kind of change in another[221]. Power always presupposes energy. It derives from energy. We also use the word 'power' to mean 'capacity', as for example when we say that someone has the power of speech.

The other characteristic natural phenomenon is change, the alteration that material bodies, physical things, undergo. That material bodies exist and that they undergo change is something that people are made aware of in their everyday lives. From everyday experience you can be perfectly certain that, for example, water exists and that it both freezes and evaporates.

Physical things exist independently of our perception. We perceive them with our senses. And we perceive the changes in them with our senses. Your sense of sight, for example, tells you that the apple you left on the corner of your desk three days ago is rotting. With our senses, in other words, we perceive that certain processes are occurring, that certain changes are happening[222]. The world of direct experience is a chaos of impressions. Our minds reduce this chaos to order, and thus the foundations of the natural sciences are laid.

— You have been talking about material bodies, about matter. I would like you to tell me what you think matter is, because of all the books I have read on the subject, no two define it in quite the same way.

That, my friend, is one of the hardest things of all: to define what we mean by matter.

VIEWS OF MATTER

People have been thinking about what you today call 'matter' for thousands of years. The Chaldeans, the Babylonians, the Egyptians and other Eastern peoples pondered the subject in order to solve everyday problems, often of vital importance. The ancient Greek philosophers took a different approach. They addressed the problem of 'matter' in a purely philosophical spirit. They attempted through reasoning to identify the basic, fundamental characteristics of matter, to describe its different properties, and to interpret the various phenomena associated with it.

Democritus put the mindset of the ancient Greek philosophers into words when he said that he would rather find the cause of a phenomenon than become the king of Persia[223].

Before my time the Greek word for 'matter', *hyle*, meant a woodland. Interestingly, this word survives in English in the name of the tree-frog, *hyla*. The English word 'matter' comes from the Latin *materia*, again meaning 'timber', and consequently the substance of which things were made. The word my predecessors used for 'matter' was *on*, 'that which is'.

I was the first one to give a definition of matter, and I think that it is very much the same as any modern definition. Matter, as I am sure you would agree, is whatever has objective existence and is perceived either with the senses or with scientific instruments, the substance that constitutes the observable universe and forms the basis of all objective phenomena. I defined matter as "that which is not actually, but is potentially, an individual thing" [224].

I believed from the beginning in the indestructibility of matter. Material bodies, I said, are made of one substance, and while material substances undergo change the original, the primal, substance remains the same[225]. And in *On Generation and Corruption* I say that while matter is essential for there to be a material body, in some special cases it is possible for something material to come from nothing[226]. In certain conditions, that is, it is possible to create matter out of nothing, or, as you would say, it is possible to create matter from energy.

—Democritus though, says that atoms, which are matter, neither disappear nor are created out of nothing. Do you not accept his atomic theory?

On the contrary.

THE ATOMIC THEORY

The atomic theory is an admirable notion. What I thought was that atoms are indivisible simply because we did not have the means to divide them, and not because they are something solid, compact, massive. In my tract *On the Soul* I say that even if we consider Democritus' spherical atoms to be absolutely small, there will still be something in them that causes motion and something that moves. Nor in fact did Democritus exclude the possibility that his atoms might be composed of other smaller particles. Plato, for his part, thought that the atoms of matter were indivisible and that they were flat[227].

I thought that matter is composed of the same basic substance, wherever it is found. This is formulated in the *Physics*, in the famous phrase "all is one". I call it famous, because it was used by many who came after me, albeit with different meanings. The alchemists took it as their motto, and depicted it as a circle formed by a serpent biting its tail. That serpent symbolised the recycling of matter.

THE PRIMARY ELEMENTS OF MATTER

One of the most interesting intellectual inventions of the ancient Greek philosophers in relation to matter is the introduction of the concept of primary elements. This was one of the main contributions of the Ionian philosophers.

What the ancient Greek philosophers thought about the primary elements of material bodies may sometimes be inaccurate, but the idea that they first conceived and the thought that they first put into words, namely that the numberless multitude of different material bodies (gases, liquids and solids) must all come from simple primary substances, what we would now call chemical elements, reveals a remarkable perception of the whole problem of matter, especially for their time. It would, therefore, be quite fair to say that those ancient sages laid the foundations for the natural sciences.

In my view the primary element and the beginning of all that is, is that from which they were produced and to which they return when they decay. Later, summing up the opinions of different philosophers, I gave a somewhat different definition: the primary elements of matter, I decided, are the smallest possible parts into which material bodies can be divided; these particles must, however, have the same properties as the initial material bodies.

As you will realise, those particles correspond to what you now call molecules, which are defined as the smallest identifiable unit into which a pure substance can be divided and still retain the composition and chemical properties of that substance. It is true that I was at first perplexed by the primary elements spoken of by my teacher, Plato, and the other philosophers. Later, I realised that some considered the elements to be matter while others thought they were energy. There was also a third group who thought that the elements were both matter and energy.

In the end, I accepted the four elements proposed by Empedocles, *earth, water, air, fire*, for I thought that there cannot be just one element, but every element must have an opposite. I also thought there could not be an infinity of elements, because then it would be difficult for man to know them all.

THE CHEMICAL COMPOUNDS

Where I disagree with other philosophers of my day is that even when the elements unite and form what you would call a chemical compound, they do not lose their entity. In order to illustrate what I meant, I used two simple examples. A man who is a musician does not stop being a man; that is, he does not lose his human substance. Or when we say that a statue was made from bronze, on no account do we mean we believe that the bronze has lost its bronzeness.

I also held that for us to identify a substance we have to know not only of which elements it is compounded but also in what proportions[228].

As a chemistry student you know that in order to describe a chemical compound, in order to decide what a substance is, you have to know both what chemical elements it is composed of and in what proportion. You may, for example, have found out by analysis that a substance is composed of hydrogen and oxygen, but that is not enough to tell you what it is, for there are two well-known compounds made of only hydrogen and oxygen. In order to know which one you have, you have to know the proportion of oxygen to hydrogen in it: if you have two parts of hydrogen to one part of oxygen, you have water; if you have equal parts of each (two and two), you have hydrogen peroxide, which is quite a different thing!

As you know, something similar is true of all chemical compounds. That is, the molecules of any chemical compound are composed of a certain number of chemical elements in certain proportions, linked in a certain way[229].

Is that not precisely the law of definite proportions formulated by Joseph-Louis Proust in 1794?

MIXTURE AND CHEMICAL COMPOUND

As a chemistry student you will also know for a chemical compound to exist certain substances (reagents) must first mingle and then react; that is, a chemical phenomenon must occur. Up until my time the difference between the simple mixing and the chemical reaction of the different substances was unclear[230]. I may fairly say that I was the first to attempt to clarify when the mixing of two substances yields a mixture and when it produces a chemical compound.

I think I put it fairly clearly in my treatise *On Generation and Corruption*: when certain material bodies are powdered and mixed in such a way that the particles of one substance cannot be distinguished from those of the other, then we say that they form a mixture. Is that not how you define a mixture today?

– It is, indeed.

I also observed that the several components of a mixture retain their own particular properties even when mixed together. This is stated in *On Generation and Corruption*: the components of the mixture, I said in that book, retain their characteristics just as they were before being mixed together; they retain, that is, their essential entity. But if they alter, they cease to form a mixture because they have lost their original characteristics, they no longer have the properties they had before the alteration occurred.

This observation of mine, as I am sure you will have realised, refers to the characteristic difference between mixtures and chemical substances. I also observed that a mixture can be separated into its components again[231].

Another thing I point out is that it is possible for one person to discern the components of a mixture but not another: to one, that is, it may appear heterogeneous and to the other homogeneous, as you would say today. It is possible, too, that a mixture appearing homogenous to the average person is heterogeneous in the eyes of the keener-sighted, just as the mythical Lynceus[232] could spot things invisible to others among the rocks and trees, and even under the earth. The characteristic feature of a mixture, I repeat, is that it is of uniform composition throughout —homogeneous, to use your word.

Speaking of chemical elements, remember how you described Copernicus as a bit dishonest because you thought that he had omitted any reference to Aristarchus in connection with the heliocentric system? Well, I wonder what you'll think of Berzelius.

THE SYMBOLS OF THE CHEMICAL ELEMENTS

As you may know, the symbols for the chemical elements were established in 1811 by one of the fathers of modern chemistry, the Swede Jacob Berzelius.. The system of notation he developed used the capitalised first letter of the Latin name of the element: for example, the element nitrogen is symbolised by the capital letter N, carbon by C, and so on. This was exactly what the ancient Greeks had done. Their elements were the four primary elements of Empedocles, and they symbolised them by the first letter of the word: Γ for earth (Γη) Υ for water (Υδορ), A for air (Αηρ) and Π for fire (Πυρ).

Berzelius claimed to have been a great admirer of mine, so he cannot have been unaware of those symbols.

Well, never mind. What else did you want me to tell you?

Well, we seem to have finished with Alexander the Great, and with your theories on matters of enduring interest to us humans. What I would like, if you don't mind, is a brief commentary on the life and works of the most important ancient Greek philosophers.

I have no objection whatsoever; in fact, it will be a pleasure. But who shall we begin with? If we decide to take them in order of importance, I am going to find myself in a spot, because each one made his mark in different areas of philosophy. Not to mention the trouble I am going to be in up here —you cannot imagine what fuddy-duddies they have become! Or how irritating: each one thinks he's the most important and they keep buttonholing you to insist that time has proved them right. So if you don't mind I think we'll start with Socrates, my spiritual grandfather, and continue with Plato, my own teacher. What do you say?

That's fine with me.

Right, then, let's begin with Socrates.

SOCRATES

You can get some idea of what an awe-inspiring figure Socrates was from the words that were used to describe him: the most excellent, the most just, the most wise, and suchlike. It is also telling that Plato described himself as a devout student of Socrates.

When I was young, about your age, in fact, I had the good fortune to be able to listen to Socrates in person. That was when I was at Plato's Academy, where he was universally admired and revered. That sort of climate was bound to affect my thinking, and this is apparent in my writings, even in those where I wanted to express some criticism of his views.

Socrates was devoted to philosophy and largely indifferent to material things. He lived a very ascetic life, and his fortitude and endurance in the face of hunger, thirst and cold became legendary.

His modesty, too, was proverbial. His famous dictum, "The only thing I know is that I know nothing", says it all. With those few words he describes the man who knows a great deal, realises how much there is that he doesn't know and, being objective and unpretentious, has no hesitation is saying so. Unlike the uneducated, and worse still the semi-educated, who are arrogant.

Socrates believed in God and in the immortality of the soul. He said, in fact, that God sees all, hears all, is everywhere present, and has a care for all.

But we know that he was accused of impiety and in fact was tried and condemned to death.

Yes, it is true that Socrates was condemned to death. But

he was accused of neglecting the gods worshipped in Athens, rather than of impiety. The charge was of "the practice of religious novelties" and "corrupting the young".

Socrates was the most down-to-earth of philosophers. He was a very simple man, without extravagances of any kind, either in his dress or in his behaviour. He taught things that liberated the mind, but he did not despise the things of this world.

Socrates wrote nothing. All that we know of him comes from Xenophon and Plato. He may not actually have spoken a single word of all that Plato ascribes to him in the dialogues, but they must be true to his spirit, since Plato was one of his most faithful students. As for what Xenophon tells us about Socrates, the most trustworthy part is likely what he copied from Plato.

Socrates was short and exceedingly ugly. He was born in 470 BC in a suburb of Athens. His family was a modest one, and not particularly well off; his father was a stonecutter and his mother a midwife. He studied with Anaxagoras, Archelaus and the music teacher Damon.

He was, apparently, a man of great charm and magical eloquence, and his students were devoted to him. In a passage in the *Symposium* Plato has one of them, Alcibiades, describe the effect of listening to him teach: "When I hear him speak, my heart dances."

Socrates married at the age of fifty, solely because he wanted a child. When someone asked his opinion on whether or not he should marry, Socrates advised him to do as he wished, because either way he would regret it[234].

His wife, Xanthippe, had no interests outside her household. When Socrates, that most eloquent of men, returned home he had little to say to her. His silence infuriated her, and once after much shouting she picked up the water jug in her rage and hurled it at his head. At which Socrates merely said that he was not surprised that such thunderings had brought rain[235]. He and Xanthippe had one son, called Lamprocles.

Socrates also had two other sons, Sophroniscus and Menexenus; their mother was Myrto, the daughter of Aristides the Just. Plutarch tells us that he married her out of pity, for she was destitute, but whether this was a legal marriage or not we do not know.

Socrates, at least as an older man, had no interest in the stars or in nature in general. When invited to accompany some friends on a trip into the countryside, he answered that he always wanted to learn new things, and therefore preferred to stay in the city where people always had something to say, which was not the case with fields and trees[236].

—*What was the famous Socratic method of teaching?*

THE SOCRATIC METHOD

Socrates did not lecture. Rather than stating and expounding on his own positions, he asked judiciously devised questions to lead others to reach his conclusions for themselves. He described himself as being like a midwife, helping others give birth to thought, ideas, wisdom[237].

Socrates wrote nothing himself, and had little liking for long treatises. He compared books to paintings, remarking that just as a portrait of a man will not respond to your greeting, so written words will not answer your questions.

Some people have suggested, in the light of this attitude, that perhaps Socrates had never actually learned to read or write.

—*Hold on a minute, is it possible that a man of such genius, such a gifted man as Socrates, was illiterate? I can't believe it!*

It's not so unthinkable. I'm sure you must know brilliant people (of a certain age) who recoil from the idea of learning to use a computer. Don't forget that in those days most citizens were illiterate. Plutarch[238] tells a lovely story of a man who on a voting day asked Aristides, not knowing who he was, to write his ballot for him, proposing that Aristides be ostracised. Aristides did so, and then asked the man if he knew who this Aristides was, that he wanted to ostracise.

The man said no, he was simply tired of hearing him called Aristides the Just everywhere he went. As you can see, democracy has its drawbacks.

Socrates was a good citizen. He served in the army, and with another two thousand Athenians went off to fight at Potidaea, which had risen against Athens. Plato tells us, through the mouth of Alcibiades in the *Symposium*, that Socrates displayed a rare indifference to the hardships of campaigning and always fought bravely. He also took part in the Amphipolis campaign. Many were surprised to see that such a peaceful man, and a man of such great wisdom, could also be a fine fighter[239].

It is a fact that Socrates was a patriot and in general a dutiful citizen, and he was not afraid of death. This was clear in everything he said and did at the time of his trial.

THE TRIAL OF SOCRATES

Throughout his trial Socrates displayed a proud detachment that infuriated many of the Athenians. This was apparent in the voting on his sentence: the first time there were two hundred and eighty votes against him, the second time three hundred and sixty, with one hundred and forty in his favour. Why was there a second vote? Well, like any condemned person, Socrates had the right to counter-propose a lighter sentence. Instead of which, he stated that his entire life had been so virtuous that he merited a seat at the Prytaneion, the public table where the state honoured Olympic victors. This reply incensed the court and, as we have seen, he was sentenced to death by an increased majority.

Hearing this final sentence pronounced, Socrates turned to the people and remarked that he was old enough that, had they but had a little patience, time would have passed the same sentence on him before long; that is, he told them that essentially they were not punishing him at all. Then he began to express his thoughts about death.

The charge of impiety was brought against Socrates by an

insignificant young poet named Meletus. The charge could be brought against any Athenian who indicated even the slightest doubt about the existence of the established pantheon[240]. An accusation of impiety was a popular way of getting rid of highly placed persons or nuisances.

The trial of Socrates took place in February of 399 BC. So many people flocked to hear the proceedings that, as Plutarch recounts, the narrow streets of Athens were totally choked. In the vicinity of the courthouse order was maintained by the public slaves, a sort of municipal police force. To keep the crowd away from the jurors, the public slaves held ropes freshly soaked in red paint in front of the entranceways. Anyone who came too close would get paint on his clothes, proof positive that he had tried to force an entrance. The penalty for this was withholding of the annual compensation paid for attendance at the public assembly.

— *What were the real reasons for the trial and condemnation of Socrates?*

He made a lot of people feel stupid, for it must be admitted that he could be sarcastic at times. Even his "I know that I know nothing" annoyed people, for they it made them think that they must be intellectually naked indeed.

Socrates was not executed immediately, as was the custom, because the sacred ship that had taken the Athenian delegation to Delos for the annual festival celebrating the birthday of Apollo and Artemis had not yet returned, and no executions could take place before that pilgrimage ended. In the meanwhile, Crito, a rich Athenian and faithful friend of Socrates, visited him repeatedly in his prison.

– *What did Crito say to Socrates on these visits?*

What was said between Crito and Socrates in the prison on the day before his death is, I think, exceptionally important and a text that everyone should know. It is recorded in the *Crito*, which Plato wrote when he was still very young, and which I think is a very faithful expression of Socrates' beliefs.

The work begins with Crito arriving early one morning at the prison, full of affection and fear for his friend, to tell

Socrates that the sacred ship has been sighted and the execution will therefore take place the next day.

Crito urges Socrates to escape. This would not be difficult to arrange, since Crito had plenty of money to bribe the guards with, and there were many others who would willingly help as well. He even offered to spirit Socrates away to Thessaly, where he had many friends. Bribery was a way of life in ancient Athens — and I fear things have not greatly changed since.

Crito used every argument he could think of to persuade Socrates to agree: the charges were false; the decision was unjust; the sentence was unfair; Socrates had a duty to support his family. He even argued that he and some other of their friends could be reproached for unwillingness to put up the money necessary to bribe the guards! Socrates remained firm, however: he could not act against his principles, and his whole life had been spent in teaching, with his words and by his actions, that the first duty of the citizen is to obey the laws of the state.

There follows a dialogue in which the arguments on either side are expressed in a masterly way. The discussion encapsulates the quintessence of morality and the concept of duty. One particularly captivating feature of this dialogue is that Plato has Socrates engaging in debate with the laws themselves. The whole thing is so magnificent that I think it is worth reading word for word, and I would advise you to study it. So boot up your printer and print out this passage from the Crito[241]. And please make copies for your classmates — you'll be doing your country a service.

THE DIALOGUE BETWEEN SOCRATES AND CRITO

SOCRATES: Well, look at it this way. If the laws and the community of the city came to us when we were about to run away from here, or whatever it should be called, and standing over us were to ask, "Tell me, Socrates, what are you intending to do? By attempting this deed, aren't you planning to do nothing other than destroy us, the laws, and the civic community, as much as you can? Or does it seem possible to you that any city where the verdicts reached have no force but are made powerless and corrupted by private citizens could continue to exist and not be in ruins?"

What will we say, Crito, to these questions and others like them? Because there is a lot more a person could say, especially an orator, on behalf of this law we're destroying, which establishes the verdicts that have been decided as sovereign. Or will we say to them that "The city treated us unjustly and did not decide the case properly"? Will we say this, or something like it?

CRITO: By Zeus, that's what we'll say, Socrates

SOCRATES: What if the laws then said, "Socrates, did we agree on this, we and you, to honour the decisions that the city makes?" And if we were surprised to hear them say this, perhaps they would say, "Socrates, don't be surprised at what we're saying but answer, since you are used to participating in questioning and answering. Come, then, what reason can you give us and the city for trying to destroy us? Did we not, to begin with, give birth to you? And wasn't it through us that your father married your mother and conceived you? So show those of us, the laws concerning marriages, what fault you find that keeps them from being good?" "I find no fault with them," I would say.

"What about the laws concerning the upbringing and education of children, by which you too were raised? Or didn't those of us, the laws established on this matter, give good instructions when they directed your father to educate you in the arts and gymnastics?" "They did," I would say.

"Well, then. Since you have been born and brought up and educated, could you say that you were not our offspring and slave from the beginning, both you and your ancestors? And if this is so, do you suppose that justice between you and us is based on equality, and do you think that whatever we might try to do to you, it is just for you to do these things to us in return? Justice between you and your father, or your master if you happened to have one, was not based on equality, so that you could not do whatever you had suffered in return, neither speak back when crossed nor strike back when struck nor many other such things. Will you be allowed to do this to your homeland and the laws, so that, if we try to destroy you, thinking this to be just, you will then try to destroy us the laws and your homeland in return with as much power as you have and claim that you're acting justly in doing so, the man who truly cares about virtue?

Are you so wise that it has slipped your mind that the homeland is deserving of more honour and reverence and worship than your mother and father and all of your other ancestors? And is held in higher esteem both by the gods and by men of good sense? And that when she is angry you should show her more respect and compliance and obedience than your father, and either convince her or do what she commands, and suffer without complaining if she orders you to suffer something? And that whether it is to be beaten or imprisoned, or to be wounded and killed if she leads you into war, you must do it? And that justice is like this, and that you must not be daunted or withdraw or abandon your position, but at war and in the courts and everywhere you must do what the city and the homeland orders, or convince her by appealing to what is naturally just? And that it is not holy to use force against one's mother and father, and it is so much worse to do so against one's homeland?" What will we say to this, Crito? That the laws speak the truth? Or not?

CRITO: It looks so to me..

SOCRATES: "Consider, then, Socrates" the laws might say, "whether we speak the truth about the following: that it is not just for you to try to do to us what you're now attempting. For we gave birth to you, brought you up, educated you, and gave you and all the other citizens everything we could that's good, and yet even so we pronounce that we have given the power to any Athenian who wishes, when he has been admitted as an adult and sees the affairs of the city and us the laws and is not pleased with us, to take his possessions and leave for wherever he wants. And if any among you wants to live in a colony because we and the city do not satisfy him, or if he wants to go somewhere else and live as a foreigner, none of us laws stands in the way or forbids him from taking his possessions with him and leaving for wherever he wants.

But whoever remains with us, having observed how we decide lawsuits and take care of other civic matters, we claim this man by his action has now made an agreement with us to do what we command him to do, and we claim that anyone who does not obey is guilty three times over, because he disobeys us who gave birth to him, and who raised him, and because, despite agreeing to be subject to us, he does not obey us or persuade us if we are doing something improper, and although we give him an alternative and don't angrily press him to do what we order but instead we allow either of two possibilities, either to persuade us or to comply, he does neither of these.

We say that you especially will be liable to these charges, Socrates, if indeed you carry out your plans, and you not least of the Athenians but most of all." If, then, I would say, "How do you mean?", perhaps they would scold me justly, saying that I have made this agreement more than other Athenians. They might say, "Socrates, we have great evidence for this, that we and the city satisfy you. For you would never have lived here more than all of the other Athenians unless it seemed particularly good to you, and you never left the city for a festival, except once to Isthmos, but never to anywhere else, except on military duty, not did you ever make another trip like other Athenians, nor did any urge seize you to get to know a different city or other laws, but we and our city were sufficient for you.

So intently did you choose us and agree to be governed by us that, in particular, because your city was satisfactory to you, you had children in it. Moreover, at your trial you could have proposed exile, if you had wished, and what you're now trying to do to the city without her consent, you could have done then with her consent. At the time, you prided yourself on not being angry if you had to die, and you chose death, you said, in preference to exile. But now you neither feel shame in the face of those words nor have you any respect for us, the laws. By trying to destroy us you are doing what the most despicable slave would do, trying to run away contrary to the contract and the agreement by which you agreed to be governed by us. So answer us first on the particular point of whether or not we speak the truth in claiming that you agreed to be governed by us in deed and not merely in words." What can we say to this, Crito? Mustn't we agree?

CRITO: We must, Socrates.

SOCRATES: "Aren't you", they might say, "going against your contract and agreement with ourselves, which you were not forced to agree to nor deceived about nor compelled to decide upon in a short time but over seventy years, in which time you could have gone away if we did not satisfy you and these agreements did not appear just to you. You did not prefer Sparta nor Crete, each of which you claim is well-governed, nor any other of the Hellenic cities or the foreign ones, but you left it less than the lame and the blind and the other disabled people. Evidently the city and also we the laws were so much more pleasing to you than to other Athenians, for is a city without laws satisfactory to anyone? Now then, won't you keep to your agreement? You will, if you are convinced by us, at any rate, Socrates; and at least you won't look ridiculous by leaving the city.

Just think about what good it would do you and your friends if you break it and do wrong in one of these ways. It's pretty clear that your friends will risk exile along with you and disenfranchisement from the city and confiscation of their property. And if you first go to one of the closest cities, to Thebes or Megara — since both are well-governed — you would be an enemy, Socrates, of those governments, and all those who care about their cities will regard you suspiciously, thinking that you are a destroyer of the laws. And you will confirm the opinion of the judges in thinking that they judged the case correctly, since whoever is a destroyer of the laws would certainly be considered in some ways a destroyer of young and foolish men.

Will you flee, then, from well-governed cities and from the most civilised people? Is it worth it to you to live like this? Will you associate with them, Socrates, and feel no shame when talking with them? What will you say, Socrates —what you said here, that virtue and justice are the most valuable for humans and lawfulness and the laws? And you don't think the conduct of this Socrates will appear shameful? One should think so.

But will you leave these places and go to Crito's friends in Thessaly, since there is plenty of disorder and disobedience there? They might listen with pleasure to you, about how you amusingly ran away from prison wearing some costume or a peasant's vest or something else of the sort that runaways typically dress themselves in, altering your appearance. But still, will no one say that an old man, who probably only has a short time left in his life, was so greedy in his desire to live that he dared to violate the greatest laws? Perhaps not, if you do not annoy anyone. You yourself will surely spend your life sucking up to everyone and being a slave. What else will you do but feast in Thessaly, as though you had travelled to Thessaly for dinner. And those speeches, the ones about justice and the other virtues, where will they be?

Is it for the sake of your children that you want to live, so that you can raise and educate them? What are you going to do in that case? You'll raise and educate them by bringing them to Thessaly and making them outsiders, so that they will enjoy that benefit too? Or if not that, will they grow up better if they are raised and educated with you alive but away from them, because your friends will take care of them? Is it that if you go to Thessaly, they'll look after them, but if you go to Hades they won't? If those who claim to be your friends are any good, you must believe that they will.

So be convinced by us who brought you up, Socrates, and

do not put children or life or anything else ahead of justice, so that when you go to Hades you will be able to provide all this as your defence to those who rule there. Since neither in this world, nor in the next when you arrive, will this action be thought better or more just or more pious for you and your friends to do. But as it is you leave us, if indeed you depart, having been done an injustice not by us, the laws, but by men. If you return the injustice, however, and repay the harm and flee in shame, having violated your agreement and contract with us and harmed those who least of all should be harmed, yourself, your friends, your homeland, and us, we will make life hard for you while you're alive, and then our brothers, the laws in Hades, will not receive you favourably, knowing that you also tried to destroy us as far as you were able. So do not be persuaded by Crito to do what he says instead of what we say."

Rest assured, my dear friend Crito, that this is what I seem to hear, just as the Corybantes seem to hear the pipes; and this sound, from these words, resonates within me and makes me unable to hear anything else. So be aware that, based on what I currently believe, at least, if you speak in opposition to this, you will speak in vain. Nevertheless, if you honestly think you can do something more, then speak.

CRITO: No, Socrates. I am unable to speak.

SOCRATES: Then let it be, Crito, and let us act this way, since this is where the god leads us*.

This is truly a grand speech that Socrates has made. A veritable hymn to morality and the concept of duty.

It's amazing. So powerful, and yet so charming. The whole basis of political philosophy is right there. This dialogue alone is enough to establish Socrates as one of the most enlightened minds of all time. Now I want to hear what you can tell me about Plato.

* * *

* Dialogue reproduced from the translation by Cathal Woods & Ryan Pack.

PLATO

I spent twenty years with Plato, and he taught me a lot. He was my teacher at the Academy in Athens — Plato's Academy, as you call it today. There was a fair age difference between us, about forty years. He had considerable esteem for me, let me teach rhetoric in the Academy. It was there, at the Academy, that I experienced the almost sensuous pleasure of thinking.

Later, I was accused of being unfeeling towards him, and of repudiating his ideas. I don't think I did anything of the kind. Disagreeing with someone, even your teacher, does not make you unsympathetic.

Something I once said in this regard is still remembered: *Plato is dear to me, but dearer still is truth.* In fact, I still hear people using the expression, which of course simply means that we must seek and defend the truth even at the cost of displeasing those closest to us. Plato would not have disagreed. In any case, none of the ancient Greek philosophers merely repeated what their teachers had taught them: they went further, developed their own views, sometimes radically different. I don't call that disrespect.

Didn't my own student, Theophrastus, who took over the Lyceum from me, express his own ideas? That didn't surprise me in the least, I can assure you. There's nothing wrong with that. What's wrong is ingratitude, or appropriating other people's ideas.

—Who, in your view, was *Plato's spiritual father?*

That, I think, is a meaningless question in the case of a philosopher of Plato's stature. In any case, it is a fact that he was in some sort a disciple of Socrates and was, naturally, greatly influenced by him. I think I mentioned earlier that he himself described himself as a devout student of his. Plato's first teacher was apparently the less well-known Cratylus, who taught him Heracleitus' theories of matter.

Plato used to say that ideas live in an eternal and perfect world of which, he thought, our natural world is an incomplete imitation. He also thought that there was little point in wasting time studying the natural world. I, of course, take just the opposite view: far from scorning the physical world in which we live I think that it is essential that we study it. This does not, of course, mean that I do not respect the world of ideas. It has been said that Plato was a mystic as well as a philosopher, while I, as well as a philosopher, was also a scientist.

For Plato, philosophy was a rebirth of the soul, which leads to the harmonious co-existence of all things, serves all the needs of this life, and leads to spiritual goods. Plato believed in the immortality of the soul and in metempsychosis. He used to say, in fact, that the soul can be demoted or promoted, passing into an inferior or a superior dwelling-place, depending on its previous life. As he explains it in the Timaeus, if someone has failed to live his appointed time well he will be changed into a woman at the next birth, and if he fails again, into a beast[242]. Elsewhere he writes that we do not remember the experiences of our previous life, because before returning to earth all souls must drink of the waters of Lethe.

For Plato ethics is the science that shows us what is good and what is bad and how we must act to attain the former and avoid the latter, He conceived of happiness as the acquisition of intellectual good. In my opinion, this is something ungraspable, something valid only in metaphysics. The real good is to know yourself and then to harmonise yourself with the needs of your nature.

Plato is a colossus of world history. He was born in 428 BC into a noble Athenian family. At first, he wanted to become a politician, but was soon disenchanted with politicians and political life. He was also disillusioned with democracy, after seeing what it did to Socrates, the man whom he admired above all others. Socrates was the man who inspired his devotion to the art of dialectic and the reason why he abandoned poetry for philosophy.

Like almost all the Greek philosophers, he travelled a good deal. He visited Sicily, and made a special trip to Mount

Etna, to see the place where Empedocles threw himself into the crater.

In Sicily he met Dion, the brother-in-law of Dionysius the Elder, Tyrant of Syracuse. Dionysius was delighted with Plato and invited him to remain in the palace and teach. Plato, however, disliked the Epicurean atmosphere of the court, and in the end a disagreement with the tyrant resulted in his being literally dragged down to the port and shipped off to Aegina. During the journey he was taken prisoner by pirates and sold as a slave, but was eventually ransomed by a rich admirer from Cyrene, in North Africa, who recognised him, purchased him, and gave him a large sum of money. With this capital Plato bought some land in Athens and founded his famous Academy.

PLATO'S ACADEMY

Plato had the words "Let no one ignorant of geometry enter" inscribed over the doorway of his Academy. Geometry, in his view, led from practical knowledge to the world of abstract thinking.

The Academy occupied a beautiful garden near the sanctuary dedicated to the legendary hero Academus, in the present-day district of Kolonos. Students came to the Academy, to Plato, from all over Greece and beyond. He even had some female students, for like Socrates he recognised the intellectual and moral equality of men and women —which is odd, when you remember his theories on metempsychosis. The founding of Academy was one of the most important events in the ancient world.

Plato died at the age of eighty-one, and was buried in the grove of the hero Academus. His Academy continued, under the direction of his nephew Speusippus, although everyone agreed that I was the most prominent person in the school.

After he founded the Academy, Plato had little time for writing. Some of his famous dialogues must have been written before that time, while other important works, such as the *Symposium*, the *Phaedo* and the *Parmenides* were written in the early days of the Academy.

Plato spent his latter years writing books on physics, cosmology and aspects of political philosophy, which is the subject of his famous *Republic*.

Plato is one of the few ancient Greek philosophers whose work has been preserved virtually in its entirety.

PLATO'S REPUBLIC

Plato's works have a rare literary beauty. They are written in the form of dialogues, which he developed into an ideal vehicle for expressing his philosophical ideas. The *Republic* is a good example of their style and structure. In it, Socrates attempts to describe the ideal state to a group of friends, who, in the opening scene, are talking about justice[243]. After listening to various opinions, Socrates joins in. Since justice, he says, can only have meaning and substance within the framework of some organised society, a state, it is useful to see what brings the state into existence. The state arises out of human needs, for no man is self-sufficient. What are the basic human needs? Food, clothing and shelter. Consequently, a state requires farmers, builders, weavers and shoemakers. Each of those craftsmen, however, needs tools to work with — ploughs, chisels, looms, awls. Carpenters and smiths are therefore required as well, to make these tools. Perhaps, too, a country may produce an oversupply of some material goods and not enough of others; in these cases they will need to trade with neighbouring countries, to sell their surplus and purchase what is lacking; this means that merchants and seafarers are also needed[244]. And these are just the very basic requirements of human existence. But the citizens of a prosperous society will also want certain comforts, certain refinements, a certain luxury, delicacies on the table, perfumes and jewellery to wear when they go to the theatre. Our society must therefore also have jewellers, musicians, dancers, actors, and so on.

Now, to meet all these needs, Socrates continued, the state has to prosper and flourish. And that would be a temptation for its neighbours. They would plot against it, which might lead to war. Our state will therefore also require soldiers and arms[245]. And there must also be laws regulating the obligations and duties of the citizens and rulers to see that they are applied.

In the Republic Plato also says that anyone born into a certain class of citizens must remain there. Only in exceptional circumstances, for example extraordinary services rendered to the state, or a heinous offence against its laws, can he rise to a higher class or fall to a lower one.

If a citizen of the higher classes realises that his child is unsatisfactory, he must make him a labourer, no matter how difficult this is for him to bear. Similarly, if a labourer's child displays exceptional qualities, then the leaders should have an obligation to raise him to a higher class.

He also recommends that public servants live communally and have no private possessions, for the handling of the state's finances would be a temptation. Of course, their salaries should be sufficient to enable them to live decently. Astonishingly for his time, he suggested that there ought to be female public servants as well as male, who should receive the same training as the men and, like the men, live communally and own no property. He also tossed out the idea that women should not have their own husbands, but the best of each sex should mate with the best of the other, not necessarily forming permanent couples. The children would thus not know who their parents were, and so that the public servants, who in time of war would also staff the army, would not have family at home to worry about and could thus devote all their care and attention to the state.

The children of the most illustrious couples would be suckled by the mothers with the richest milk. The children of inferior couples would be accommodated in other, second-class, nurseries.

—I can hardly believe my ears! Could men like Plato and Socrates actually have said such things, and in such a highly developed society as that of Classical Athens? It's unreal. It makes them sound like Hitler, who wanted to create a pure Aryan race.

Why do you find that surprising? There was nothing new about the idea. Have you not heard that in Sparta malformed infants were thrown into a gorge, for the sake of improving the race? It was influenced by the Spartans that Plato spoke of the abolition of private property, communal living, and other such communistic ideas. He had known the Spartans as conquerors at first hand, as a young man of twenty, and saw Sparta as the model of a powerful state. He agreed with nationalisation and collective life. For these ideas he was —much later— accused of glamorising communistic and totalitarian regimes and denounced as an enemy of open society and democracy. Some saw him as a forerunner of Marx and Engels. In the final analysis I don't think Plato was against democracy, he just took every opportunity to stress its pros and cons[246]. You must also remember that the things Plato has Socrates say in the different dialogues may not necessarily reflect his real thinking. Diogenes Laertius tells us that once when Plato was reading one of these dialogues Socrates, who was present, interjected "What nonsense that young fellow puts in my mouth!"[247].

We often hear the phrase "Platonic love" used to describe a non-romantic, non-sexual relationship between a man and a woman. Where did this meaning come from, and what did Plato actually think of love?

PLATONIC LOVE

I can't imagine where that impression of Platonic love came from. What I do know is that Plato believed a consummated love to be a very beautiful thing, whose object is the perpetuation of the species. He talks of love in the Symposium, which is one of the loveliest works of literature of any age.

In the Symposium, Plato recounts a discussion among friends at a banquet hosted by the poet Agathon, who is celebrating a victory in a dramatic contest. One of those present, although a little late in arriving, is Socrates. At the beginning of the discussion, as was the custom, each person expressed his thoughts about love:

- The one who loves is happier than the one who is loved.
- Loves are of two kinds: the earthy, the natural love of Aphrodite Pandemos, and the celestial, the intellectual love of Aphrodite Urania.
- Humans normally seek the natural sort of love. That is, men pursue women to enjoy their bodies, heedless of their mental capacities. Celestial love is cerebral, its primary motives are intellectual. Perhaps this is what is known as Platonic love.

Celestial love can, naturally, exist between men. It is not homosexuality, though, because there is no sexual contact.

Another guest at the banquet said that there is a qualitative opposition in nature (male-female), but that love intervenes to soften the oppositions and restore harmony.

Once they had all had their say, Socrates spoke up.

- The object of love is the reproduction of the beautiful.
- The beautiful and the good are the same.
- The human mind can, like the body, conceive and bear fruit.
- All men desire to become happy and immortal, achieving the beautiful and the good.
- Some think that they can ensure immortality by acquiring glory, some by making love to beautiful women.
- Others think that immortality is achieved through engagement with things of the mind.

If there is nothing else you want to ask about Plato, I suggest we move on to Epicurus, an important philosopher who lived after Socrates.

—No, there is nothing more I want to ask. But with your permission I'd like to tell you about something I read the other day. It was an interview the British novelist Kazuo Ishiguro gave a journalist writing for To Vima newspaper just after his book "The Buried Giant" was published in Greek.

In this interview Ishiguro said: "Plato was a pivotal figure for me, because I read him when I was a young man studying philosophy. His works had a tremendous influence on me. Not so much the "Republic", but the "Platonic Dialogues". What happens in the dialogues is that there is some man who is very pleased with himself and his opinions. And then Socrates comes along, joins in the discussion, and by the end of the conversation the first man has been brought to realise that the values he had been defending are essentially unfounded. This also happens in many of my books. Plato, I think, is still inherently part of everything I write, even today."

That's it, that's all I wanted to say. So let's get on with Epicurus.

EPICURUS

Epicurus was a disputed figure. In his own day, he had devoted followers and equally devoted enemies. Typical of the reactions he provoked are the opinions of a pair of Romans. The poet Lucretius cites many of his ideas in the *De rerum natura*, and hails him as a god: "He was a god, yes, a god, who with his art seized life from the towering waves and the depths of darkness and brought it into a quiet harbour under clear skies". Cicero, however, had a very different opinion of him, and described an Epicurean as coming from the pigsty rather than the school[248].

I have to say that I think Cicero was exaggerating and being unfair. As is often the case in such situations, the truth lies somewhere in the middle. Epicurean thinking often reflects the idealism of Plato, but more closely agrees with my philosophy.

Epicurus was born in Samos in 341 BC, a time when the autonomy of the cities was greatly diminished. He was a teacher, and turned to philosophy when the works of Democritus came into his hands[249]. Eventually he settled in Athens and opened a school of his own. He had no superstitious fear of the gods, and disapproved of the mystery cults, which had become very popular.

One of his main interests was physics. He adopted a number of positions, usually borrowed from earlier philosophers. Two that spring to mind are "The universe is infinite, unchanging, and therefore eternal" and "The material bodies are infinite in number and are in continual interaction".

He should certainly be remembered for his theory of matter: "Nothing comes from nothing and nothing is lost", a view that was confirmed experimentally by Lavoisier many centuries later.

The aim of Epicurean philosophy is to deliver man from his passions and make his life happy. He talked about what is good and what is evil, about happiness and pleasure, about the good, about virtue and friendship.

He thought that a happy life could be achieved by freedom from pain and enjoyment of pleasure. His ethics, I have to say, were not utilitarian. The pleasure he extolled and for which he is criticised was not necessarily of the flesh.

His school, which was known as "The Garden", was a democratic community, whose members were bound by religious and social ties as well as by friendship.

His maxim was "Pass unnoticed" — which, I may say, young man, is a very wise precept to live by if you want to succeed. No one likes an egoist, a show-off, a person who is always pushing himself forward.

Epicurus was one of those philosophers who profess another, better, world, without suggesting how to achieve it. He did not ask his students to give all their belongings to the brotherhood, as did Pythagoras, on the grounds that "Friends have all things in common." Epicurus died in Athens at the age of seventy-two.

He was a prolific writer. I shall set down for you a number of his *Principal Doctrines*, sayings relating mainly to ethics from the book of the same name.

- Any bodily pain is bearable, because extreme pain does not last long, while chronic pain is mild.
- It is impossible to live a pleasant life without living wisely and honourably and justly, and it is impossible to live wisely and honourably and justly without living pleasantly.
- No pleasure is a bad thing in itself, but the things which

produce certain pleasures entail disturbances many times greater than the pleasures themselves.

- The wealth required by nature is limited and is easy to procure; but the wealth required by vain ideals has no bounds.
- The just man is most free from disturbance, while the unjust is full of the utmost disturbance.
- Of our desires some are natural and necessary, like hunger and thirst, others are natural but not necessary, like those for extravagant meals; and others are neither natural nor necessary, but are due to vanity, like victors' crowns and the raising of statues.
- Natural justice is a pledge of reciprocal benefit, to prevent one man from harming or being harmed by another.
- It is not the young man who is happy, but the old man who has lived a good life, because the young man does not know what life may have in store for him, while the old man has garnered pleasant memories with which to live.
- Let us try to make the next journey better than the last, and rejoice without excess when we reach the end.
- We respond to the troubles of friends not with lamentations but with action.
- In a philosophical discussion the winner is the one who learns the most. That is, the one who disagreed and was persuaded by the other.
- Self-sufficiency is a greater good than wealth.
- The greatest fruit of self-sufficiency is freedom.
- If you desire to make Pythocles rich, do not give him more things but curb his desires.
- We should be grateful to nature who made the accessible necessary and the inaccessible unnecessary.

You've certainly given me a whole new impression of the Epicureans! Could we now, do you think, talk a little about the pre-Socratic philosophers, who gave so much to the exact sciences?

I'd be delighted. Many of them were very important indeed, and of course very well known.

I think the best way of approaching them is chronologically, starting with the earliest. Although that is not as easy as it sounds, since their precise dates are not absolutely certain. For example, Diogenes Laertius tells us that Thales died during the fifty-eighth Olympiad. The Olympiad, as you may know, was a four-year period beginning from each celebration of the Olympic Games. This was a generally accepted way of reckoning dates in Ancient Greece, but not very precise, since the dates of the Olympiads themselves can only be calculated indirectly. For the record, the first Olympiad was reckoned to have begun in 776 BC, in your terms. What I'm getting at is that no one knows exactly when any of these philosophers were born.

What I would suggest, then, is that we simply follow the generally accepted chronological order for the pre-Socratic philosophers, if you have no objection.

— *That's fine with me.*

In that case, print out the list of pre-Socratic philosophers with their indicative dates of birth, and keep it handy for reference purposes. So we begin, then, with Thales.

THE PRE-SOCRATIC PHILOSOPHERS**

THALES of Miletus	640 BC
ANAXIMANDER of Miletus	610 BC
ANAXIMENES of Miletus	585 BC
PYTHAGORAS of Samos	580 BC
HERACLEITUS of Ephesus	540 BC
PARMENIDES of Elis	515 BC
ANAXAGORAS of Clazomenae	500 BC
EMPEDOCLES of Acragas	494 BC
LEUCIPPUS of Miletus	480 BC
DEMOCRITUS of Abdera	400 BC

** *The birth dates are merely indicative*

THALES

Thales was born in the Ionian city of Miletus, in roughly 640 BC, and died during a heat wave at the age of ninety while watching an athletic competition. He was one of the Seven Wise Men of Ancient Greece and was the actually the first to have been called "the Wise" [250].

He studied, as you would say today, with Egyptian and Chaldean priests, who expounded on astronomy, mathematics and navigation.

He never married. Tradition has it that when his mother —like all mothers everywhere— would press him to take a wife, his standard answer was "it is not yet time", until the day he switched it to "it is no longer time".

Also, when asked why he did not want to have children, he said, "Out of love for them." [251] Which I take to mean that he did not think himself a good candidate for such a serious matter as raising children.

Thales laid the foundations of scientific research in the natural sciences. He was the first to disregard the mythological stories of the creation of the world and made the great leap to belief that the universe is formed from a single material substance.

—*Is that enough to justify his place among the Seven Wise Men of Ancient Greece?*

That theory is not the only reason for his inclusion, but it is certainly one of them. His undisputed achievements in various scientific domains are numerous.

In astronomy, among other things he predicted, many months before the event, through a series of mathematical calculations, the eclipse of the sun that occurred on 28 May 585 BC[252].

In a campaign against the Persians the army of King Croesus of Lydia found itself unable to cross the river Halys. Thales, who happened to be in Croesus' camp, engineered a diversion of the river that reduced its width by half and thus enabled Croesus' men to cross[253].

This Croesus was a fabulously wealthy king. Herodotus tells the story of how the Athenian lawgiver Solon was asked whether there existed a more fortunate man than Croesus in the whole world. Solon answered "Call not a man happy until he die." How right Solon was is shown by the fact that not long afterwards Croesus was taken prisoner by the Persians and burnt alive.

—*What was Thales' general philosophy?*

I shall repeat some of his sayings for you to give you an idea of his general views on life, and his wit.

Thales had been saying that death is no different from life. "Then why do you not die?", someone asked. The answer came back promptly: "Have I not just been telling you that there is no difference?"

When someone asked him which came first, night or day, he answered "Night, but only by a day".

To an adulterer who asked whether he should swear that he never committed adultery he replied that a false oath is a worse crime.

When asked how we should live well and justly, he replied, "Avoid doing what you would blame others for doing." He also disapproved of unfair enrichment and permitting criticism of those one admired. He also said that it is very difficult to know oneself, although some ascribe that saying to Chilon, another of the Seven Wise Men. He was also wont to advise "Nothing to excess", or, moderation in all things, but then so did —and do— most wise men[254].

—*I have heard that, much as the ancient philosophers were admired by their contemporaries, people were often of two minds about them, because although wise they were also impractical: they discovered wonderful things, wrote beautiful books, formulated amazing theories, but paid no attention to their own interests, their own material welfare, and remained poor, often living on handouts or the patronage of a wealthy student.*

That is true. Many people thought they were daft[255], for that very reason. And when Thales heard such comments about himself, that his poverty was proof that philosophy was of no use, he decided he would show them that he could perfectly well make money if he wanted to. He hadn't bothered before, because it was not something he was interested in. So, what did he do?

Based on his astronomical skills and observations of the weather he knew that there would be a bumper crop of olives in the coming year, so he borrowed some money and leased all the olive presses in the area. When the harvest fulfilled his prediction and olive presses were consequently in great demand, Thales rented them out at a higher price and made himself a tidy profit,[256] thus proving that philosophers could turn their knowledge to good practical effect if they wanted to. This demonstration gave his compatriots a whole new idea of him.

—*What else did he do?*

He was the first to calculate the height of the pyramids, using a very simple method: he compared the length of their shadow to the length of his own at a moment when his shadow matched his height[257].

He advised navigators to steer by the Little Bear[258]. As you probably know, the North Star is the last star in the tail of the Little Bear.

According to Proclus, it was Thales who demonstrated that the angles at the base of an isosceles triangle are equal and, according to Eudemus, that the opposite angles formed by the intersection of two straight lines are also equal.

I used the word 'daft' a few minutes ago in connection with philosophers. It is true that it can often be applied to people who live by their intellect. They devote endless effort, time, and often money, to clarifying or writing something for the benefit of their students, knowing from the outset that this will bring them no material advantage. All they want from their students is some recognition. I'm telling you this as a teacher, Alexander, in the hope that you will not be one of those students who are a disappointment to their teachers.

I will tell you a story about Thales in this regard. According to the Roman philosopher Apuleius, when he was already an old man Thales calculated the trajectory of the sun. When he communicated this discovery to his student Mandrolytus of Priene, he was very excited and asked Thales how much he should pay him for this lesson.

"I will consider myself very well paid", replied Thales, "if when you teach this to others you do not present it as your own discovery, but acknowledge it as mine"[259]. It seems that Thales must have had bitter experience of this sort of thing in the past.

Diogenes Laertius says that Thales was the first of the Ionian philosophers to make a systematic study of what is known as natural philosophy.

Natural philosophy developed in Ionia, an ancient region comprising the central section of the west coast of what is now Turkey, with the islands of Chios and Samos. The Ionian philosophers were principally concerned with the origin of the cosmos and the primary components of matter and material things. Thales believed that it was important to observe one's surroundings and try to draw conclusions from observed phenomena, and sought to find natural causes to explain those phenomena rather than attribute them to the gods.

The basic building block of matter, he thought, the original substance out of which all others are formed, is water[260]. Whatever gave him that idea, you may well ask. And yet it is not so foolish a notion. His conclusion is based on the observation that seed is moist but dries out quickly, losing its properties, and that all living creatures contain water. He also thought that the earth floats on water.

As I note in my book On the Soul, Thales knew of electricity, having observed the appearance of static electricity when things are rubbed against amber, which the Greeks called *electron*. He also knew of magnetism, having seen that magnetite, a mineral that occurs on that coast, attracted iron[261].

—*I can see that you have considerable admiration for Thales. To us the idea that all things come from water sounds ridiculous, because we know that they come from compounds of the ninety chemical elements found in nature.*

I know. Thales' theory sounds very naïve today, but if you remember that he was the first to move away from mythological accounts of the origin of things, you will realise how important his contribution was to science generally and to the concept of the origin of matter in particular.

Now, if I am not mistaken, the next name on your list of Wise Men is Anaximander.

Yes, it's Anaximander.

Right, then, let's continue with him.

ANAXIMANDER

Anaximander was unquestionably one of the greatest intellects in human history. He was a student of Thales, and therefore one of those we call natural philosophers. In his view the primary element of matter is something he called *apeiron*, "unlimited". Some form of matter that is unlimited and imperishable. But definitely not water, as Thales thought.

— *There was, in other words, a disagreement between teacher and student?*

I don't think I would call it a disagreement, or at least not a radical one. Don't forget that before Thales all ideas about the origins of everything were mythological: everything was the work of one or another of the gods.

The disagreement over the primary element of matter is between Thales and his predecessors, not between Thales and Anaximander, both of whom proposed some material substance as the primary element. We don't know what Thales would have thought about Anaximander's theories. He might well have adopted them. For one of the best things that can happen to a teacher is to leave behind him students who equal or excel him. The opposite is disappointing, and a sign of failure.

Anaximander was interested in many things and is credited with many discoveries. He was the first to invent a sundial, which as you know is simply a post hammered into the ground which shows the time of day by the length and direction of its shadow, which changes as the sun moves across the heaven from east to west.

He was the first to make a map that was really useful to sailors, because apart from what any map contains it also had "useful guides". He noted, for example, what peoples the traveller would encounter in each place, and other information about different geographical regions.

Obviously, in order to draw detailed maps filled with useful information, Anaximander must have travelled considerably. He is said to have founded a colony on the Black Sea, which he called Apollonia; and he also drew a map of the heavens.

He held that the Earth is neither suspended nor supported, but floats freely at the centre of the universe.

On one occasion he warned the Spartans to leave their city because he predicted that there would be an earthquake. Cicero tells us that the earthquake did indeed occur, and was so great that it destroyed the whole city and toppled a great chunk off the top of Mount Taygetus.

Anaximander was born in Miletus in 610 BC and lived for sixty-three years. He was the first to write a treatise On nature or On the nature of things, part of which is preserved by the neo-Platonist philosopher Simplicius. It contains Anaximander's theory that everything in the world comes from an imperceptible substance which he called *apeiron*. Everything is composed of *apeiron* and everything returns to *apeiron* when it decomposes. Or as the Book of Genesis puts it, "Dust you are and to dust you will return." Anaximander, in other words, believed that all material things are composed of and decompose into the same elements.

— *What did he think this apeiron was? Does the word refer to a quantity of matter or is it the name of some specific matter?*

In my view, as I explain in my *Physics*, none of the primary elements of matter can exist in unlimited quantity. Elsewhere I become even more categorical and state that nothing exists in infinite quantity. Anaximander was not, I think, referring to quantity. His *apeiron* is an undefined entity, of which he thought that everything in the vast universe was composed.

Some of your contemporaries identify Anaximander's *apeiron* with hydrogen, which they think was the first chemical element formed after the creation of the universe (the Big Bang). It is thought that hydrogen was created in unimaginable quantity and that all the other chemical elements derive from it; this theory is now accepted. And now, following your list, let's move on to Anaximenes.

ANAXIMENES

Anaximenes was a student of Anaximander, who had been a student of Thales, both monists as we have seen, and like them he too asserts that there is only one kind of ultimate substance. This, he thought, was air[262], and went on to say that, when rarefied, air becomes fire (heat) and, when condensed, water (cooling).

Air, he said, encompasses everything — "Just as our soul, being air, holds us together, so do breath and air encompass the whole world" — and is in constant motion. With this infinite and constant motion it undergoes change. It may thin and become fire or thicken and become first wind, then cloud, then water, then earth, and finally stone.

Few people today know much about Anaximenes and his theories, but anyone who has taken chemistry at school will probably have heard of a manometer, an instrument for measuring the pressure of gases and vapours. Who would guess, though, that the word 'manometer' comes from the Greek word *manosis*, meaning rarefaction or thinning, which was used by Anaximenes to explain his theory?

According to Pliny, Anaximenes demonstrated the first sundial, in Sparta, asserted that the moon takes its light from the sun, and explained eclipses. So you see, Alexander, that Anaximenes, too, added his bit to the structure of what we called natural philosophy.

And now, who is next on our list?
According to the table, it is Pythagoras.

PYTHAGORAS

The master said it, and that's that. These words illustrate the spirit that reigned among the disciples in the famous School that Pythagoras founded at Croton in southern Italy. The "he" was, of course, Pythagoras, and the phrase demonstrates the no-argument acceptance of and obedience to the master's authority. Pythagoras considered himself the incarnation of Apollo on earth. He was a legend in his lifetime.

The School of Pythagoras differed in its mode of operation from the other schools of philosophy. It was characterised by severe discipline, austerity, and exaggerated respect for one's seniors. Self-criticism was practised daily. The work of the School followed a certain ceremonial, which was kept secret from outsiders.

The Pythagorean School was effectively a religious brotherhood, and his teachings had religious and moral parameters.

Pythagoras left no written texts. What we know about him and his theories come from the writings of the Pythagoreans, his disciples, which however also contain some of their own ideas.. That is why in my books I do not refer to Pythagoras, but to the Pythagoreans.

If you were to ask me what lies at the heart of Pythagoras' cosmology, I would answer without a moment's hesitation that it is number, mathematics.

Pythagoras, say his disciples, concluded that numbers have a functional significance as a result of observing the harmony that exists in the natural world; this he thought, was evident in the movements of the earth and stars, and also in musical sounds. He believed that this harmony obeyed certain mathematical relations; he also believed that number plays a leading role in the creation of all that exists.

But let us take his career from the beginning. When he came of age, he wanted to study mathematics, and therefore approached the most famous teachers of mathematics of that age, who were the Egyptian priests.

They, for some reason, were unwilling to accept him; perhaps it was his extreme intelligence, or possibly a degree of insolence on his part. Whatever the reason, they subjected him to increasingly difficult examinations, all of which he passed with flying colours, as you would say. In the end he was accepted as an equal, admitted into their circle, and allowed to share their knowledge[263].

Having learned all he could in Egypt, there seemed to be nothing more to gain by remaining there, so Pythagoras decided to travel to other lands and learn what he could of other customs and other sciences. Thus, he learned astronomy from the Chaldeans, geometry from the Phoenicians, and occult sciences from the Magi, an ancient Persian clan specialising in cultic activities.

After years of travelling and pursuing his studies in the East, Pythagoras returned to Samos. But the dissolute manners prevailing there were not to his taste, and so he went on to Croton, in southern Italy, where he settled and began teaching.

He founded a school that was very like a secret society. Something like the Masons. Its members, the students, had to abide by rules and comply with orders that were odd, to say the least, or allegorical. For example, they were forbidden to eat broad beans, and when they got up in the morning they had to make sure they left no imprint of their body on the mattress.

What do you think Pythagoras meant by those rules?

Well, he may have been equating the imprint on the mattress with too many hours spent lying in bed —a thing to be discouraged. But why he had to do it indirectly instead of saying it straight out, well, that is just the way secret societies work.

But why such an aversion to broad beans?

It may be that he was susceptible to favism, a hereditary disorder associated with the lack of a certain enzyme, triggered by eating broad beans. It results in severe anaemia, jaundice and haemorrhaging in various organs. If Pythagoras had had such an attack, it is understandable that he didn't even want to hear the word mentioned.

You may have gathered that Pythagoras was not what you might call unassuming. He began every lesson with the words "I swear by the air I breathe and the water I drink that I will not tolerate any objection to what I shall tell you." [264]

He divided his students into two groups, based on their intellectual capacity: those who could actively approach knowledge and those who could merely attend his classes.

He spoke in arithmetical codes and used many symbols, so that only the initiated would be able to understand him. He attached great importance to the solidarity that he thought should exist among the members of the community. Some even ascribed supernatural powers to him: for example, he was said to have been seen simultaneously in Croton and in Metapontum.

His students looked upon him with awe and admiration. Although when I say 'looked upon', that is merely a figure of speech, because when he taught it was always from behind a curtain. Only a select few were allowed into his presence. They even avoided pronouncing his name; it was always "ipse dixit", "he [the master] said…".

These eccentricities began to irritate people, and such feeling grew up against him in Croton that he was forced to leave. He apparently went to the Temple of the Muses in Metapontum, still in Sicily, where he refused to eat and subsequently died. How long did he live? Here, too, opinions vary. Some say around seventy years, others ninety, others a hundred and fifty. The veil of mystery that shrouded his whole life covered him to the end.

When asked by the tyrant of Phlius, an ancient city in the Peloponnese, who he was, Pythagoras replied "A philosopher". This was the first time the word had been heard.

The Pythagorean school of philosophy had many of the features of a religious movement. His followers believed in metempsychosis. Pythagoras himself held that he had already lived four previous lives in various bodies; in the intervals, he temporarily inhabited a plant or animal. Such opinions were probably the result of his many years in the East. Don't smile, you must be aware that there are still religions that believe in the transmigration of the soul. The soul, they thought, moves from body to body, going to a higher or lower class of creature depending on the life just lived.

Pythagoras thought that "all things are numbers",[265] and that number lies at the heart of matter and regulates its properties.

—*Wait a minute, now. That can't be right. I could understand the primary element being water, or air, or an aether, or something else with substance, but number? Number is non-material, a symbol.*

You've hit the nail on the head with that last word. Number for Pythagoras as the primary element of nature symbolises something else. You're a chemistry student — can you tell me what atomic number is and what it means to you?

—*Atomic number is the number of protons in the nucleus of an atom. This number is the same as the number of electrons surrounding the nucleus, which determine the properties of the atoms, of matter.*

There you are, then. Pythagoras' theory isn't looking quite so silly, is it?

Pythagoras believed that everything, even "the motion of the stars and the harmony of sounds", is determined by numbers. That surprises you? Well, you're not alone, it's a thought that startles many people. But it's true, for all that. The stars in their courses do obey mathematical rules, and musical harmony fits into mathematical patterns. Many composers have used mathematics in their music, one famous modern example being Yannis Xenakis. Pythagoras also discovered that there is a constant ratio between the length of a lyre's strings and the fundamental musical chords. This excited him so much that he declared that "The principles of mathematics are the principles of everything."

Pythagoras is thought to have been the first to use the word 'mathematics', by which he meant what we would now call a general science[266].

THE MATHEMATICAL STRUCTURE
OF THE GREEK LANGUAGE

May I interrupt here to tell you about something I read lately that made quite an impression on me?. It was a book on the mathematical decoding of the Greek language, by Vasilios Argyropoulos, who says that certain Ancient Greek words are not random formations but have a mathematical structure, and that the correlation of letters and numbers can even yield mathematical constants. Let me give you an example.

Everyone knows that if you divide the length of the circumference of any circle by the length of its diameter, you always get the same number, 3.14, which is universally symbolised by the Greek letter π. That is:

$$\frac{\text{length of circumference of circle}}{\text{diameter}} = 3{,}14 = \pi.$$

Now, if you replace each letter of the Greek words for length (μήκος), circumference (περιφέρεια), circle (κύκλος) and diameter (διάμετρος) as they appear in the numerator and the denominator with its corresponding number (see table; the Greeks did not have Arabic numerals, but used the letters of the alphabet to represent numbers), you get:

μήκος: $40 + 8 + 20 + 70 + 200 = 338$

περιφέρειας: $80 + 5 + 100 + 10 + 500 + 5 + 100$
$$+ 5 + 10 + 1 + 200 = 1016$$

κύκλου: $20 + 400 + 20 + 30 + 70 + 400 = 940$

διάμετρος: $4 + 10 + 1 + 40 + 5 + 300 + 100 + 70 + 200 = 730.$

Adding the numerical values of each word gives us:

$$\frac{338 + 1016 + 940}{730} = 3.14 = \pi.$$

Isn't that amazing? You can't tell me that's just chance.

No, it's not just chance. You're quite right to be amazed.

Those Greek words for length, diameter and circumference existed, of course, long before the time of Archimedes, but he was the first to calculate the value 3.14 for π.

The results of the mathematical exploring done by the Pythagoreans became widely known after the School was closed and its students dispersed to different Greek cities.

TABLE OF GREEK LETTERS
AND THEIR NUMBER EQUIVALENTS

α′	1	ιε′	16	ν′	50
β′	2	ις′	17	ξ′	60
γ′	3	ιζ′	18	ο′	70
δ′	4	ιη′	19	π′	80
ε′	5	ιθ′	20	ϟ′	90
ς′	6	κ′	21	ρ′	100
ζ′	7	κα′	22	σ′	200
η′	8	κβ′	23	τ′	300
θ′	9	κγ′	24	υ′	400
ι′	10	κδ′	25	φ′	500
ια′	11	κε′	29	χ′	600
ιβ′	12	κθ′	20	ψ′	700
ιγ′	13	λ′	30	ω′	800
ιδ′	14	μ′	40		

PYTHAGOREAN THEOREM

Do you know what Pythagoras did when he discovered the famous theorem that has made his name familiar to every schoolchild? Apparently (or so we are told by Iamblichus) he was so excited that he offered a sacrifice of one hundred oxen!

The Pythagorean theorem states that: "In a right-angled triangle, the square of the hypotenuse is equal to the sum of the squares of the other two sides" [267].

Another theorem attributed to the Pythagoreans is that the sum of the angles of any triangle equals two right angles.

Pythagoras was greatly honoured after his death. Coins and medals displaying his head were struck, and images of him appear in churches and in the works of great Renaissance painters.

I think that by now you should have a good basic picture of the life and work of Pythagoras.

I think I have. Now, next on our list is Heracleitus. He, I seem to remember, was called "the Obscure". Was he that difficult to understand?

HERACLEITUS

He tended to speak in riddles, and his statements were often very unclear. For example, take the famous pronouncement: "a man cannot step into the same river twice" [268]. Now, whatever does he mean by that? Why could you not step into a river any number of times?

—It certainly seems to be a riddle. But surely what he meant was not the river itself but the flow of water. Of course you can step into a river at the same place again and again, but the water flowing past you will not be the same.

That is certainly a plausible explanation, and chimes with his basic idea that nothing is stationary, all is in flux, everything that exists is in constant motion. The phrase is used a lot in your day, I notice, not just for matter and material things, but to suggest the instability of emotions, philosophical views, political and economic situations, and so on.

Another of his favourite expressions was that nothing is constant except change. Heracleitus believed that things exist in a state of a constant flux and transformation. Even the most apparently solid and unchanging things are not inert: mountains erode, iron rusts, and we grow old.

Heracleitus was also the man who said "Everything comes into being through strife", and "war is the father of all" [269]. He said, too, that the truest harmony comes from opposites, and went on to explain that "only when we fall sick do we appreciate the value of health, only when we are hungry do we savour the food, and only when we are weary are we grateful for rest".

Heracleitus had little respect for physicians. He suffered from dropsy, and after visiting a doctor is reported to have said "Not only do they cut and burn you but they expect to be paid for it". He also mocked those who prayed in front of statues, saying that this was like talking to the house rather than those who live in it.

He left just one book, and it was poorly written and very hard to understand. Myself, I think he was perfectly capable of having done so on purpose, so that only the very few, the truly percipient, would understand it. Because, as he said, "Whatever you say to the masses is going to go straight over their heads. It's like talking to the deaf." Which he put in one of his obscure turns of phrase: those present are absent.

The fact is, that since there is virtually no punctuation in his texts, it is often hard to know whether a given word belongs with the one before it or the one after it[270].

—*You're giving me the impression that Heracleitus was something of a disputed figure. Is that your opinion?*

Not in the least. But he was not popular in his day; his reputation was only established later. There are still important figures who revere him. Nietzsche, for example, who was a devoted student of the ancient Greek philosopher, thought himself a reincarnation of Heracleitus. He may perhaps have been as fond of his way of expressing his ideas as of those ideas themselves.

Heracleitus belonged to an aristocratic family and was undoubtedly what you would call an intellectual; the result was that he had no time for ordinary folk. He was particularly disdainful of the uneducated and the ignorant. Which he thought most men were. He despised the multitude.

It is not known whether Heracleitus studied with any famous teacher. He himself said he was self-educated.

He was not interested in wealth or fame. And he scathingly criticised his fellow-citizens of Ephesus for banishing Hermodorus, an admirable governor of the city and the 'most estimable man among them', simply for being beyond reproach in all he did. Malicious envy has, as you can see, long been a characteristic of many Greeks.

What about the natural sciences? Did Heracleitus make a contribution in that field?

First of all, he believed fire to be the primordial element, out of which all else had arisen[271]. All things come from fire, he said, and as fire all things end[272]. Yes, I know how peculiar that sounds to you. I suspect that you are wondering how it is possible for a substance to be created from fire and to end up as fire.

Well, just think about it for a moment. What would you, as a chemistry student, say if I told you that what Heracleitus called "Fire" is simply what you today call energy? Is it not now universally accepted that energy can be transformed into matter and conversely, matter into energy. Einstein even reduced that concept to a formula, in his famous equation. It is, therefore, perfectly possible for energy to produce particles of matter and particles of matter to yield energy.

All right, but how do you account for what he said about fire being transmitted in 'psegmata', little 'particles', and not continuously?

The definition of a quantum in modern physics is a 'discrete natural unit, or packet, of energy or other physical property'. I think you have your answer right there. Heracleitus' 'particles of fire' are what you would now call quanta of energy.

So why, if a term already existed, with Heracleitus' word 'psegmata', are quanta not called that?

The term existed, certainly, but apparently the man who rediscovered Heracleitus' theory some fifteen hundred years later either did not know it or simply did not like it.

—I guess that's as good a place as any to leave Heracleitus. What can you tell me about the next pre-Socratic on our list, Parmenides?

PARMENIDES

Parmenides was an important, but at the same time a very modest man. His name became a byword for a conservative and decent way of life[273]. He believed that every human act has its own specific object, and that the object is what determines the importance of the act.

Parmenides was also a famous lawgiver. When his fellow-citizens came of age they swore by the "Laws of Parmenides". He was born in Elea, in southern Italy, and the school he founded there was one of the principal schools of pre-Socratic philosophy.

Parmenides abandoned the monism of the Ionian philosophers and argued that matter is composed of two primary elements, fire and earth. In my opinion, Parmenides really thought of those elements as *heat* and *cold*, for which he used the words *fire* and *earth*. In other words, Parmenides used the word 'fire' to signify the properties of fire, and the word 'earth' to signify the properties of solids.

— *Not a very interesting character. Shall we move on, then, to Anaxagoras? I've read that he was the teacher of Socrates, Pericles and Euripides, which suggests that he must have been an important person.*

"Like master, like pupil", you mean? Well, there is a good bit of truth in that.

ANAXAGORAS

Anaxagoras regarded *mind*, which he thought to be unchanging, as the beginning and source of everything[274]. He thus made a distinction between mind and soul. A king or a rich man is not, he said, a happy man, although he allowed that he would not be surprised if a person who considered himself happy was thought by the world to be unhappy[275], because most people equate happiness with material things.

In that, of course, he was quite right[276], and in general I agree with much of what Anaxagoras said - for example, that order exists in nature.

What I do not agree with is the notion of an aether, which he posited as the source, and basic substance of all things[277]. This aether was not, of course, what you chemists mean by an ether; it was more like a rarefied air.

Despite his errors there can be no doubt that Anaxagoras was a man of genius. Take this saying, for example: The earth is the mother of the plants and the sun is their father[278]. That is, the moist earth (the mother) generates the plant and the sun (the father) nourishes it and makes it grow.

How many centuries did it take for scientists to realise that plants get the nourishment that sustains them through the process of photosynthesis, which takes place only by day and only in the presence of sunlight?

Anaxagoras was born into a wealthy family in Clazomenae, a city near present-day Izmir, sometime around 500 BC. When he came of age, he gave all he possessed to his relatives, so that he would have no worries.

He liked to go and sit alone and contemplate the sky from the top of some nearby mountain. One of his fellow-citizens reproached him for not loving his native city, since he had abandoned it for a mountaintop. "You are quite wrong," he replied, "I adore my native place" and pointed at the sky. The heavens, he believed, were the common fatherland of all men.

He learned much about the universe from the occult writings of Egyptian priests. This enabled him to predict an eclipse of the sun, an earthquake (from the cloudiness of the water in a well) and the fall of a meteorite[279].

Once he appeared at the Olympic Games with a leather mantle over his head, as if expecting a downpour, although the sky was perfectly clear. Before his neighbours had finished cracking jokes at his expense, the heavens opened and everyone —except himself— was drenched.

He also maintained that sound is transmitted through the air by means of successive percussions. As you know from your physics, sound is transmitted by successive compressions and rarefactions of the air.

While still a young man he moved to Athens, where he founded a school of philosophy, and where he became the friend, as well as the teacher, of the famous Athenian statesman Pericles. This did not prevent him from being prosecuted on the usual charge of impiety and banished. Not even Pericles, for all his power, could intervene in the workings of justice.

While in exile, someone condoled with him upon having lost the Athenians. "It is not I who have lost the Athenians," he replied "but the Athenians who have lost me"[280]. When Athenian friends said how sorry they were that he would be ending his days in a foreign land, he merely remarked that "the descent to Hades is the same from every place". When his period of exile was over he returned to Athens, where he was prosecuted again, this time because a slave "confessed", after a severe beating, that he had heard Anaxagoras say that the sun was a fiery rock revolving in the heavens.

To anyone who complained of the fee he charged for his lessons he replied "Those who wish light put oil in their lamps." [281] He said something similar to Pericles as well.

Like most ancient Greek philosophers Anaxagoras speculated on the fundamental elements of matter and how they were activated. In his view they were neither one, as Thales, Anaximander, Anaximenes and Heracleitus had thought, nor four, as Empedocles later suggested, but infinite in number. These primordial particles, which he called "homeomers", were infinitesimal specks of matter that had their own characteristics, their own properties. They were identical in quality, and invisible, and could perhaps be compared to what we call molecules. He believed that these homeomers were set in order by reason, which played a role not unlike that which you ascribe to DNA, in determining the unfolding of the life of which it is a part. A governing role, not a creative one. Anaxagoras also said that reason has nothing to do with chance, because reason "knows what it is doing".

Anaxagoras believed that the stars are fiery rocks and the moon a cold one, which is illuminated by the sun. The winds are produced by the thinning of the air caused by the heat of the sun. This, of course, is very close to the truth. Lightning comes from clouds clashing together (he was quite right on that score). The comets are flaming planets, and the sun is larger than the region of the Peloponnese. He was right there too!

He also said that human beings are superior to all others only because they have hands. For me, that is backwards: it is because man is superior to all other animals that the Creator gave him hands, because he would be able to make use of them[282].

Anaxagoras died at Lampsacus, a city on the coast of Asia Minor, of starvation following a hunger strike.

— Next on our list is Empedocles. Those of us who study the exact sciences have considerable respect for him, because with his theory of four basic elements, earth, air, water and fire, he came closest to what we believe today. Isn't that right?

You are right that he gave a new dimension to thinking about the elements. And yes, his theories were a major step towards reality.

EMPEDOCLES

Empedocles was a larger-than-life figure. First of all, he was a poet, and some of the more obscure passages in his writings on matter can be ascribed to an excess of poetic licence. For example, he says that Love (philia, or what you would call chemical affinity) is what brings the elements together and creates chemical compounds, and Strife (neikos) what separates them. He even goes a step farther, and adds that philia is the cause of the creation of good things and neikos of the bad. A bit too poetical for the exact sciences, don't you think?

Having said that, I must admit that your word "affinity" (as in chemical affinity) has something of the same romantic cast.

The problem with Empedocles was that while his thinking was sound and his ideas good, he did not express them clearly. Mainly because he didn't use the right words. That is why his works have not had the recognition they deserve. They resemble an untrained soldier in battle, who may succeed in hitting an enemy, but not effectively[283].

— You said earlier that he was a remarkable personality. Why did you describe him that way?

First of all he was considered a poetic genius. Your own Kostis Palamas was a great admirer of his.

In his book On Nature, Empedocles describes things through imagery. For example, he calls the sea the "sweat of the earth"[284], and in describing the birth of a child speaks of the infant emerging from the cleft in the meadows of Aphrodite, avoiding the bald word pudenda[285].

Empedocles was a prolific writer. He even wrote tragedies, but thinking them unworthy of his intellect he had his sister burn them.

He was, as well, the subject of many legends, and held to be a miracle-worker and a sorcerer. The accounts of the end of his life are truly in the realm of legend, for some say that he fell from his chariot and was killed, others that he ascended to Mount Olympus, and yet others that he leaped into the crater of Mount Etna and was vaporised.

The famous thinker Nietzsche, who was a great admirer of Wagner, thought that the soul of Empedocles had found a new home in the body of the German dramatic composer. This was something Nietzsche tended to do, find a similarity between the personality of a modern intellectual and some ancient Greek. Perhaps he did it to show that he was familiar with the classics. Or maybe he believed it.

Empedocles was born into a wealthy family in the Sicilian city of Acragas in 494 BC. His views on religion were much like those of the Pythagoreans. He believed in metempsychosis and he hated broad beans.

He knew something about centrifugal force, for he mentions that if you tie a beaker of water to a string and whirl it about, the water will not spill.

He was also interested in medicine. When a pestilence broke out in Selinus, Empedocles realised that it came from the stagnant waters of a small stream that ran through the city. He paid for labourers to dig drainage channels to divert the water, and the epidemic began to subside. After that he was treated as a god[286].

He also cured a woman from Acragas who had a disease of the womb. She could scarcely breathe and everyone had given her up for dead, but Empedocles made her well. After this, thinking that his fame could go no higher, he withdrew from public view. That is when he was said to have leaped into the crater of Mount Etna,

—*I'm anxious to hear what you are going to say about Leucippus and Democritus, the originators of the atomic theory.*

The name Democritus is found in many places, but the name Leucippus only occurs together with that of Democritus.

LEUCIPPUS - DEMOCRITUS

There are many who, like Epicurus, deny that there ever was a philosopher called Leucippus. Because his existence is wholly identified with the theory of atomism, it was thought that the name Leucippus was a pseudonym of Democritus. I mention him many times, especially in my book *On Generation and Corruption*. In my opinion, Leucippus existed. He was born between 490 and 470 BC, possibly at Miletus, possibly at Abdera or even Elea. Some say he travelled much, and finally settled in Abdera, where he taught philosophy. Democritus does not mention him in any of his works. They say that it was Leucippus who first said that the primary constituent of matter is the atom.

Democritus is a much more definite figure than the shadowy Leucippus. He was born in Abdera in Thrace in 460 BC, and died at a very great age — some say he lived to be over a hundred. And while Leucippus, if he existed at all, passed unnoticed, there are plenty of stories about Democritus.

—*I'd like to hear some of them.*

I am more than happy to oblige. Democritus was called the Laughing Philosopher, because he was a very cheerful man. This seems to have been the result of a sense of mental and material self-sufficiency that left him happy and peaceful. One of his favourite sayings, in fact, is that the rich man is one who is contented with what he has.

Democritus had a wife who was tiny. Someone once asked him how it happened that a man who was both handsome and famous should have married such a little squib of a woman. Democritus answered: "Since I had to suffer that misfortune, I made sure it was as small as possible."

It is said that Democritus blinded himself, by exposing

his eyes to the sun's rays reflected off a silver shield, because —he said— natural sight interferes with the sight of the soul.

In his old age Democritus began to weary of life. He even wrote in one of his books: "Long life is a long death"[287]. And so he decided it was time to leave this world, and began slowly and steadily to reduce the amount he ate. When he was at the point of death, his sister pleaded with him not to die that day, because then she would not be able to take part in the Thesmophoria, a women's festival on the Pnyx. Since he could no longer eat, Democritus asked for fresh loaves to be brought to him continuously, so he could smell them. In this way he managed to live for three days longer, and his sister was able to attend the Thesmophoria.

There was a philosopher in Athens who heard about Democritus' theory of atoms, and was taken aback at the idea that all material bodies are composed of atoms in constant motion. How could the piece of white marble he was holding in his hand be made of ceaselessly moving particles which none of his senses was able to perceive? So he went to Abdera and asked Democritus to explain.

Democritus took him out to a hillside where a flock of sheep was grazing. They watched for a while as the sheep drifted around the pasture, as sheep do. Then they went to a hill on the other side of the valley, a considerable distance away. There Democritus pointed to a white patch on the hillside they had just come from, and asked the man what it was. The Athenian answered that it was the flock of sheep they had just been watching. Democritus then asked if he could see any sheep moving. "No," replied the Athenian, "I cannot make out any individual sheep." "I am sure" said Democritus "that you don't doubt that the sheep are still moving as they graze, just as they were before. But we are too far away to see them." This, he went on to explain, is precisely what happens with the atoms: they are too small for us to see or distinguish their movements.

According to Democritus, atoms are so small as to be imperceptible, but it is from combinations of different atoms that all perceptible things are made. There were those who asked scornfully how Democritus could insist that these little particles existed, when he couldn't see them. He answered them with a pair of concrete images: a wet cloth hung out in the sunshine dries without our being aware of the evaporation of the water that is taking place, and a perfume jar left open fills the room with its fragrance, although we see no change or movement in the jar nor any particles of scent in the air. Think too, he said, of motes of dust in a room, which can only be seen when a sunbeam falls upon them, and then we distinguish not only the particles but their movement as well[288].

As a chemistry student you know that atoms and even molecules are so small that they cannot be seen without an electron microscope.

To give you some idea of the size of an atom, think of the whole population of the world, all eight billion of you, working for ten hours a day, three hundred and sixty-five days a year, each putting one atom of copper in a scale every second: it would take roughly three hundred and sixty-one thousand years to weigh out one gramme of copper.

—*That last story about Democritus brings to mind the much-debated question of experiments in Ancient Greece. There seems to be a general idea that the ancient Greeks disliked conducting experiments. Is that true?*

There is some truth in what you say, but if you think that an experiment can properly be defined as the deliberate, controlled reproduction of a sequence of acts in a natural or manmade setting for the purpose of studying a specific phenomenon, then I can assure you that the ancient Greeks did indeed perform experiments.

THE EXPERIMENT IN ANCIENT GREECE

Tell me, son, my observation that the evaporation of water produces a cooling effect —was that not the product of experimentation? Did I not have to repeat the phenomenon in specific conditions? Or my conclusion that the temperature of boiling water remains the same —was that not the result of a series of experiments?

The great laboratory for the ancient Greeks was of course nature. That is where they experimented. But that does not mean that they did not also conduct experiments indoors. The paints used to decorate the palace of Knossos or the tombs at Vergina could not have lasted for two and a half thousand years if they had been prepared without testing. How likely is it that your modern paints, developed at considerable expense and with much experimenting in up-to-date laboratories, will last two and half thousand years?

It is true that experiments requiring manipulations and manual labour were assigned to women and resident aliens, who were considered second-class citizens, but the results were studied by the free citizens.

And since you brought up the question, there is a common belief that the ancient Greeks had their heads in the clouds, since they spurned actual experimenting and wanted to work everything out with the power of their intellect alone. That is simply not true. The ancient Greeks greatly admired anyone who could turn his knowledge to practical account in the service of his fellowmen. They also had a high regard for productive labour: metalworking, for example, they held in high esteem.

The production of iron, copper, lead and silver from their ores was a lucrative art, and the different processes were a well-guarded secret. The art of metalworking was placed under the protection of Hermes Kedroos: this is the source of the phrase "hermetically closed", meaning sealed airtight. The name of Hermes also gave us the word "armoire".

THE LIFE OF DEMOCRITUS

Democritus came from a wealthy family. When his father died, he asked for his share of the estate in cash, and set off to travel. He visited Ethiopia, the lands around the Red Sea, even India, and of course spent some time in Athens. He is said to have travelled more than any of his contemporaries. As was the custom in those days he studied astronomy with the Chaldeans, mathematics with the Egyptians, and theology with the Magi (a tribe of Medes, you may remember).

Democritus considered himself an authority in five domains: philosophy, ethics, art, mathematics and the natural sciences.

Plato, who couldn't abide Democritus, say in the *Erastai* that he (Democritus) is like the athlete who is crowned victor in the pentathlon without having won any of the individual events —meaning, of course, that Democritus had not mastered any of the fields in which he thought he was an expert[289].

Democritus wrote many books, but very few have survived. They were generally very well received, except by Plato, who had so little opinion of him that he never even referred to him by name.

Would you say that Democritus was the father of the atomic theory? Or the shadowy Leucippus, who we assume was his teacher?

I think, both. Both are very correctly described as atomists, but I think it must have been Leucippus who originated the theory while Democritus established it. In my books, whenever I speak of the atomic theory I mention them both.

One of the fundamental questions treated by both Leucippus and Democritus is that of the primary component of matter. Their answer was that matter cannot be divided indefinitely and that all material bodies are composed of infinitesimally small particles, which are indivisible,. The word atom comes from the Greek prefix *a-*, meaning not, and the Greek verb *temno*, meaning to cut.

ATOMIC THEORY

According to Democritus, atoms have the following characteristics[290]:

- They are physically indivisible.

- They are infinitesimally small, but of different sizes.
- They are so small that they are invisible.
- They are infinite in number.
- They are self-existent, not having come from something else.
- They are indestructible.
- They are solid, hard and incompressible.
- They are in constant swirling motion.
- They are uniform in nature.

That is, the primordial atoms posited by Democritus are very similar to what we now accept atoms to be!

Another thing worth noting is Democritus' view that the basic building blocks of matter enclose opposing forces. As you know, in the atom there exists a repulsive force between proton and proton and electron and electron.

Although with his atomic theory and his general convictions Democritus was undoubtedly a materialist, that is, one of the school who believe that all facts are causally dependent upon or even reducible to, physical processes, he held that spiritual goods are better than material[291] and told people to do no wrong, "not for fear of punishment, but because it is wrong."

—*What else can you tell me about Democritus, his atomic theory, and his views on the natural sciences generally.*

First of all, as a chemistry student you must be aware that Democritus' atomic theory has not only been proved right but has triumphed. This is illustrated, for example, in the words of the famous French mathematician, philosopher and economist Cournot (1801-1877), who said that "None of the ideas that antiquity has bequeathed to us has had a greater or even a similar success than the atomic theory of matter".

This does not, of course, mean that there were no dissenters, either among the great philosophers of the period or important scientists of the 19th century, when chemistry was beginning to take shape as a science.

One of those was the great French academician and chemist Marcellin Berthelot, who ridiculed the atomist position and was even opposed to introducing the teaching of atomic theory into French secondary schools (1884). It almost beggars belief that at the threshold of the 20th century such an eminent chemist could have been so wrong —for this, remember, was just sixty years before the atom bomb that destroyed Hiroshima.

And since you want my opinion, I will just make another couple of comments.

One is on his belief that an atom can be transmuted into a different atom. He thought that atoms, the primary constituents of matter, have different properties because they differ in size and shape. His contemporaries thought that this was a weakness in his theory, but today as you know Democritus has been completely vindicated.

The other concerns the real failing in his teaching, although he was not the only one to think this way, which was his reduction of all the senses to touch. He believed, that is, that all the senses operate by means of some kind of physical contact[292]. This, of course, has been proven to be incorrect.

And now, I think, it is time for you to get some rest. We have been talking for hours, and you are, after all, convalescing.

Once again you are right —I hadn't realised how tired I was! But I feel very privileged to have had this long conversation with you. Thank you!

* *
*

REFERENCES

1. Aristotle, *Politics*, 1252a.
2. Plato, *Protagoras*, 219 b-d.
3. Aristotle, *Politics*, 1253a 26.
4. Aristotle, *Politics*, 1253a 27-29.
5. Aristotle, *Politics*, 1253a 31-33.
6. Aristotle, *Politics*, 1252a 28-29.
7. Aristotle, *Politics*, 1281a 34-35.
8. Aristotle, *Politics*, 1252b 34.
9. Aristotle, *Politics*, 1253a 3.
10. Aristotle, *Politics*, 1252a 26-27.
11. Aristotle, *Politics*, 1252a 26-31.
12. Aristotle, *Nicomachean Ethics*, 1162a 16-24.
13. Aristotle, *Politics*, 1253a 15-16.
14. Aristotle, *Politics*, 1252b 31-33.
15. Aristotle, *Politics*, 1278b 15.
16. Aristotle, *Nicomachean Ethics*, 1097b.
17. Aristotle, *Politics*, 1253a 2-3.
18. Aristotle, *Politics*, 1253a 7-10.
19. Aristotle, *Politics*, 1253a 10-18.
20. Aristotle, *Nicomachean Ethics*, 1134b.
21. Xenophon, *Memorabilia*, I 6.
22. Philostratus, *Lives of the Sophists*, I 3.
23. Diogenes Laertius, *Lives of Eminent Philosophers*, II, IV.
24. Diogenes Laertius, *Lives of Eminent Philosophers*, II, VIII.
25. L. De Crescenzo, The History of Greek Philosophy. Grove, 1992.
26. Plutarch, *The Education of Children*, 7, 4.
27. Aristotle, *Politics*, 1295b.
28. Aristotle, *Politics*, 1268a.
29. Aristotle, *Politics*, 1261a.

30. F. W. Bain, *Body and Soul* (W.D. Ross, Aristotle, ch. 4, n. 76).

31. Aristotle, *History of Animals*, 52lb.

32. Aristotle, *Generation of Animals*, 733a.

33. Aristotle, *History of Animals*, 52lb.

34. Aristotle, *History of Animals*, 566b.

35. Aristotle, *History of Animals*, 513a- 515a.

36. Aristotle, *Generation of Animals*, 718b 32- 719 a2.

37. Aristotle, *History of Animals*, 486, *Parts of Animals*,
    639b, 2-5, 695b, 20-25.

38. Aristotle, *Parts of Animals*, 659a, 662a, 688a, 690a.

39. Aristotle, *Parts of Animals*, 663a, *History of Animals*, 487b 26.

40. Aristotle, *History of Animals*, 588 a.

41. Aristotle, *Generation of Animals*, l, 1.

42. Aristotle, *Generation of Animals*, 722b.

43. Aristotle, *Generation of Animals*, 723b.

44. Aristotle, *Generation of Animals*, 723a.

45. Aristotle, *Generation of Animals*, 726b.

46. Aristotle, *Generation of Animals*, 730b, 10-21, 731a 21.

47. Aristotle, *Generation of Animals*, 740a, 5-23.

48. Aristotle, *Generation of Animals*, 736a.

49. Aristotle, *Generation of Animals*, 736b 27, 737a 1.

50. Aristotle, *Generation of Animals*, 740a, 4, 3.

51. Aristotle, *On the Heavens*, 271a.

52. Aristotle, *History of Animals*, 502b, Aristotle,
    Parts of Animals, 669b, 670b.

53. Aristotle, *Generation of Animals*, 640a.

54. Aristotle, *Generation of Animals*, 639b.

55. Aristotle, *Generation of Animals*, 640b.

56. Aristotle, *Generation of Animals*, 640a.

57. Aristotle, *Generation of Animals*, 696b.

58. Fragment 16 (Rose).

59. Aristotle, *Physics*, 242a.

60. Aristotle, *Metaphysics*, 1074a-b.

61. Aristotle, *Metaphysics*, 1074a-b.

62. Aristotle, *Metaphysics*, 1074a.

63. Aristotle, *Metaphysics*, 1074a-b.

64. Aristotle, *Eudemean Ethics*, 1244b.

65. Aristotle, *Metaphysics*, 1075b.

66. Aristotle, *Eudemean Ethics*, 1244b.

67. Fragment 14 (Diels-Kranz).

68. Botsford & Robinson, *Ancient Greek History*, MIET, Athens 1979, p. 376 (in Greek).

69. Aristotle, *Nicomachean Ethics*, 1156a.

70. Aristotle, *Nicomachean Ethics*, 1166a.

71. Aristotle, *Nicomachean Ethics*, 1161b.

72. Aristotle, *Nicomachean Ethics*, 1099b.

73. Fragment 52 (Diels-Kranz).

74. Aristotle, *Nicomachean Ethics*, 1100a.

75. Aristotle, *Politics*, 1290b.

76. Aristotle, *Politics*, 1291b.

77. Aristotle, *Politics*, 1310a.

78. Aristotle, *Politics*, 1302a.

79. Aristotle, *Politics*, 1296a.

80. Aristotle, *Politics*, 1286a.

81. Aristotle, *Politics*, 1332b.

82. Aristotle, *Politics*, 1281a.

83. Aristotle, *Politics*, 1291a.

84. Aristotle, *Politics*, 1292a.

85. Aristotle, *Politics*, 1307b.

86. Aristotle, *Nicomachean Ethics*, 1102a.

87. Aristotle, *Politics*, 1310a.

88. Aristotle, *Politics*, 1253b.

89. Aristotle, *Politics*, 1276b.

90. Aristotle, *Politics*, 1276b.

91. Aristotle, *Politics*, 1277b.

92. Aristotle, *Politics*, 1276b.

93. Aristotle, *Nicomachean Ethics*, 1102a.

94. Aristotle, *Nicomachean Ethics*, 1107a.

95. Aristotle, *Nicomachean Ethics*, 1176b.

96. Aristotle, *Nicomachean Ethics*, 1105b.

97. Aristotle, *Nicomachean Ethics*, 1140b.

98. Aristotle, *Nicomachean Ethics*, 1103b.

99. Aristotle, *Eudemean Ethics*, 1216a.

100. Aristotle, *Politics*, 1310a.

101. Aristotle, *Nicomachean Ethics*, 1103b.

102. Aristotle, *Nicomachean Ethics*, 1179b.

103. Aristotle, *Politics*, 1310a.

104. Aristotle, *Politics*, 1309a.

105. Aristotle, *Politics*, 1253b.

106. Thucydides, *History of the Peloponnesian War*, 8-9.

107. L. De Crescenzo, *The History of Greek Philosophy: The Pre-Socratics*. Grove, 1992.

108. Plato, *Meno*, 73c.

109. Plato, *Gorgias*, 452d-e.

110. Plato, *Republic*, 473c,484a, 485b.

111. Aristotle, *Nicomachean Ethics*, 1180a.

112. Francis Wolff, *Aristotle and Politics*, PUG, 4th edition, 2008.

113. Aristotle, *Nicomachean Ethics*, 1180b.

114. Aristotle, *Nicomachean Ethics*, 1181a.

115. Aristotle, *Politics*, 1337a.

116. Aristotle, *Nicomachean Ethics*, 1103a.

117. Aristotle, *Nicomachean Ethics*, 1105b.

118. Aristotle, *On the Soul*, 425a.

119. Aristotle, *Metaphysics*, 980a.

120. Aristotle, *Metaphysics*, 981a.

121. Aristotle, *Nicomachean Ethics*, 1105b.

122. Aristotle, *On the Soul*, 425a.

123. Aristotle, *Metaphysics*, 980a.

124. Aristotle, *Metaphysics*, 981a.

125. Aristotle, *Nicomachean Ethics*, 1106b.

126. Aristotle, *Nicomachean Ethics*, 1107b.

127. Aristotle, *Nicomachean Ethics*, 1109a.

128. Aristotle, *Nicomachean Ethics*, 1113b.

129. Aristotle, *Nicomachean Ethics*, 1114b.

130. Aristotle, *Eudemean Ethics*, 1216b.

131. Aristotle, *Politics*, 1281a.

132. Aristotle, *Politics*, 1282b.

133. Aristotle, *Politics*, 1283a.

134. Aristotle, *Politics*, 1283b.

135. Aristotle, *Politics*, 1278b.

136. Aristotle, *Politics*, 1278b.

137. Aristotle, *Politics*, 1279b.

138. Aristotle, *Politics*, 1282a.

139. Aristotle, *Politics*, 1282a.

140. Aristotle, *Politics*, 1287a.

141. Aristotle, *Politics*, 1263a.

142. Aristotle, *Politics*, 1267a.

143. Aristotle, *Politics*, 1263a.

144. Aristotle, *Politics*, 1267a.

145. Aristotle, *Politics*, 1266b.

146. Fragment 52 (Diels-Kranz).

147. Aristotle, *Nicomachean Ethics*, 1133a.

148. Aristotle, *Politics*, 1257b.

149. Aristotle, *Politics*, 1317b.

150. Aristotle, *Politics*, 1254a.

151. T. Valala, *Provoles ston Aristotele*, p. 330 (in Greek).

152. Aristotle, *Nicomachean Ethics*, 1123b.

153. Aristotle, *Nicomachean Ethics*, 1127b.

154. Aristotle, *Nicomachean Ethics*, 1175a.

155. Aristotle, *Politics*, 1252a.

156. Aristotle, *Nicomachean Ethics*, 1162a.

157. I. Goudelis, *Erotike philia stin Archaia Ellada*, 1999 (in Greek).

158. Aristotle, *Poetics*, 1451b.

159. Aristotle, *Poetics*, 1449b.

160. Aristotle, *Nicomachean Ethics*, 1096a.

161. I. Sikoutris, *Platonos Symposion*, Kollaros, Athens 1986 (in Greek).

162. Aristotle, *Nicomachean Ethics*, 1099a.

163. Aristotle, *Nicomachean Ethics*, 1101a.

164. J. M. Zemb, *Aristoteles*, Hamburg 1967 (in German).

165. Aristotle, *Rhetoric*, 1356b.

166. Aristotle, *Rhetoric*, 1404b.

167. Aristotle, *Rhetoric*, 1359b.

168. Aristotle, *Metaphysics*, 1005b.

169. Aristotle, *Prior Analytics*, 24a.

170. Aristotle, *Prior Analytics*, 41a, 50a.

171. Aristotle, *Metaphysics*, 1006b.

172. Aristotle, *Posterior Analytics*, 89b

173. Aristotle, *Nicomachean Ethics*, 1103b.

174. Aristotle, *Nicomachean Ethics*, 1107a.

175. Aristotle, *Nicomachean Ethics*, 1117b.

176. Aristotle, *Nicomachean Ethics*, 1118b.

177. Aristotle, *Nicomachean Ethics*, 1104b.

178. Aristotle, *Nicomachean Ethics*, 1174b.

179. Aristotle, *Nicomachean Ethics*, 1178a.

180. Aristotle, *Nicomachean Ethics*, 1111b.

181. Aristotle, *Nicomachean Ethics*, 1102b.

182. Aristotle, *Nicomachean Ethics*, 1148b, 1149a.

183. Aristotle, *Nicomachean Ethics*, 1109b.

184. Aristotle, *Nicomachean Ethics*, 1115a.

185. Aristotle, *Nicomachean Ethics*, 1100b.

186. Aristotle, *Nicomachean Ethics*, 1123a.

187. Aristotle, *Nicomachean Ethics*, 1125a.

188. Aristotle, *On the Soul*, 402a.

189. Aristotle, *On the Soul*, 432a.

190. Aristotle, *On the Soul*, 430a.

191. Aristotle, *On the Soul*, 407b.

192. Aristotle, *On the Soul*, 425b.

193. Aristotle, *On the Soul*, 408b.

194. Aristotle, *On the Soul*, 427b.

195. Aristotle, *On the Soul*, 428b.

196. Aristotle, *On Dreams*, 459a, 459b.

197. Aristotle, *On the Senses and Their Objects*, 437b.

198. Aristotle, *On the Soul*, 424a, 426a.

199. Aristotle, *On the Soul*, 435b.

200. Aristotle, *On Sleep*, 454b, 455a.

201. Aristotle, *On the Senses and Their Objects*, 436b, 437b.

202. Aristotle, *On the Senses and Their Objects*, 440b.

203. Aristotle, *On the Senses and Their Objects*, 438b.

204. Aristotle, *On the Senses and Their Objects*, 443a.

205. Aristotle, *On the Senses and Their Objects*, 441a.

206. Aristotle, *On the Senses and Their Objects*, 447b.

207. Aristotle, *On the Heavens*, 296a.

208. Aristotle, *Metaphysics*, 1073a.

209. Aristotle, *On the Heavens*, 270b.

209ᵃ. N. Spyrou, *Iones philosophoi kai kosmologike episteme*, *Apoplous* [periodical], Samos 1998 (in Greek).

210. Aristotle, *Meteorology*, 338a, 347b.

211. Aristotle, *Meteorology*, 346b.

212. Aristotle, *Meteorology*, 347a.

213. Aristotle, *Meteorology*, 356a.

214. Aristotle, *Meteorology*, 358b.

215. G. Manousakis-G. Kazektzidis, *I goetia tis epistemis stin Archaia Ellada*. Patakis, Athens 1998 (in Greek).

216. E. Schrödinger, *Nature and the Greeks*, CUP, 2914.

217. Aristotle, *Metaphysics*, 980a.

218. Aristotle, *Metaphysics*, 1010a.

219. Aristotle, *Physics*, 257a.

220. Aristotle, *Physics*, 200b.

221. Aristotle, *Metaphysics*, 1045b, 1046b.

222. Aristotle, *Physics*, 245b.

223. Fragment 118 (Diels-Kranz).

224. Aristotle, *Metaphysics*, 1042a.

225. Aristotle, *Physics*, 191β.

226. Aristotle, *On Generation and Corruption*, 317b.

227. Aristotle, *On Generation and Corruption*, 325b.

228. Aristotle, *Physics*, 187b.

229. Aristotle, *On Generation and Corruption*, 333b.

230. Aristotle, *On Generation and Corruption*, 322b.

231. Aristotle, *On Generation and Corruption*, 327b.

232. Aristotle, *On Generation and Corruption*, 388a.

233. Plato, *Symposium*, 217b-a- 219c.

234. Diogenes Laertius, *Lives of Eminent Philosophers*, II.V.33.

235. Diogenes Laertius, *Lives of Eminent Philosophers*, II.V.36.

236. Plato, *Phaedrus*, 230b-c.

237. Plato, *Theaetetus*, 151e.

238. Plutarch, *Aristides*, 7.

239. Plato, *Symposium*, 219c-220d.

240. Xenophon, A1, 1 221b.

241. Plato, *Crito*, 50b.

242. Plato, *Timaeus*, 42b-d.

243. Plato, *Republic*, 433a.

244. Plato, *Republic*, 369a-371c.

245. Plato, *Republic*, 372d-374a.

246. Plato, *Republic*, 291d.

247. Diogenes Laertius, *Lives of Eminent Philosophers*, III. 35.

248. Epicurus, *Principal Doctrines*.

249. Apollodorus, *On the Life of Epicurus*.

250. Plato, *Protagoras*, 343a.

251. Diogenes Laertius, *Lives of Eminent Philosophers*, 1.26.

252. Herodotus, *History*, I. 75.

253. Herodotus, *History*, I. 75.

254. *Thales, Anaximander, Anaximenes*. Exantas, Athens, p. 54.

255. Aristotle, *Nicomachean Ethics*, 1141b.

256. Aristotle, *Politics*, 14, 1259a.

257. Pliny, *Natural History*, XXXVI 82.

258. Diogenes Laertius, *Lives of Eminent Philosophers*, 1.27.

259. Apuleius, Flor. 18, pp. 10, 37.

260. Aristotle, *Metaphysics*, 983b.

261. Aristotle, *On the Soul*, 405a.

262. Aristotle, *Physics*, 204a.

263. Porphyry, *Life of Pythagoras*, 7.

264. Diogenes Laertius, *Lives of Eminent Philosophers*, VIII.11.

265. Aristotle, *Metaphysics*, 985a.

266. V. Spandagos-R. Spandagou-D. Traulou, *Oi mathematikoi tis archaias Ellados*. Aethra, Athens. (in Greek)

267. Euclid, *Elements*, 1, 47.

268. Aristotle, *Metaphysics*, 1010a.

269. Fragment 53 (Diels-Kranz).

270. Aristotle, *Rhetoric*, 1407b.

271. Aristotle, *Metaphysics*, 984a.

272. Aristotle, *Physics*, 205a.

273. A. Hatzikakidis, *Aristotelike telologia*, Athens 1994.(in Greek)

274. Aristotle, *On the Soul*, 405a.

275. Aristotle, *Nicomachean Ethics*, 1179a.

276. Aristotle, *Eudemean Ethics*, 1215b.

277. Aristotle, *Physics*, 252a.

278. Aristotle, *On Plants*, 817a.

279. Pliny, *Natural History*, II 149-50.

280. Diogenes Laertius, *Lives of Eminent Philosophers*, II 10.

281. Plutarch, *Pericles*, 16.

282. Aristotle, *Parts of Animals*, 1068a.

283. Aristotle, *Parts of Animals*, 985a.

284. Fragment 55 (Diels-Kranz).

285. Fragment 46 (Diels-Kranz).

286. Diogenes Laertius, *Lives of Eminent Philosophers*,
     On abstention, IV 21.

287. Porphyrios, *On the abstention*, IV 21.

288. Aristotle, *On the Soul*, 404a.

289. Plato, *Rival Lovers*, 136a.

290. Aristotle, *On Generation and Corruption*, 314a,
     Simplicius, *Physics*, 925.

291. Aristotle, *On the Senses and Their Objects*, 442a.

* * *

THIS
FIRST EDITION OF
WITH ARISTOTLE ONLINE
ORIGINALLY WRITTEN IN GREEK
WAS TRANSLATED BY
JANET KONIORDOS
AND DESIGNED BY
GEORGIOS
CHATZIVANTSIDES